FLIGHT DREAMS

FLIGHT DREAMS

MICHAEL CRAFT

Kensington Books

http://www.kensingtonbooks.com

KENSINGTON BOOKS are published by

Kensington Publishing Corp.
850 Third Avenue
New York, NY 10022

Library of Congress Card Catalog Number: 96-079076
ISBN 1-57566-174-8

First Printing: June, 1997
10 9 8 7 6 5 4 3 2 1

Printed in the United States of America

The author thanks both Mitchell Waters and John Scognamiglio for their encouragement, wise counsel, and friendship.

The story that unfolds on the following pages is the product of an active imagination. Characters, places, and organizations named herein are largely fictitious. Any similarity to real-world counterparts, however, is hardly coincidental, and readers are invited to draw any conclusions they wish, inflammatory or droll.

—MC

Encore
bien sûr
à Léon

PART ONE

OCTOBER

S	M	T	W	T	F	S
				1	2	3
4	5	6	7	8	9	10
11	12	13	14	15	16	17
18	19	20	21	22	23	24
25	26	27	28	29	30	31

$100 MILLION AT STAKE
Missing airline heiress will be declared dead in three months

By Mark Manning
Journal Investigative Reporter

OCTOBER 1, CHICAGO IL— Three months from today, January 1, will mark seven years since the unexplained disappearance of Helena Carter, sole heir to the late Ridgely Carter, founder of CarterAir. Considered by many analysts to be the nation's most profitable regional airline, the privately held corporation holds cash reserves estimated in excess of one hundred million dollars.

Should Mrs. Carter's disappearance remain unexplained on January 1, she will be declared legally dead, and her fortune will be distributed according to the terms of a will bequeathing the bulk of her estate to the Roman Catholic Archdiocese of Chicago and a substantial sum to the Federated Cat Clubs of America (FCCA).

Mrs. Carter disappeared from the grounds of her Bluff Shores estate, north of Chicago, on New Year's Day nearly seven years ago. The police investigation has been stymied from the start. If the heiress was abducted from her home, her captor left no evidence of the deed. If, on the other hand, Mrs. Carter disappeared of her own volition, she left no clues as to her motive or destination.

Jerry Klein, chief operating officer of CarterAir and executor of Helena Carter's estate, has recently persuaded the courts to allow the estate to increase its reward offer to a half-million dollars for information leading to knowledge of the whereabouts of the heiress, whether living or dead. Police have dismissed numerous new leads generated by the offer, characterizing the informants as either cranks or frauds.

With the approach of the seven-year deadline, wide speculation has grown that Mrs. Carter was murdered, and one of this city's news organizations has openly named a suspect amid rhetorical calls for justice. The *Journal*'s investigation, however, has revealed no evidence to corroborate these accusations, and it is the position of this newspaper that Helena Carter must logically be presumed alive. ❏

Thursday, October 1

"**I** see trees." The hushed voice speaks slowly through the phone. "I see a large house surrounded by trees."

Mark Manning laughs. Confident that there is no need to take notes, he caps his pet pen, an antique Mont Blanc.

"I fail to see what's so funny, Mr. Manning." The voice is indignant. "I'm only trying to help. This information could be useful to your stories."

"Sorry," Manning says indifferently, "but it's a safe guess that any wealthy person would live in a big house. And most houses have trees around them." He closes his note pad and adds it to the tidy clutter on his desk in the newsroom of the *Chicago Journal.*

"But I see these things so *clearly,*" the voice persists. "With a little help from you, Mr. Manning, we could find her body."

"She *is* dead, then? Do you see that?" He stares at his computer terminal, transfixed for a moment by the rhythmic winking of its cursor.

"Certainly," the voice responds, as if clueing-in an ignorant child. "Everyone knows *that*, Mr. Manning. It's common knowledge."

"Thanks for calling," says Manning, bringing the conversation to an abrupt close. "I'm on deadline right now and can't talk any longer."

He hears a little squawk from the receiver as he tosses it back on top of the phone. He lights a cigarette with a small brass lighter that he flicks, extinguishes, and returns in a single motion to the pocket of a crisp blue oxford-cloth shirt.

"Hey, handsome, deadline was nearly an hour ago," says a taunting voice from behind. Daryl, a copy kid, overheard the end of Manning's call and now sidles into the reporter's cubicle. With an easy familiarity, he perches on the desk and asks, "How many does that make?"

"Three this morning," says Manning, disgruntled. He rolls his chair back from the desk, loosens his tie, and unbuttons his collar. "Every time my byline appears over anything pertaining to Helena Carter, I get a flurry of calls from these damned mystics." He tosses up a leg and plops his foot next to the computer. Reflections from a fluorescent work lamp glisten as wavy bands in the polished cordovan of his shoe.

"Then why'd you write it?" asks the college intern, fanning his hands in disapproval of the cigarette smoke. He flares his nostrils, exaggerating the "demure Negroid features" that are sometimes the subject of his coy patter.

"Because today is October first. In three months the estate will be settled—unless she reappears before then."

"She can't very well reappear from the grave, can she?" asks Daryl, scrutinizing a hangnail at arm's length.

"Of course not. But I don't think she's dead. I think she disappeared of her own free will."

"Sure, Mark, the old gal could've run away for lots of reasons— maybe she's just screwy." Daryl swirls a finger at his temple. "Isn't it more likely, though, that she's been killed?"

"There was no motive to kill her."

"A *hundred million dollars* isn't a motive? Look, doll, I'm the first to concede that you know more about this case than anyone else does. You've been on this story from the start, and there isn't a paper in the country that hasn't picked up your stuff, byline and all."

"What about the *Post?*" Manning quips.

"I stand corrected. The tabloid across the street has not run your byline, but then, they've got Humphrey Hasting, and he's writing exactly the kind of sensational fluff they're famous for. But you, Mark, are the expert. My God—how many reporters get calls from a chief detective asking for clarification of details of his own case? So I bow to your expertise. Does that please you?"

Manning answers with a shrug. He plants the cigarette in the corner of his mouth and joins his hands behind his head, stretching lithely.

His is not the body of most thirty-nine-year-olds. Lean and

muscled, he's in better shape than most at twenty-five. The well-defined planes of his face hint at the precise workings of an analytical mind, as if made visible through the piercing clarity of uncommonly green eyes. His hair, now peppered with those first dashes of gray, is worn a bit short for the fashion of the day, imparting a military attractiveness to his bearing—an impression made all the more vivid by the pleated khaki slacks he always wears.

Daryl crosses his arms, preparing to rest his case. "So how can you say—knowing everything you know—that a hundred million dollars is not sufficient motive for murder?"

Reaching to flick the ash of his cigarette, Manning sits forward in his chair with a sigh that seems to say, All right, I'll explain this just once.

"Helena Carter's will was located without difficulty shortly after she disappeared. It took some doing for a flock of 'interested parties' to persuade the courts to open the will of someone not known to be dead, but it was indeed opened, primarily for any light it might shed on motives for murder. All that was learned, though, is that the document simply does not raise any suspicions or point to any suspects."

"But, Mark, the old girl must have been crackers. No one in his right mind leaves that kind of fortune to be split between an animal pound and a church."

"Not a 'pound,' Daryl. It's a federation of cat clubs. Carter was a cat-lady; she bred them. She was also a devout Catholic. The stipulations of her will were well thought out, and she employed top legal talent to implement them; she was no madwoman. She never had kids, but saw to it that her one surviving sister would be cared for by means of carefully constructed trusts. Yes, she decided that the bulk of her legacy would be used to endow organizations that were significant to her, but I don't think that's *crazy.*"

"Look, Mark, it doesn't matter if she was nuts or not. Point is, whoever murdered her obviously didn't know *what* was in the will. He apparently thought there might be something in it for himself."

"Who?"

"*I* don't know. How about the houseman that Hasting and the *Post* keep harping on?"

"Daryl, people can *fry* for knocking off little old ladies. And if that lady happens to be sole heir to a highly profitable airline, representing one of the fattest fortunes to grace the North Shore suburbs of Chicago, you can bet that the effort to find and fry the culprit will be intense. Why would anyone choose to jeopardize the contented fulfillment of his twilight years on the mere hunch that it might be worth his while? Would you?"

"Of course not, but *I'm* not a murderer. Such people do exist, though, and they're not all as logical as you. Maybe the guy's dumb. It just *seems* that Helena Carter was murdered."

Manning tells him, "You don't *seem* to have produced a body. You don't *seem* to have come up with a suspect or even a reasonable motive. On the basis of what I do know—not what I think, or believe, or would like to believe, but *know*—I'm convinced that Helena Carter is alive."

"If you could prove it, you'd be a half-million dollars richer," Daryl reminds him. "And I know just the man you could spend it on."

Manning ignores Daryl's come-on, telling him, "The reward isn't the only consideration. If I could prove that Helena Carter is alive, there'd be a Partridge Prize waiting for me next year."

"The coveted Brass Bird," Daryl waxes rhapsodic, "investigative journalism's highest award." Then he beads Manning with a get-real stare. "*If* you could prove that she's alive."

They are silent. Both have stated their positions, and it is clear that no convincing has been done.

Daryl enjoys these encounters. He and Manning often engage in such banter, and the cagey sparring implies a sort of intimacy. It is not a physical intimacy—though Daryl has made it plain enough he would welcome the possibility—but simply a professional closeness. Daryl is a journalism student at Northwestern and, in spite of his flighty manner, is committed to making a career of it. He sees Manning as the *Journal*'s star reporter and constantly seeks ways to prove his own potential.

The efforts have not gone unnoticed by Manning, who encourages the kid and treats him more like an equal than a gofer. In moments of honest introspection, Manning also recognizes that Daryl intrigues him. While he feels no particular attraction to Daryl, he admires the young man's openness. Thirty-nine and still single, Manning wonders for a moment whether his next birthday might trigger something he doesn't care to face.

Suppressing these thoughts, he curls his lips into a little smile. "Well, enough of that."

Daryl mirrors Manning's smile. He asks, "How old was she . . . *is* she?"

"She just turned fifty-six," says Manning. "She was forty-nine when she disappeared, a young widow, but most people think of her as elderly—guess it fits the image of a rich North Shore matron. Everything I've learned about her, though, paints a picture of a spry, spirited woman."

Daryl checks his watch and affects a lisp: "Speaking of spry and spirited, you'd better get your ass in gear. Gordon wanted to see you ten minutes ago."

Gordon Smith, the *Journal*'s managing editor, is not a man to be kept waiting. Manning sits bolt upright and snuffs out his cigarette, asking, "Why the hell didn't you say so?"

"Well, I did—just now."

Manning has already shrugged into his jacket. He tightens his tie as he trots down the aisle toward the newsroom's front offices.

The *Journal*'s previous managing editor opted for a late retirement; it was general consensus that he waited too long. Gordon Smith, as city editor, was heir apparent, so when the promotion finally came, it surprised no one.

Smith has accepted the mantle of authority gracefully, but with little inner joy. Some years earlier, when he became city editor, he yearned for the creative involvement of a reporter. "Reporting is what newspaper work is all *about*," he confided to his wife when she wondered aloud one night why his success had brought on a mild despondency. Now that he is managing editor, he misses the duties of city editor, and reporting seems all the more removed from his life.

Nonetheless, he enjoys playing the role in which he now finds himself cast. He has acquired a wardrobe of three-piece suits, which he wears at all times. Arriving at his *Journal* office, he hangs up his jacket, unbuttons his vest, and rolls up the sleeves of his starched white shirt. He has become the picture of a "working editor" and once joked to Manning that he planned to get suspenders and arm garters.

When Manning enters Smith's office, though, he senses at once that there will be no joking today. The editor sits peering at a blank computer screen. His expression is sullen, his complexion ashen.

"What's the matter, Gordon?" Manning asks him, forgoing any small talk.

"You know, Mark, it's funny." Smith vacantly motions for Manning to sit down. His gaze wanders out the window to the cool autumn sky arching over Lake Michigan. "You'd think it would be enough for a man to sit in his tower office, secure in the knowledge that he presides over the most respected news organization in the Midwest, leaving day-to-day reporting and editorial matters to the best staff in the business." Smith's voice, barely audible, trails off to nothing as he continues to study the sky.

"Are you talking about Nathan Cain?" asks Manning, referring to the *Journal*'s publisher.

"Who else?" Smith turns in his chair to face Manning across the desk. "Nathan has more drive and vision than any newsman I know. When he set up our foreign bureau in Ethiopia, lots of folks laughed at the idea—but now they're picking up *our* wire stories covering the hostage crisis there. Say what you will about him, but Nathan is a 'big picture' kind of guy."

"You'll get no argument from me. The *Journal* has never been stronger than it is right now with Cain at the helm. Hell, he *is* the *Journal*."

"Exactly," says the editor, at last looking Manning in the eye, "and that's what makes all of this so . . . sticky."

Apprehension colors Manning's voice. "All of what, Gordon?"

"All of this business about the Carter woman. You've once again drawn the conclusion in print that she's alive, while the rest of the world seems convinced that she was murdered. Nathan feels that your position is an embarrassment to the paper. He must be taking some heat from his buddies."

"What buddies?"

"Who knows? Probably the guys he rubs elbows with at United Way board meetings. Isn't Josh Williams on that board?"

"Ah, yes," says Manning. "Josh Williams, publisher of the *Post*, happens to be married to Humphrey Hasting's sister."

"Bingo." Smith swallows hard, then exhales before continuing. "Whatever the reason, Nathan wants the *Journal* to fall in line. He wants you to reverse your position."

"I can't do that, Gordon. I . . ."

"Mark, I agree with you. I told him so. But he's made up his mind."

"For God's sake," says Manning, exasperated, "why don't you just *edit* my stories to fit whatever policy he wants?"

"Why not, indeed. Or I could simply assign the story to someone else. I suggested that to Nathan, but he wouldn't hear of it. He's always had that odd streak—a perverse sense of gaming. He insists that the turnaround come from you personally."

"He can't *force* me to write something I don't believe."

"Of course not, but he can—and did—issue an ultimatum. Nathan Cain told me this morning that you are to reverse your Carter position in the next edition. If you don't, and if Carter doesn't reappear by New Year's, you're *out* of here. To make his wishes all the more compelling, he threatened that you'd never find work at another paper. As you're well aware, he has the power to make good on that promise."

"But *why?*" asks Manning. "What's behind his sudden interest in this story? Nathan Cain doesn't strike me as the sort of man who'll lose sleep over a bit of razzing from his colleagues."

"I don't have any answers," Smith tells him with a frustrated shrug. "Yes, Nathan's orders seem groundless, and I tried to dissuade him, but my opinions don't count—not this time. I'm just an overpaid messenger. And the message is: He calls the shots."

Stunned, Manning mumbles, "My entire adult life, I've struggled to build a reputation based on reason and integrity . . ."

Smith doesn't mince words. "Integrity isn't worth shit if you wind up losing your job—a job you're supposedly good at."

Manning thinks for a moment, but only a moment, before asking, "He doesn't leave me much choice, does he?"

"No, he doesn't."

"Then I'd better get to work and find Helena Carter."

Manning rises to leave, but pauses. With a feeble smile, he turns to ask his editor, "Did you think I'd knuckle under?"

"I hoped not, but I didn't know. Cain was sure you'd give in, but the ultimatum is no bluff. Having taken up the gauntlet, you've got to deliver."

"I know that, Gordon. I'll try not to disappoint you."

"Good luck, Mark."

Friday, October 2

Manning glances at the Roman numerals on his watch. It's nearly noon. Twenty-four hours have passed since Gordon Smith delivered their publisher's ultimatum, and Manning has wasted no time setting up a lunch date with Roxanne Exner, a lawyer—one of many—who deals with the Carter estate. He needs her help.

Michigan Avenue is already swamped with office workers who have sneaked out to enjoy the weather. Manning jostles through the crowd along the fashionable boulevard, then turns onto the shadowed side street that leads to his favorite Armenian restaurant, quickening his pace against a chilly east wind that blows from the lake.

He ducks under the tentlike awning and in through the door, his nostrils drinking in the warm smells of garlic, grape leaves, and sesame. Pausing a moment while his eyes adjust to the near-darkness of the cramped dining room, he notices Roxanne waving her fingers at him from one of the deeply coved booths.

"I'm surprised you're here already," he says while sliding in next to her.

She leans toward him, offering her cheek for a kiss, which Manning delivers. She tells him, "I don't normally lunch this early, if at all. But your call sounded rather desperate, and—as you know—I enjoy your company. I had to reschedule a few meetings, so it seems that you're indebted to me." She flashes him a sly smile, lifting her Scotch and soda in a perfunctory toast.

Manning now notices that his usual vodka on the rocks already sits before him. They touch glasses, then sip. He tells her, "For a pushy broad, you're awfully alluring."

She has to think about that one. She reflexively bristles at the mention of "broad," but she likes "pushy," and "alluring" is a bonus. On balance, she takes it as a compliment.

While she analyzes his comment, Manning studies Roxanne. They have slept together once—or was it twice? A few years younger than Manning, about thirty-five, she is single, stylish, undeniably attractive. She's a climber, a talented attorney who was recently named partner at one of the city's more prestigious firms. She occasionally provides tips or legal advice for Manning's stories. She is a friend.

Roxanne spreads a copy of the morning *Post* on the table in a pool of light cast by a Moroccan-style lantern overhead. She jabs at a story with her index finger. "Did you see this latest crap?" she asks Manning. "I've read more substantial reporting in *school* papers."

"Predictable," he answers.

"Just listen to this headline: POLICE APATHY PLAGUES CARTER CASE. Then in italic: *Will Public Ever Know Whole Story?* Byline, naturally: Humphrey Hasting. Opening paragraph: 'Deputy Chicago police superintendent Earl Murphy admitted in an exclusive interview with the *Post* that lack of incriminating evidence has hampered police efforts to find missing airline heiress Helena Carter's murderer. When asked what direction renewed efforts might take in this case, Murphy revealed that the department is currently consulting with a number of psychics and clairvoyants who have been flown to Chicago to help locate the body. The long-overdue measure is undoubtedly meant to appease a frustrated citizenry, increasingly weary of the investigative bungling that has characterized this case. . . .'"

Disgusted, Roxanne pushes the tabloid across the table and lets it flutter to the floor. "Mark, this pompous ass is just beating the bushes for a headline."

"You're preaching to the choir, Roxanne—I *know* he's a hack. But he does have a knack for stirring people up, and that makes him dangerous."

"And powerful. My God, now he's got the Chicago police squirming. What's *their* interest in this case? Carter disappeared in Bluff Shores."

"The Chicago Archdiocese stands to inherit nearly a hundred million dollars, remember, so you can bet that Archbishop Benedict has made a few phone calls to some folks in high places. Besides, the suburban police don't have the resources to mount a credible investigation. The FBI was called in at one point, but they got out fast because no one could prove that money—or a corpse—had crossed state lines. The question of jurisdiction has put a tricky knot in this case, but the underlying problem is lack of evidence."

"Lack of evidence is *your* handicap too, Mark. If you have nothing to go on, what makes you think you can find the old gal in time to save your job?"

"I'm not at all sure I can, but I wasn't left with much choice— I have to try. Will you help me?"

She reaches over their menus to pat his hand. "Of course," she tells him in a mock-soothing tone. Then, coolly, "I honestly think you're barking up the wrong tree, but if you're determined to make a martyr of yourself . . ."

"Look, Roxanne." He's annoyed. "I have no intention of sacrificing myself—whether to journalistic integrity or to the public's 'right to know.' I'm in this mess because the alternative is untenable. I'd appreciate your help."

She nods, all business now. "I understand, Mark. I've brought my files, and I see you've brought some too. What have you got?"

He spreads several manila folders on the table. "These are from the *Journal*'s morgue. They contain clippings of every story we've run about Helena Carter, as well as every photo we've shot of her. It's all dated on the back. I'm surprised there's so much— not only my own stories from the last seven years, but also a heap of material from before her disappearance." He stops short, noticing something in one of the folders.

"What've you got?" asks Roxanne, nosing across the table.

Manning lifts a picture from one of the older files and shows it to her. It was shot at a formal banquet in a ballroom at the Drake, years before Helena disappeared, while her husband, Ridgely Carter, was still alive. They gaze up from their table, and between them stands a stiff figure of a man with a forced smile, a hand perched squarely on each of the Carters' shoulders.

Roxanne looks at Manning with a blank expression that asks, So what?

He tells her, "That dapper, wooden gent posing in the background is none other than Nathan Cain."

"God," says Roxanne, taking the photo to examine it more closely, "the man who gave you this morning's ultimatum actually *knew* the Carters."

"I'm sure it's just a coincidence—Cain knows *everyone* in Chicago social circles—but still, the connection helps explain his interest in this story. What has me baffled, though, is why his interest is so sudden and intense. Nearly seven years have passed since the woman disappeared, I've written reams about the case, and Cain has never said boo . . . till today."

In a voice laced with mock suspicion, Roxanne says, "He's up to his *eyeballs* in this, Mark. You've got three months to get the dirt, so start digging." Laughing, she hands him the photo, then comments, "I'm surprised there's such a thick file on the mystery woman."

Manning explains, "Obviously, she was something of a socialite, but she also enjoyed a measure of fame among cat-people as a top-ranked breeder."

"Really? What kind of cats?"

"Some rare breed," Manning replies, riffling through a pile of photos. "Here we are. Abyssinian cats. Look at this one—really a magnificent animal, something like a little cougar."

"My, yes," Roxanne agrees. "Elegant."

"I'm driving up to Bluff Shores next week to interview Carter's sister, Margaret O'Connor. I haven't talked to her since the disappearance. She lives at the estate and looks after the cats. Maybe there's an angle there."

"Are there any color photos of the cats?"

"I think I saw one—must have been from the Sunday magazine. Here it is." Manning shows Roxanne a picture of the heiress posing with a ruddy-colored cat next to a towering trophy declaring the animal a quad-grand champion. Helena Carter beams a victorious smile; the cat gazes, bored, directly at the camera. "How about that? Carter's hair matches the cat's. She must have dyed it that goofy red."

Roxanne peers at the photo. She shakes her head. "That's not red dye, Mark. It's a natural rinse that comes from a plant or an herb or something. Been around for centuries. It's called henna."

"Whatever. And as long as I'm up at the estate, I also want to talk to Arthur Mendel, the houseman."

"What for? If you're so convinced that Carter is alive, why waste your time with suspected 'murderers'?"

Manning explains, "Even though there is no known evidence of murder, if I'm to *prove* that the woman is alive, I must first satisfy myself that any possible suspects had no involvement in her disappearance. It's a lot of grunt work. Truth is, I should have done it long ago."

"But you weren't sufficiently motivated till this morning, right?"

"Right." He laughs. "Are you getting hungry?"

Roxanne orders another drink, deciding to lunch on appetizers—hummus and raw kibbe. Manning has a lamb-and-couscous dish. During their meal, Roxanne brings Manning up to date on some accounting matters relating to the Carter estate, and they agree to meet again at her office.

Roxanne says, "As long as you have your appointment book out—are you free next Friday, a week from tonight?"

"Wide open," says Manning, perusing his calendar, in which he has marked each date with a running countdown of the days remaining till New Year's—a reminder that the clock is now steadily ticking toward his deadline. "My social life has been less than a whirl of late."

"Then *do* pencil me in. I'll have an out-of-town houseguest, an artist friend from college, and I'm throwing a fabboo cocktail party to introduce him to my crowd."

"Him?"

"Yes, Mark. He's a *friend*. The party's at my place—anytime after eight."

"I'll be there," Manning assures her, marking the date not in pencil, but in ink. Pausing a moment, he asks, "You're sure this guy isn't more than a 'friend'?"

"Don't I wish!"

The same afternoon, across the street from the *Journal*'s offices on an upper floor of the *Post* building, Humphrey Hasting waits to see Josh Williams, the *Post*'s publisher. A flamboyant dresser,

Hasting fusses with his bow tie—one of many that he always wears—a sartorial curiosity that accentuates his girth. At forty-nine, he has never married; to his considerable advantage, his sister, Ruth, has married Josh Williams.

Hasting fills an upholstered tub chair next to the secretary's desk outside his brother-in-law's office. Waiting impatiently, he sits with crossed legs, revealing tufts of black hair on white shins. Finding this position uncomfortable, he plants both feet on the carpet and leans back in the chair, staring tensely forward with a hand draped just above each knee. Ten fingers bounce in a random pattern on the burgundy polyester stretched tight around his legs—legs that make the secretary think of four links of sausage, two extending over the edge of the chair, two more dropping to the floor.

The woman is busy transcribing something from an earphone plugged in somewhere under her hair. The tapping of her fingers on the keyboard stops for a moment as she pauses to take a quick drag from the cigarette perched on a nearby ashtray.

"*Would* you put that damned thing out?" snaps Hasting while plucking several long gray pet-hairs from his slacks. "If you have no consideration for your own lungs, you might at least have a modicum of consideration for mine." He stares severely at the woman, thinking, *Modicum.* Good word. Haven't used it in a while.

"Sorry, Mr. Hasting," she says, extinguishing the cigarette.

"That's better," he sniffs, fluttering both hands to shoo smoke from his breathing space.

An electronic warble sounds from the secretary's phone. Taking the call, she tells Hasting, "Mr. Williams will see you now. Please go right in."

He gives her a curt nod that says, It's about time.

Hasting wears reading glasses with half-frames that hold crescent-shaped lenses. They look absurdly petite at the end of his bulbous nose. He removes them with a flourish, rising from his chair. The chair gives a creak of relief as he crosses the room toward Josh Williams's inner office. Hasting swings the door open and stands over the threshold, one foot poised in front of the other, brandishing his glasses like a lorgnette. "Good morning, Josh," he says bouncily, as if they were old pals meeting for a golf game.

"Morning, Hump," says Williams with a suspicious chuckle as he waves the man into the room.

Hasting inwardly fumes at the mention of his hated nickname, smiling too politely while closing the door. He walks to the desk and sits before Williams. His slacks whimper against the chair's leather seat as he settles in.

Williams is in the process of lighting his pipe, chosen from the collection displayed in racks on a credenza behind him. "Now what's this you need to see me about?" The pipe wobbles in his clenched teeth as he speaks. He strikes a hefty wooden match and, holding it over the bowl of the pipe, sucks furiously, his cheeks collapsing in rhythm with the bulging of his eyes. Sparks leap from the bowl as the tobacco crackles within.

"Well, Josh," says Hasting, replacing his glasses, "it's about the Carter woman."

"Yeah?" says the publisher. He's on his second match now and having no more success than with the first. He blows it out and flings it into a large ashtray in front of Hasting. The match twitches and curls, still smoking, smelling of sulfur. "What about her?" he asks, lighting a third.

"I think we should formulate some policy regarding this paper's position on the Helena Carter story."

"Whata-ya mean, 'position'?" He has the pipe going now—feebly, but it's lit.

"Josh, we have to take a stand," says Hasting, punctuating each word with delicate jabs at his knee.

"You don't take a stand, Hump, on a missing-person case. You just report the facts."

"But there haven't *been* any facts lately."

"What are we supposed to do—make some up?"

"Josh." He pauses, preparing to explain something very simple. "By taking a modicum of journalistic liberty, we could very well influence the outcome of this case." He cocks his head as if to ask, Don't you see?

Josh Williams sits back in his chair, fingers his pipe, thinking, then exhales. A cloud of aromatic blue smoke escapes from his teeth; two jets of it shoot down from his nostrils.

Williams has just turned sixty. He's spent most of his professional life at the *Post*, inching his way through the ranks the way
journalists used to, the way they did it when Chicago had four
thriving dailies. He's seen the *Post* through those years when it
held its own as a respectable morning tabloid—before the era of
its new owners, before the time when circulation and advertising
were the sole concerns of upper management. He sits now with
both elbows propped on the arms of his chair, still sucking his pipe.
He thinks of retirement—only five years away. "Okay, Hump," he
says quietly. "Let's have it. What are you driving at?" His pipe
has gone out.

"Don't be so morose," says Hasting, too cheery. "I'm not
driving at anything. It's just that I was talking to Ruth . . ."

"I thought so," says Williams through a loud laugh. He still
exhales smoke while talking, though the pipe has been dead for
some time.

"Ruth and I were thinking," Hasting continues, coughing
primly, "that the public deserves some answers. After all, this
thing's been going on now for—how long?—five, six years—"

"Seven," Williams interrupts. He can't resist adding, "Don't
you read the *Journal?*"

"Seven, whatever," Hasting acknowledges the correction.
"*Anyway*, people deserve some information. A nice old lady can't
just be wiped out while the police sit on their hands. This sort
of atrocity shouldn't be allowed in a free and prosperous society.
My God, there *are* possible suspects—the houseman, Arthur
Mendel, for instance, used to manage the stables at the Carter
estate, and you're surely aware of the shady company *those* people
keep. So what are the police waiting for? When do we get some
action? When will the public's yearning for justice be satisfied?"
He leans forward for a dramatic pause, then says softly, "You
know when, Josh? When *we* do something about it."

"And how do you propose to do something about it?" asks
Williams, digging in his pipe with a tool resembling a flat nail.

"We start stirring the waters. We keep the case constantly in
the public eye, right on page one. Leave no stone unturned. Get
our readers ready for blood, screaming for police action. Then"—
he leans forward confidentially—"perhaps a few well-timed *editorials* demanding that a suspect be brought to trial. I'll take care

of the reporting, Josh, then *your* boys can take over with the editorials."

"Reporting? *What* reporting, Hump? The case is at a standstill." Williams's pipe will not be revived. He turns it upside down and bangs it on the ashtray in front of Hasting. A small chunk of charred matter flies from the pipe and lands on Hasting's upper leg.

Hasting flicks the cinder off his slacks with his index finger, noticing that it has fused several fibers of the synthetic fabric into a hard tiny bead. The cinder lands near his foot, so he grinds it into the carpet, eyeing with satisfaction the smeared streak of black that trails his shoe.

He tells Williams, "Perhaps 'reporting' isn't exactly the right word. Something more like—shall we say?—informed commentary. The public can't tell the difference. Don't get me wrong; I'm well aware that it's our professional duty to *serve* the public. This just happens to be the most expedient means of fulfilling that obligation."

Williams sits silently for a moment, weighing what he has heard. He already knows the outcome of this discussion. "I suppose you've talked this through with Ruth?"

"As a matter of fact, we've discussed it at length."

"Mm-hm. And what'd she think about it?"

"Well, Josh, I must say that she didn't seem to care much about the public-service angle. I believe she made some reference to 'a rat's ass'—you *know* what a hard woman she can be. But then she mumbled something about doing wonders for circulation, or words to that effect. Ruth seems to think our readers are getting tired of Ethiopia."

He leans back and looks Williams in the eye. "In short, Josh, she says we'll do it."

Saturday, October 3
90 days till deadline

Bare cement flooring meets Manning's bare feet. Sitting on the edge of his bed, squinting at the sun rising over Lake Michigan through expansive east windows, he stretches, rubs his eyes, and brings the room into focus. "I've got to do something about this place," he tells himself aloud, albeit hoarsely.

The condominium loft, spacious and new, boasts an enviable address. But it is still unfinished and mostly unfurnished, its down payment having taxed Manning's finances to the limit less than a year ago. Rising from a restless sleep, troubled by the sudden insecurity of his job, he wonders how long there'll be money for the mortgage—let alone decorating.

With the day's first uncertain steps, Manning walks to the back wall of the loft, where a spartan row of cabinets serves as kitchen, and switches on the coffeemaker, loaded last night with bottled water and freshly ground beans. Listening to the machine start to gurgle, waiting for the first drop to appear in the glass carafe, he remembers the old admonition about "watched pots" and decides that it's a good morning for a run along the lakeshore.

He pulls on a pair of bright yellow nylon shorts, a faded Illini sweatshirt, and socks that crumple at his ankles. Putting on his Reeboks, he eyes them askance for a moment, then relaces one of them—just so. He grabs his keys and heads for the door, glancing back at the coffeepot, which is beginning to fill.

He's out the door, down the service elevator, and suddenly on the quiet side street that turns onto Lake Shore Drive. It's Saturday, still early, and traffic is light. The chilly air smells barely of fish—the spring influx of alewives has long since washed away. No wind blows, and the lake is placid. Gulls glide low over the water, their random calls breaking the stillness. The only people in sight are a few other runners headed up and down the shore. Some wear headphones, but most are content with nature's own pristine music on this waking autumn morning.

This will be an easy run, Manning decides—nothing serious today—so he skips his usual warm-up and takes off at a leisurely pace, headed north.

The intensely blue sky reminds him of fall afternoons more than twenty years ago in high school when he was a member of a ragtag running team. All students in the small school were expected to participate in at least one sport each year, and for Manning the obvious choice was cross-country, which stressed personal achievement more than team spirit. He overcame his initial dislike for running—the inevitable aches and pains of getting started—and eventually learned to enjoy it, taking quiet pride in his slow but steady progress, setting new goals. Regimented during high school, the discipline followed him into college and beyond as a matter of choice. Now approaching midlife, Manning takes greater satisfaction than ever from running. It assures him that he's not drinking too much, that he's not smoking too much—though he knows, of course, that he is. Most important, it simply tells him that he's still able to do it.

Having found his stride, he pushes harder, adjusting the rhythm of his breathing. Suddenly aware that he is clenching the keys in his hand, he loosens his grip, making an effort to relax every muscle but those in his legs. As he picks up speed, the rushing air makes beads of sweat feel icy against his brow. It parts his hair, as if with fingers, into damp, clustered strands that bob in unison with the pounding of his feet.

Manning feels his second wind, the renewed burst of energy known to all runners. His shoes seem to glide at a microdistance above the pavement. His throat begins to burn. Every muscle, every tendon, works and pulls and releases and pulls again like a machine thrown into high gear, straining beneath a sheath of taut, elastic skin. He feels the muscles of his calves and thighs bulging. The light-headed euphoria of overbreathing reminds Manning that he has always found something vaguely erotic about running, about the confusion of pleasure and pain.

Did it start in high school, with the sights and smells of the locker room, or did an unspoken fascination take root in his subconscious long before then, during those misty prepubescent years of youth? Is it possible to explain the pleasure derived from the sight of a man's *ankles*, the tick of white laces slapping his shoes?

Can those old preoccupations (preoccupations he has never knowingly pondered, for they would surely seem ludicrous, even embarrassing, if his mind would allow such questions to gel, to take on the rubbery yet distinct form of words that are actively thought) explain the indifference that has marked his sporadic intimacy with women?

His sexual history, the history that can be recalled as actual events, did not begin until college—his sophomore year—when he knew he could no longer make the excuse, to himself or to others (particularly his mother), that he was "busy." The pressure to lose his virginity in those days of liberation was intense, so he lost it. Mission accomplished.

She was pretty and loving, sufficiently more experienced than he. He performed just fine—nothing traumatic befell him—and the physical release was admittedly pleasurable. But it was not the stuff of dreams, not the culminating end-all event he'd been led to expect. And it never would be. Subsequent couplings were equally ho-hum, even with Roxanne, who was easily the most feisty and energetic of his partners.

So he never got much involved. He's been content to be wed to his career, a commitment that has brought many rewards. Earlier, in college, he preferred to concentrate on his studies, and that, too, had its rewards. That's how he explained things to his mother.

Then she died before he graduated. He grieved, of course. She was too young—lung cancer. But he felt relief (and he felt no guilt because of this) that he would no longer need to make excuses to her regarding the direction of his life. At her burial, he also felt relieved that issues of intimacy were never discussed with his father, who died when Manning was three.

An uncle, his mother's brother from Wisconsin, a wealthy printer, was at his mother's funeral. Manning hadn't seen him for—how long?—at least ten years. His uncle kissed him on the lips once as a boy, then again at the funeral. Manning wondered, standing near his mother's grave, if the man was gay.

The sun has inched higher into the sky. Traffic on the Outer Drive is brisker now, and the path along the beach is filling in with bicycles, dog-walkers, and many more runners.

Far ahead through the crowd, Manning glimpses a couple running toward him. The guy is a few years younger than Manning; his girlfriend, younger still. Even at a distance, they exude an air of vitality and playfulness that sets them apart from the others trudging by. The guy has tousled blond hair, teeth that flash white as he laughs at something. He's well muscled everywhere, as is the girl; their spandex running togs are both skimpy and flattering.

Handsome couple, Manning tells himself. I'll bet they work out together.

"Morning!" says the girl as the couple draws near.

Manning returns the greeting as they whisk by. Glancing over his shoulder for another look, he realizes with dismay that his gaze has been fixed squarely on the guy.

Sunday, October 4

89 days till deadline

Many miles away, at six in the morning, the heat is already oppressive. Incense fills the air. The pungency of burning spices and gums wafts through the little church and hangs as a blue-gray cloud above the heads of the faithful, slowly shifting strata with the meager whiffs of air admitted through ventilating windows cranked wide at the base of each stained-glass Gothic arch.

October sometimes brings relief, but not today. The early sun pierces the eastern windows, making brilliant the colored shards of martyrs' blood and fishermen's robes. The filtered light seems to magnify the heat rather than quell it, causing both flesh and clothing to stick to the varnished pews. Many in the congregation choose to kneel rather than make contact with the benches. The combination of heat and the midnight communion-fast can cause the less hardy to faint during the Sunday service, but that prospect is least likely at the first Mass of the day, so the church will be filled.

Four altar boys—ruddy-faced Indian brothers garbed in scarlet cassocks and fine lace surplices—busy themselves in the sanctuary, preparing for High Mass. They light six candles at the main altar and many more at the side altar that enshrines a painted statue of the Virgin Mary. Wide-eyed, a child in the congregation points toward the waves of heat that rise from the candles and cause the plaster saint to hula on her pedestal.

From its cramped loft, the choir sings Gregorian chants *a capella*. The climate, joined by what the members of the little parish term "the dark years of neglect," has rendered the organ irreparably silent.

The congregation is now gathered, all facing reverently forward. Though they don't look like rebels, they are, united in purpose from many walks of life. Most are either quite old or very young. This place was chosen as a new home by the older members of the community because it represents something familiar, something that was once part of their lives, but lost. To the young, this place represents something they never knew; they yearn for the "purity" of older ways, finding it more compatible with the idealism of youth. Conspicuously absent from the crowd are the middle-aged, the mainstream, the people who shape and inhabit the world at large.

There is a girl of about twenty with long straight hair. Beaming a smile that makes her plain face pretty, she struggles with an infant who is annoyed by the heat.

An old black man kneels near the back of the church. He has a proud bearing that belies the poverty suggested by his worn but spotless clothes. He fingers a rosary, its beads clicking against the slick surface of the pew in front of him.

There is an Indian woman with a weathered face topped by a braided crown of jet-black hair. She keeps a stern eye on three children who sit silently, wagging their legs.

A young man kneels piously with his wife sitting next to him. He is bookish-looking with freckles and wire-rimmed glasses. Sunken cheeks and a long horsey chin amplify his humorless features. He prays to a wrathful God.

His wife, by contrast, seems almost amused by his sobriety, harboring secrets about him that these other people could never guess. He brought her to this place, and she has maintained a girlish cheerfulness—while anyone else might have left him.

In a pew near the front of the church, center aisle, is a woman who neither kneels nor prays, but sits reading a popular novel, waiting for the service to begin.

The choir stops.

Silence is broken by the bell that hangs in the doorway from the sacristy to the sanctuary. The first of the altar boys has pulled its tasseled cord once, sharply, and the clang brings the congregation to their feet. An odd noise fills the church—the sound of damp clothing peeled from the pews.

The little procession approaches the altar. Behind the four boys walks the priest, a man in his late fifties, perhaps sixty. The zeal that flashes in his blue eyes reflects a lifelong dedication to his calling. The same dedication, though, has worsened the toll of his years, and the flash of his eyes is tempered with an aging milkiness. His hair is still a radiant gold, touched with lighter strands of gray and white. He wears it long and full, revealing a streak of vanity in his austere mien. The effect of his hair is all the more pronounced against the lavish brocade of the chasuble he wears. His walk seems too slow, even for the stately procession; the boys measure their steps carefully so as not to leave him behind.

The five now stand at the foot of the stairs that lead to the altar. They genuflect, the priest with more effort than the boys, then recite the opening dialogue of the liturgy, bowing in turn, striking their breasts as they confess their mortal weaknesses.

The priest mounts the stairs and opens the huge leather-bound altar missal. He turns to face the people, stretching out his arms in a gesture suggesting the crucified Christ. *"Dominos vobiscum,"* The Lord be with you, he sings in a monotone.

The liturgy continues with the expected regularity of an ancient, never-changing rite, the Tridentine rite. The priest turns to invite the congregation to pray at intervals specified by the rubrics, the red print, of the missal. Each time he turns, his face is more heavily beaded with sweat. After reading the Epistle and Gospel in Latin, the priest descends the stairs and approaches the pulpit. While the people seat themselves to hear his comments, he studies the faces that stare back at him.

A pearl of sweat glistens at the tip of his nose. It hangs there for interminable seconds, then drops. The people watch as another shimmering bead begins to form in its place. The priest deigns neither to mop his brow nor to brush the tiny salt-pool from his page of handwritten notes. Minuscule veins of blue ink grow at the edge of the pool.

The lady with the novel flaps a silk fan. She is the only one present to take action against the heat; the others suffer passively, racking up purgatorial credits in some celestial ledger. She eyes the priest with a wry smile. Come on, Father, she thinks. You're losing your audience. Better get on with it.

"My brothers and sisters," he finally says. His voice is soothing and firm. "Let us today rededicate ourselves to the beliefs, the ideals, the *truths* that we professed when we founded this community. Ever mindful of the Blessed Virgin Mary, who was assumed into heaven—taken there bodily by her Son, our Savior—we rededicate ourselves to the truths that inspired us to name our community Assumption, a name that serves to remind us of what the world has lost, of what *we* have found.

"We have come to this place for many reasons, but the shared event that unites us was a crisis of faith—a crisis generated by change, heretical change, over which we had no control. Now they wring their hands and preach against the dangers of schism, but it is they, not we, who have pushed this confrontation to the brink. Each of us present has been touched by the spirit of the Lord in a special way, and now we are reborn to that which was so carelessly lost.

"For us, then, a major battle in the fight for personal salvation has already been won. We have known God's saving grace, and we have seen His light. Like Christ the good shepherd, we must now be mindful of our brothers and sisters who have gone astray, of the forces that have misguided them, and of their dire need of our prayers.

"Let us, then, remember in our prayers the troubled Church of Rome, now riddled with the heresies of change and doctrinal inconsistency. Let us pray that the Church Universal may return to the truths of which it was once sole guardian, that the people whom God has called to be His own may once again know the peace and unity that faith alone can bring.

"Faith. It is faith alone that binds us. And it is on our faith alone that we shall one day be judged.

"My friends, I want to relate to you an incident that took place last year as I lay somewhere in that netherworld between life and death. The heart attack, as you know, was a mild one. It was the lengthy trip to the hospital, the lack of immediate care, that complicated my misfortune. Serious damage was done to the heart, I am told, and it is unlikely that I could survive another attack. The doctors presumed that I would not come back to you, that life in Assumption was a hardship I would dare not risk. When I informed them of my intention to the contrary, they said, 'But Father McMullen, you must slow down. Your heart has sent a message to your body.' So I told them, 'Then my soul will send a message to my heart.' And that message is: Faith is the power that makes us whole."

He pauses for a moment, then concludes, "My dear friends, I shall burden you with no more of my prolixity today—it is far too warm. May the blessing of almighty God descend upon all of you and remain with you always."

Father James McMullen then returns to the altar and performs the rite of sacrifice that symbolically reenacts Christ's death. The liturgy proceeds steadily toward the solemn climax of consecration, the moment at which the sacramental bread and wine are transformed for the faithful into the body and blood of Christ. It is the moment of the Mass for which Father McMullen was ordained, the focus of all his priestly powers.

It is the moment at which he will summon the physical presence of God.

It is also the moment at which he will be haunted by a recurring, unshakable memory.

He bows low over the chalice. *"Hic est enim calix sanguinis mei,"* This is the cup of My blood, he whispers. As he genuflects in adoration, an altar boy rings the tiny silver consecration bell. But as the priest peers into the golden goblet of wine-turned-blood, he hears another bell—a louder one, an alarm—and sees himself many years ago rushing down the long hall past a row of identical doors till he reaches the one he knows he must open. He grips the knob with fingers colder than the brass itself, then sees inside the room.

White sheets fall to the floor from the steel-framed bed, drenched with the still-warm blood of the boy who lies there, his eyes frozen wide with terror, his throat gaping open, savagely slashed.

Monday, October 5

88 days till deadline

By Monday morning, the long autumn rains have settled over the Midwest. Manning drives north on Sheridan Road toward the Carter estate in Bluff Shores. The pavement glistens black beneath dense trees, their wet foliage hanging low against a formless sky.

Something Italian—something frivolous and operatic—warbles from the radio and fills the car's chilly interior, a contrast that Manning finds more irritating than uplifting. The motors of the windshield wipers whir with each swipe of the blades, syncopated with the tempo of the music. Mercifully, the aria climaxes and dies.

"Good morning, friends and neighbors, wherever you are . . ." It is the drawling radio voice of Bud Stirkham, a local commentator cut from the same philosophical cloth as Humphrey Hasting. In contrast to Hasting's eloquently affected manner, though, Stirkham's gravelly style is that of a down-home aw-shucks man of the people.

". . . and if the crisis in Ethiopia isn't enough to shake your faith in *international* diplomacy, just look at the antics of officials here at home in their clumsy efforts to snag airline heiress Helena Carter's killer. This spirit of apathy and indifference extends even to the *Chicago Journal*, which historically prides itself as watchdog of the public interest . . ."

"Ranting demagogue," Manning mutters to the radio as he switches it off. Shaking his head as if to clear it of Stirkham's words, he slows the car at an intersection, peering through the rain at a street sign. He turns off Sheridan Road onto a quiet thoroughfare that leads him past unmarked roads to the vast, secluded estates perched on the lakefront.

Manning slows the car as it approaches a driveway marked by a white rail fence and a country mailbox labeled with block letters: CARTER. Turning onto the winding drive, he is struck by how flawlessly everything is maintained—fencing, ornamental trees, beds of fall flowers. Things have certainly been kept in order, as if for Helena Carter's imminent return. Rounding a curve of the wooded drive, he finds himself in view of the house, the lake, and a widespread freshly mowed lawn that glows electric green against the blur of a dark sky.

Parking near the front of the house, Manning checks the pockets of his trench coat for pen and notebook before stepping out into the rain. He ducks into his collar, dashes to the door, and rings the bell. As he waits, the lake roils beyond.

When the heavy enameled door at last cracks open, a stooped man in his sixties peers out for a moment, then swings the door wide, saying, "Good morning, Mr. Manning. We've been expecting you."

Manning steps into the checkered-tile entry hall and removes his coat. He fumbles in the pockets for his pen and steno book, studying the little man as they exchange small talk. A uniformed butler would fit this setting to a tee, but the man is dressed in freshly pressed work clothes—chambray shirt and wash pants. His manner is friendly and homey, not the least pretentious. Then Manning remembers. "You're Arthur Mendel," he tells the man. This is the nefarious houseman, the cunning majordomo whom Humphrey Hasting seems determined to bring to justice.

"I'm flattered that you remember," says Arthur. "It's been nearly seven years. And the day you were here, the day after Mrs. Carter disappeared, things were a bit hectic." Chuckling at his own understatement, he takes Manning's coat and leads him through the house, saying, "Miss O'Connor was happy to get your call. She's waiting for you in the parlor." Arthur opens a paneled walnut door to let Manning pass, closing it behind him.

The room is intimate in scale, designed for small groups of guests. Comfortable stuffed furniture faces a hickory fire framed by a mantel of coral-streaked marble. On a low table before it, a silver coffee service reflects the flames. Two cups and saucers flank a tray of pastries.

"I didn't know if you'd have eaten," says a voice, its speaker hidden by the chintz-covered wings of a plump chair. "I get the impression that young people don't bother with breakfast." Margaret O'Connor, sister of the missing heiress, rises to face her visitor, offering her hand as he steps forward. She is a small woman, tastefully dressed—perhaps too formally for the early hour. Her hair has been freshly, primly coiffed, with no attempt to hide the gray that now ousts the brown.

"You're too kind, Miss O'Connor," Manning tells her, taking her hand.

"Won't you please call me Margaret, Mr. Manning? I find 'Miss' a touch unbecoming for a woman of my age." She winks at him.

By Manning's calculation, she is only forty-eight years old, eight years younger than her sister, but she does, in truth, exude a spinsterly air. He is charmed by her candor. "I'd be delighted, Margaret. Please call me Mark."

"I'd like that *very* much," she answers, patting his hand. "May I offer you anything?"

"Just coffee, thank you."

They settle themselves, she serves, and they relax for a moment before beginning the interview. "Will you mind if I take a few notes?" Manning asks, opening his book.

She dismisses the question with a wave of her hand. "Of course not. That's why you're here."

A cat appears from around the base of Manning's chair, brushing the length of its body along his cuff. Its huge gold almond-shaped eyes look up at him; Manning's green eyes stare back at the animal. The cat's dense brown fur seems vibrantly orange in the glow of the fire. Each hair is tipped with darker shades of brown or black, like the coat of a wild animal. Its lithe body, long front legs, and big tufted ears give the cat a regal, hieroglyphic bearing. It cocks its head and emits a quiet, inquisitive meow.

"That's the cat," says Manning, transfixed by the animal's gaze.

"What cat, Mark?"

"The cat in the magazine with your sister—when they won the big award."

"Heavens no," Margaret tells him with a laugh. "That was this cat's grandfather. He's gone. This is Fred."

"Fred?" he asks with a tone suggesting he expected something more exotic. He leans forward and extends a hand to stroke the cat's head. Fred nuzzles forward, erupting into a well-tuned purr. At that moment, a second cat appears from behind the chair.

"And who's this?" Manning asks.

"Ethel."

"Married?"

"No," says Margaret, feigning shock. "They're brother and sister!"

They both laugh heartily while Fred and Ethel explore Manning's shoes. Finding little worth sniffing, the cats turn their tails to Manning and drop themselves in front of the fire, Fred sprawling, Ethel curled.

"They're beautiful," says Manning. "I've never seen an Abyssinian—at least not until last week when I saw that magazine picture."

"I'm not surprised," she tells him. "Abyssinians are still rare. The breeding is controlled, and the litters are small."

Manning sips his coffee. A burning log shifts in the grate and pops, spraying sparks, breaking a momentary lull. Manning tells Margaret, "Your home is in a much calmer state than when I last saw it, the day after the disappearance."

"Oh, I remember it well. Such a commotion it was," she tells him, fluttering both hands. *"I* was in something of a state that day. What with the shock and the uncertainty and the police and the lawyers and *reporters*—no offense, Mark, but it *was* an ordeal." She thinks for a moment, then adds, "You, however, were very considerate." She reaches over and pats his knee.

"I'm glad to hear that I behaved myself." He finishes his coffee and sets the cup on the table. "Tell me, Margaret. It's been nearly seven years since Helena disappeared. Surely you've given the mystery a lot of thought. Do you have any idea what may have happened?"

She sighs demurely, shaking her head. "I'm afraid I don't. So many people seem so sure that Helen is dead, sometimes I almost wish I could believe that—'closure,' you know. But I simply can't imagine why anyone would want to harm Helen. Sure, there's the money"—she gestures vacantly at their surroundings—"but it hasn't done anyone any good."

"If she's not dead, where do you think she might be?"

"I don't have any idea at all. Not anymore." She pauses in thought. "I used to have a . . . *theory*, but it was only an empty hunch."

"What was it?"

"It seems silly now. I'd prefer that you not write about this."

Manning sets his pen and notebook on the table.

Margaret tells him, "I'm sure you already know that Helen was very religious. I found it amazing—sort of inconsistent—that she could combine her staunch faith with so many worldly interests. Actually, I thought she took the whole church thing a bit *too* seriously, but that's not an opinion I felt I could express to her.

"We were, of course, brought up Catholic. Papa was a railroad man—a hard worker and a good looker and a pretty good drinker too. All told, he was a fine father. He always showed real love and affection for Mama, Helen, and me. But he wanted a big family. After the twins were gone, Mama just put her foot down and said she was through trying. Well, that never set well with Papa, and we always sensed that he felt sort of cheated. We were comfortable enough, living down near the rail yards, but never what you'd call 'well off.' I think he hoped that another child—a son—might grow up to be a doctor or a professor or maybe a tycoon, and that would have made him the happiest man around."

She pauses a moment, picks up her coffee cup, then returns it to the table without drinking. She tells Manning, "He seemed to take comfort in the church. It was a lasting force of goodness in his life, as it had been for *his* father when he came over from Ireland. He took the church much more seriously than Mama, which Helen and I found kind of strange because it was just the opposite in all our friends' families.

"As we were growing up, Mama used to sit down with Helen and me after school sometimes, before Papa got home. She'd explain things to us—woman things, you know. She'd put on a big grin and tell us that even though Papa wanted a rich, successful son, there was no reason he couldn't have rich, successful daughters. She'd explain how hard it was for a woman to make any kind of business success out of herself—and in those days, it was true. But then she leaned real close to tell us a secret. Helen and

I listened with eyes as big as saucers while she told us how we *could* be successful in a way that would do Papa proud. Pretty little girls like us, she said, should have no problem going out and finding a couple of nice, rich husbands. Helen and I giggled and bit our knuckles, it all sounded so naughty."

She picks up the cup again, sips from it, then holds it in her lap, coddling it with both hands. "Well, I don't have to tell you that Helen managed to go out and do exactly what Mama said. I tried, too, but was never so lucky. When Helen found Ridgely Carter, Mama told her that she should call herself *Helena* because it sounded more sophisticated. Papa died before the wedding. Helen moved out when she married, of course, so I ended up staying home with Mama. Money wasn't a problem. We had Papa's railroad pension, and Helen was always generous when any special need came up. Then Mama died. That was the end of the pension. I was uneducated, unemployed, and—at thirty, I assumed—forever single."

Margaret returns her cup to the table, setting it in its saucer with a decisive clank. "So Helen and Ridgely took me in. They were always sweet about it, but I couldn't help feeling that I had invaded their home. 'Nonsense,' Ridgely used to tell me, 'with all the guests and hired help we have around here, we'll hardly even notice another face in the halls.' And he was right. Those were good years, while Ridgely was alive. Helen married him for his money—make no mistake about that—but he loved her from the start, and her love for him grew and grew as the years went by. It was a happy home, *mostly*, in spite of that nasty episode with Arthur's gambling. Ridgely was wonderful, always. He tried to teach us all something about managing money. It's a good thing he did—when he died, Helen got everything.

"She'd been religious all her life, and Ridgely's death seemed to boost her zeal. It's funny. Mama always said we had to marry rich—and Helen did. Papa always said we had to keep our faith— and Helen did. I don't know if Helen was accommodating, clever, or just plain obedient. She *was* clever, smart as a whip, got top marks in school. I was a little awed by her; it seems I've always lived in her shadow. She's eight years older than me, and when you're a child, that's a big difference. She was kind of a second

Mama. Now that she's gone, it's left to me to look after her house and take care of her cats."

She has spoken softly, without rancor, making flat observations. Her reminiscing has been a bittersweet amusement on this dark, wet morning in front of the fire. "Lord, how I can babble," she says. "That's what you get for asking me to start talking." She pours more coffee.

Manning says, "It was fascinating. But, Margaret . . ." He is reluctant to tell her that the point of their discussion has slipped her mind. "You said that you once had a theory about where your sister might be."

She places her fingers over her mouth, eyes popping, then laughs. "I knew I was driving at *something*. After Ridgely died, Helen got involved with our local parish, Saint Jerome's. She struck up a friendship with our pastor, Father Matthew Carey—such a handsome young priest. Helen joined several church committees and ended up on the parish council. She and Father Carey really liked each other—you could tell from the way they had fun together, at first—but more and more they found themselves at odds.

"It started with minor issues that came up at council meetings, and eventually their differences grew to the point where Helen referred to herself as the 'loyal opposition.' I'm not sure what it was all about—her church activities weren't of much interest to me—but it had something to do with all the changes brought on by the Vatican Council in the sixties. I got the impression that she'd have preferred for them to keep the Church the way she knew it as a girl."

The pace of Margaret's speech quickens as she leans toward Manning to tell him, "Helen mentioned several times—and it was unusual because we rarely discussed religion—some sort of movement in the Catholic Church to go back to the old ways. There's a European bishop or cardinal who's leading the movement—he's been in the news from time to time. And there's a little community, a *town*, somewhere in the West where these people go to live and to have the Church the way they want it.

"I never thought Helen was so serious about her beliefs that she would consider going to such a place, but after she disappeared, I wasn't so sure. So I talked to Father Carey about it, and he said that the same idea had crossed his mind. He told me that he once knew the priest who eventually became leader of this little town, and he offered to write to see what he could learn. A couple of weeks later, he phoned me to say he received a letter from the other priest. There was no one out there who could be Helen."

Margaret leans back in her chair, concluding, "And that was the end of my theory, Mark. It was only a hunch."

"Would you mind," Manning asks, "if I talked to Father Carey myself?"

"Of course not. If you think there's any chance he could lead you to Helen, by all means, go see him. He's really very nice." She studies Manning curiously for a moment, then adds, "I think you two will like each other."

He jots down the names of the priest and the parish, then says, "I know you've been asked these questions many times, but could you recall for me exactly what happened when your sister disappeared? When did you realize she was gone? How did you know she was missing?"

Margaret O'Connor nestles farther into her chair, seemingly swallowed by its upholstery. Wringing her hands, she says, "It was New Year's Day and horribly cold. The morning began as usual. I took a warm bath, then dressed and went down to the kitchen to join Helen for coffee. We usually met there around seven o'clock, but it was later that morning because we'd stayed up the night before to see in the New Year. Helen wasn't there yet, so I started the coffee and then went to the basement to feed the cats—the new cattery was still being built back then, and the cats were kept downstairs. While making the rounds, I noticed that Abe was missing. Abe is the cat you saw in the magazine; he was Helen's prime stud, the best breeding stock in the country. So I got a little panicky . . ."

"Excuse me, Margaret, but how did you know Abe was missing? Couldn't he have been anywhere in the house?"

"Oh no, Mark. Fred and Ethel"—she gestures toward the cats lying by the fire—"are pets. We've always kept one or two cats as altered house pets. The breeding stock, the show cats, are kept in the cattery. They never leave their cages, except to breed or to show. But Abe was gone."

"How much was Abe worth?"

"Heavens, you don't *sell* a cat like Abe."

"But if you *had* to sell him for some reason, how much would you expect to get? Roughly."

"Many thousands of dollars, certainly. Abe had recently been judged the finest Abyssinian in the country—possibly the world. He was priceless. Then I noticed Eve's cage empty too."

"Eve?" he asks, guessing the answer.

"Eve was Helen's prime queen."

"Worth about the same as Abe?"

"Almost. Studs are generally more valuable."

Manning is taking notes so quickly now, his writing is reduced to a scribble. More to himself than to the woman, he says, "We all knew that a wealthy heiress had disappeared and that a couple of cats were missing with her, but no one understood just 'who' those cats were."

Margaret continues, "So I ran upstairs to tell Helen. I stood at her door, pounding on it and shouting that something terrible had happened. Finally, I opened the door, not knowing what to expect, afraid of what I might find." She stares into an indefinite space beyond Manning's shoulder.

"What did you find?" he asks softly.

She looks at him as though snapping out of a trance. "Nothing," she says with a shrug. "Helen wasn't there. Her room was in order. I glanced through her closets, but nothing seemed to be missing."

"What did you assume, then, about the cats and your sister?"

"I assumed they were together," she tells him, stating the obvious conclusion. "It was unusual, but nothing worth phoning the police about—not yet. A bit later, Arthur came to the house for his duties."

"Your houseman, Arthur Mendel?"

"He's been with the Carter family forever, and now he's the only permanent staff left on the estate. He lives in quarters near the cattery, where the old stable used to be. When he came to the house that morning, I told him about Helen and the two cats. He said he hadn't driven Helen anywhere, and as we talked, we both got worried. By evening, Helen still wasn't back, so we decided to call the police if we didn't hear from her by midnight.

And that's what we did. You know the rest; you were here with the others the next day."

Manning asks, "Did the police question you about the cats?"

"Not much. I told them the cats were missing, but I didn't want to make too much of a fuss over it—we were all concerned about *Helen*, and it seemed trivial to dwell on the cats. Do you think that makes any difference?"

Manning's pen jabs the page with a period at the end of a note. "I'm not sure. Any new angle is worth exploring." He flips a fresh page open. "Margaret, may I ask a personal question about your sister? Did Helen dye her hair? A friend who saw the magazine picture said that it looked as if she used a henna rinse. The color seemed to match Abe."

Margaret chuckles, raising one brow confidentially. "Your friend is very observant. Yes, Helen used a henna rinse, trying to match the rich Abyssinian hue. I suppose it was part vanity— Helen's hair was grayer than mine," she says, dabbing at her temples with her fingers. "But there was more to it than that. Henna has been used as a hair color for a long, long time. Cleopatra used it. And I'm sure you've noticed how the Abyssinian resembles the sacred cat of ancient Egypt. Helen was intrigued by that connection. She felt it might be useful in her campaigns."

"What campaigns?" asks Manning.

"'Campaigning' is what they call touring a cat for the top national awards. It's a full-time job, involving lots of time, travel, money, and—what do they call it?—public relations. I guess you'd say that Helen's henna hair was a gimmick."

Manning nods, finishes a note, then asks, "After the initial shock of your sister's disappearance wore off, were you able to determine if anything other than the cats was missing, like clothes or money? What I'm getting at is this: Do you think she could have taken enough with her to keep her comfortable for this long?"

"Helen has closet after closet of clothes. I'm not *sure* if anything is missing, but it's possible. There were plenty of jewels and furs, too; Ridgely loved to lavish her with beautiful things. But valuables like that were catalogued and put in safe deposit shortly after she disappeared. As far as money is concerned, I never knew much about her finances—investments, savings, and such—we didn't need to talk about money. You could ask Jerry Klein about it. He runs CarterAir and looks after the estate."

Manning has dutifully recorded her comments. He caps his pen and is about to slip it into his pocket when something occurs to him. "One more thing, Margaret. When you were telling me about growing up with Helen, you made some reference to 'the twins.' Who were you talking about?"

"Our brothers. We had a pair of twin brothers."

"You *did?*" Manning riffles through his notes, confirming that this detail has escaped him. "In all the time I've been covering this story, I've never heard anything about brothers."

"I'd be surprised if you had," she tells him. "They've been gone for over forty years. They went away to school, and something bad happened—I don't know what—I was too young to understand. One of them died, and the other disappeared. The boys were a few years older than Helen, and I was quite young when it all happened."

"What were their names?" asks Manning.

"I honestly don't remember. Isn't that remarkable? I was very young when they were still at home, and they were *never* discussed afterward."

On his pad, Manning notes in the margin: *Repressed memories. Heavy denial.*

Margaret adds, "My single vivid recollection of them still gives me the chills. One of the boys was interested in Indian lore and had a hatchet with a stone blade that he treasured above all other possessions. One day, Helen and I were playing with him in a vacant lot behind the house. He caught a garden snake, which terrified me enough. Then, with his hatchet, *he chopped off its head.* It made me sick—literally. Mama couldn't get the bile stains out of my dress, so she threw it away. It had pictures of kittens and puppies on it. I loved that little dress—it was my favorite."

Her story has ended. She lapses into a long silence, preoccupied with her thoughts of the past, thoughts that have not even scratched her consciousness for many years. She has said enough.

Quietly, Manning caps his pen, closes his notebook, and reaches down to the floor to rub one of the cats behind its ears. Fred gazes up at Manning with an expression that looks like an appreciative grin, then breaks into a rumbling purr. Ethel interrupts her nap long enough to open her eyes a slit, wondering what has roused Fred.

Manning rises. "Don't get up," he tells Margaret. "I've taken enough of your time today, and I truly appreciate the information you've shared with me. You've been most helpful." He steps to her chair and clasps one of her hands with both of his. "I'll see myself out, Margaret. Thanks again."

He crosses the room, opens the door, and glances back before leaving. Margaret sits perfectly still, facing the fireplace, eyes fixed on the flames, as if trying to discern some meaning from their ethereal, random dance.

In the hall, Arthur Mendel awaits Manning with his trench coat. "You won't need to wear this home," he says. "The rain has finally stopped."

"Thank you, Arthur," says Manning, taking the coat. "I wonder if you'd have time to walk me out to the car. Miss O'Connor mentioned that there's a separate cattery building on the grounds. Could you show me where it is?"

"I'd be delighted," Arthur tells him, ushering him out the front door. They walk past Manning's car to the side of the house, and Arthur points to a low L-shaped building on a bluff at the rear of the estate. The sky has lightened some, and whitecaps roll landward from the heaving gray surface of the lake. Arthur asks, "Would you like to stroll back there for a closer look?"

"Sure," says Manning.

Arthur leads the way along a flagstone path. Though the rain has stopped, a raw wind drives mist from the lake, and Manning struggles to don the coat he carried, its flapping folds of khaki tamed as he cinches the belt with a taut knot. Approaching the building, Arthur says, "Care to look inside?"

"Not today, thanks," says Manning, huddling under the broad eaves at the juncture of the building's two wings. "Actually, I just wanted to talk with you privately, Arthur. May I ask you a few questions?"

"Certainly." The older man's quick response reveals that he's flattered by the famed reporter's attention.

Manning tells him, "I hope this won't embarrass you, and I raise the issue only because there are people who might construe it as being related to Mrs. Carter's disappearance."

With a tone now colored by wariness, Arthur responds, "Yes?"

"During my conversation with Miss O'Connor this morning, she mentioned something that surprised me. She said that after she came to live here with Mr. Carter and her sister, the estate proved to be a happy home, except for a 'nasty episode with Arthur's gambling' . . ."

"What!" says Arthur, stepping backward. His expression suggests betrayal. "I can't *believe* she'd mention that, not after the way she threw the household into a tizzy with *her* loose ways. Don't let her kid you, Mr. Manning. She may come across as Miss Prim-and-Proper, but let me tell you . . ."

He stops. He's said too much. He buries his mouth in his hands, regains his composure, then forces a smile and tells Manning, "I'm sorry. That was inappropriate—I hope you'll kindly disregard those remarks. What Miss O'Connor told you is quite correct."

"Did the gambling problems relate to the horses?"

"I'm afraid so, yes. As you may know, Mr. Carter enjoyed horses and maintained a stable that I looked after—it was right here, in fact, before the cattery was built. He never raced them, but enjoyed the track, and we both had a passing acquaintance with a lot of pros out there—jockeys, trainers, and such. Mr. Carter placed an occasional bet—it was the social thing to do— but *I* got a little too deep in it. I lost more than I won, and I borrowed from the wrong people. Some threats were made, and it came to Mr. Carter's attention, which scared me more than the threats. But he was always a perfect gentleman, and he proved to be my best friend."

"What did he do?" Manning asks.

The mist has collected in Arthur's hair, streamed to his brows, and now drips down his cheeks. There may be tears too—Manning isn't sure. Arthur smiles through the water on his face, saying, "Ridgely Carter paid off my debts, suggested I stay away from the track, and never mentioned it again. I never bet on another horse, and I don't think he did either."

Manning turns from Arthur. Pondering the horizon over the lake, he asks him, "Do you know there's a . . . 'notion' going around that implicates you in Mrs. Carter's disappearance?"

"I hear things—like everybody else."

Manning turns to him. "This horse business won't look good,

Arthur. It *doesn't* look good. It's news to me, and I don't know what to make of it."

Arthur touches Manning's arm. "It doesn't mean *anything*," he assures him. "It happened. It wasn't very nice. But then it was *over*. I lost all interest in racing. Mr. Carter didn't even seem to care about his *own* horses after that. Later, after he died, Mrs. Carter agreed with me that there was no point in maintaining a stable on the property. So we had it torn down. Mrs. Carter wanted to use the space for her cattery. It was under construction when she disappeared. And here it stands." Arthur gestures with both hands toward the sturdy foundation of the building.

Manning pauses to think, checks his watch, then says, "Okay, Arthur. I need to get back to the city. Thanks so much."

"My pleasure, Mr. Manning. If I can help in any way, you know where to find me."

They shake hands and step out from under the eaves, beginning their trek to Manning's car. They have ventured only a few yards from the cattery when Manning glances back for another look at it. The longer of its two wings stands where the stable must have been, making use of the old brick footings. The shorter wing, however, was built atop a massive new foundation of concrete.

Wednesday, October 7

86 days till deadline

Manning is driving north again from Chicago to Bluff Shores. When he phoned Father Matthew Carey yesterday to schedule an interview, the priest told him that he would be away from the parish most of Wednesday, but Manning was welcome to come talk awhile after the six-thirty Mass.

Manning glances at the dashboard clock just as it flashes *7:00 AM.* Having pulled himself out of bed earlier than usual today, he doesn't feel quite awake. He hasn't even turned on the radio, riding in silence, immersed in uneasy thoughts. He hasn't set foot in a church for years, except in the line of duty—covering protests, for instance, or politicians' funerals.

He turns onto Saint Jerome's parish property. The pine-flanked entry reminds him more of a country club than a church. In the distance he can see the main building. It is round—a mammoth cylinder of light-colored brick with a shallow, conical roof that peaks not with a steeple but with a skylight. Its only "windows" are colored glass blocks randomly piercing the walls.

Local critics have likened the building to a host of other structures ranging from a bullring to a nuclear reactor. Researching the parish in the *Journal*'s morgue yesterday, Manning learned that the church was built several years after the closing of the Second Vatican Council, not because the old building needed replacement, but simply because the wealthy parishioners wanted to erect an edifice better suited to the new modes of worship decreed by their changing church.

Manning drives past the school, the convent, the rectory—all of more traditional design than the church—and pulls his car into the parking lot near the hulking architectural oddity. Only a few other cars are parked there, perhaps a dozen, all in prime spaces, their bumpers almost touching the building. He reflexively checks his pockets for his notebook and Mont Blanc, then gets out of the car.

The October monsoon has broken, if only briefly, and Manning is able to walk at leisure, without darting for cover. His cordovan oxfords crunch the still-wet gravel. Hungry unseen birds gab noisily from the trees in the belated cloud-clogged dawn.

As Manning enters the building's vestibule, an enormous sculpted bronze door closes silently behind him, hushing the birds. A ventilating system whispers from nowhere, and the carpeting underfoot heightens the pervasive sense of quiet. Pulling open one of the glass doors etched with an abstraction of the Trinity, he steps into the church proper. The vaulted room yawns before him as if to suck him toward its center, where a monolithic slab of black marble serves as the altar. The overall effect is impressively dramatic, and Manning settles into a rear pew near the door to study the church's interior while waiting for the service to end.

Manning tries to remember his last nonworking church visit. Ten years ago? No, fifteen? Can it possibly be that long since the gnawing suspicion became a firm reality for him? It has been *that long* since all the moral crises of his youth were washed clean. Suddenly gone were all the ethical dilemmas and doctrinal controversies and denominational nitpicking, all the guilt and doubts and *complications* that had cluttered his life. Years and years have passed since the realization formed in his brain and finally screamed to him with the voice of reason and logic and common sense—the voice that *would be heard*—that he simply no longer could believe in the existence of God.

He's been *free* that long. Why, he wonders, did it not happen sooner? Santa Claus died for him when he was six. The unwelcome knowledge that the benevolent old giver of gifts was merely a myth came as a disappointment, of course, but he soon got over it, knowing even then, even that young, that a grasp of reality—seeing things the way they *are*, not simply as one would like them to be—was ultimately far more satisfying, more liberating than living a game, living a lie. Things *fit*.

If Santa died so painlessly when Manning was six, how did God manage to linger for another twenty years?

How'd He do it? He had the forces of indoctrination and the

momentum of blind faith on His side, that's how. When Manning was six, he was deemed old enough to share the winking truth of the fairy tale that is Santa; he was also deemed old enough for recruitment into the larger fantasy, the big one. Parochial school, first communion, altar boy, confirmation—he was set down a path that narrowed at every step. He was told by his mother, his teachers, and society at large that he would frolic in heaven if he believed, that he would burn in hell if he did not. Is it any wonder that his life was thwarted and ruled by mysticism for twenty years? The *miracle* is that he managed to see the light at all, that he managed to slough off the nonsense and to recognize the majesty and power of reason.

Manning glances at the long liturgical banners swaying in the currents of air that circulate through the rafters. This church looks so different from those he knew in his youth. Do they all look like this now?

His attention shifts to the service, which is nearing its end. Father Carey stands at the altar, vested in white. The congregation numbers less than twenty and is gathered in a circle around the altar with the priest. Manning guesses Father Carey's age to be near his own, around forty. True to Margaret O'Connor's description, he is indeed attractive, with curly brown hair and intense eyes of the same color. He has a commanding presence that seems to infatuate his parishioners. It was surely a coup for so young a man to be appointed pastor of a parish as large and affluent as Saint Jerome's, and it was probably he who convinced Helena Carter to include the church in her will. He is undoubtedly a favorite among the hierarchy, someone "to be watched," someone being groomed for bigger things. He's too polished, too slick, a manipulator, Manning tells himself.

Manning watches as Carey clasps both hands of each of the faithful during the rite of peace, as he distributes chunks of consecrated bread and passes an earthen chalice of wine, as he finally instructs his flock, "Go in peace to love and serve the Lord." As the people begin leaving the sanctuary and the priest retreats to the sacristy, Manning rises and ambles down the aisle toward the front row of pews.

A minute or two later, the priest appears again, dressed now in the traditional black suit and Roman collar. "Mark? Sorry to keep you waiting."

"Not at all, Father," Manning says, stepping forward to shake hands.

"Please—call me Matt," the priest tells him, his manner businesslike, yet warmly personal, his handshake sure and deliberate.

Manning wonders if the priest prolonged the handshake a moment longer than necessary. "Thanks, Matt. I appreciate your taking time to see me." They share a smile that seems to bond them, and Manning wonders if he has misjudged the man.

"I'm glad we could arrange it," Carey says while sitting in the front pew, motioning for Manning to join him. "It's been so long since Helena disappeared, we've all but given up hope. Lately, though, the papers are showing a renewed interest in the case. Tell me—are you on to something?"

"I don't know yet. That's why I'm here. May I ask a few questions—and take a few notes?" Manning opens his pad and unscrews the cap of his pen.

"Of course." With a chummy tone of understatement, he adds, "I understand you're under a bit of pressure from your publisher."

"That's right." Manning laughs, though a bit uncomfortably. He asks the priest, "How do you happen to know about that?"

"Just a coincidence. I was at a social function with Archbishop Benedict on Saturday, and he had been to dinner Friday night with Nathan Cain. They go way back together—committee work or something. Anyway, Mr. Cain told the archbishop about your ultimatum, and the archbishop told me."

Manning pauses, watching the priest, then asks flatly, "Really?"

"Yes." Father Carey laughs. "For heaven sake, Mark, it's not a *conspiracy*. People at that level of power and influence all know each other. In fact, the archbishop knew the Carters well—he played *golf* with Ridgely. Chances are, Nathan Cain did too."

Manning remembers the morgue photo of Cain with the Carters. He nods, deep in thought. Then he feels the priest's hand on his knee.

"Mark, I'd like to help you. But I can tell you from the outset that I have no idea what happened to Helena Carter. I'd be a wealthy man if I did."

"Do you care about wealth, Father?" asks Manning, pointedly using the clerical title.

"My remark was indiscreet, I admit. But since you ask—yes, I confess that certain earthly pleasures are highly appealing." He removes his hand from Manning's knee. "I hasten to add, though, that an interest in *money* is not necessarily contrary to my priestly calling. I'm a diocesan priest, Mark; I'm not a member of a religious order and have taken no vow of poverty. Wealth is not intrinsically evil. Indeed, much good can come from it." He gestures with both hands at the building that surrounds them, a testament to the benevolence of cash. "Does such an attitude bother you, hearing it from a priest?"

"Certainly not," Manning assures him.

"I only ask," the priest explains, "because it bothered Helena deeply. We'd become close friends, but the issue of money eventually drove us apart."

"So *that* was it," Manning says, underlining something in his notebook. "I talked to Helena's sister, Margaret, a couple of days ago, and she said that you and Helena had a falling-out."

"It's funny about money. After her husband died, her wealth began to prey on her—she didn't deserve her affluence, she married him for it, that kind of thing. It was during the course of some lengthy counseling sessions that the whole matter flared up. In an attempt to relieve her of these pointless anxieties, I confided in her my own materialistic leanings. She misinterpreted my remarks completely, and from that day forward I sensed her suspicion that I was after her legacy. It was very poor judgment on my part."

"It couldn't have done too much harm, Matt. Her will leaves the bulk of her fortune to the Archdiocese."

The priest stands and steps to the center of the sanctuary. "I was shocked to learn it. Yes, we had discussed the possibility of a major bequest—earlier." He places a hand on the altar. "But I swear by the God I serve, Mark, that I did not expect a dime for the Church—not after our money-talk. I was convinced that it would all go to The Society."

"What 'Society'? Margaret O'Connor told me that her sister had gotten interested in some conservative Catholic group. They sounded to me like a bunch of reactionaries."

"Precisely. They call themselves the Society for the Restoration of the Faith, but in church circles they're simply known as The Society. The movement's seeds were sewn back in the sixties at the Vatican Council itself. The whole upshot of Vatican II, of course, was *reform*." He whirls a hand above his head, indicating the bizarre architecture. "But there was a sizable faction of the council that wanted the church to remain unchanged. There were even those who wanted to return to earlier ways. The handwriting was on the wall, though, in favor of modernization, so most of the conservatives either stepped in line or just kept quiet. But not all of them."

Carey sits next to Manning again, explaining, "A tiny group spearheaded by the Belgian prelate, Marcel Cardinal L'Évêque, became increasingly vocal in the debates, declaring the council's proposed changes heretical—an extremely serious charge. But the council's momentum would not be stopped, and I imagine you're familiar with the direction of mainstream Catholicism since then."

"Generally," says Manning. "And L'Évêque?"

"He didn't stop. He's ancient now, but he vigorously heads an ultraconservative movement that's preaching schism. He's on a collision course with Rome, flirting with excommunication. But that would only make him a martyr to his cause, and I don't think Rome would risk it. So his numbers are growing. Slowly."

Manning rises, thinking, and strolls across the aisle to the next bank of pews. As a child, he was taught to genuflect whenever crossing the church's center, and even now he feels the subliminal tug of that training on his right knee—but he resists it. He turns to ask Father Carey, "How did Helena Carter get interested in all this?"

"There was a lot of publicity about the founding of a community in this country about ten years ago. The movement had been predominately European since its inception, so of little interest to the American church. The Society caused quite a furor, though, when it announced that it had generated enough interest—and secured sufficient funding, the source of which was never revealed—to acquire an abandoned mission town in the West. It would become their base of operation in America, reporting directly to L'Évêque. The community never really got off the ground, though, and it dropped out of the news entirely, even in church publications."

Manning sits in the nearest pew, writing in his notebook. Facing the priest across the aisle, he asks, "What do you know about the place?"

"Not much. It's called Assumption, a little town that was built in the desert somewhere in the Southwest—Arizona or New Mexico, I think—miles from any city. It's secluded, and they want to keep it that way. There's a church and a school and maybe a hundred residents at most. Their civic as well as moral leader is the pastor of the church, Father James McMullen. He's a fine man, sincere in his beliefs, though of course I feel he's gone off the deep end with them. It so happens that I took classes from him in theology and doctrinal history while I was in the seminary, so I knew him well. Years later, we were all shocked to learn that he was packing up and leaving to oversee the founding of this reactionary community in the desert. It all sounded so eerie, like a cult or some oddball sect."

Manning asks, "Helena Carter sympathized with The Society?"

Carey exhales audibly. He rises and approaches the altar again, telling the reporter, "I don't think she fully understood it as the anti-Rome doctrinal faction that it essentially is. Instead, she viewed it simply as the last stronghold of those sentimental aspects of Catholicism that many of us would like to hang on to. The Latin Mass, the meatless Fridays, the novenas and benedictions, stations of the cross, Saturdays in the confessional—all those things served to set us apart and, by doing that, to *define* us to *ourselves* in ways that were easily understood, guaranteeing salvation in no uncertain terms. That can be very comforting. Some of our people have never recovered from the loss."

"Was Helena one of those people?" asks Manning. "Did she seem inordinately anxious to return to the old ways? Do you think she'd be willing to run off and devote her life to the issue?"

"No," says the priest. He returns from the altar and stands near the pew where Manning sits. "Her preference for the old ways of the church never struck me as anything more than the wistful longings of a middle-aged widow who wanted to recapture part of the world she had known in her youth."

"Margaret told me that you wrote to Assumption to ask whether Helena might be there."

Carey sits next to Manning and explains, "Sometime after the disappearance, Margaret came to me and told me she wondered whether Helena had gone to Assumption. She didn't know anything about the place—not even its name—but apparently Helena had spoken of it at home from time to time. Since the same thought had crossed my own mind, and since I'd known Father McMullen from school, I immediately wrote to him, asking if perhaps he had a new arrival who might be Helena. He soon wrote back, regretting that he could be of no help, assuring me that there was no such woman there."

Manning asks bluntly, "Would he lie to you?"

The priest laughs, then rivets Manning with a dead-serious stare. "It's unthinkable that Jim McMullen would lie or even stretch the truth for the sake of his personal gain."

"What about the sake of the community, The Society?"

"I see what you're driving at, Mark, but I know this man well enough to let the whole matter rest on his word."

Manning turns a page of his notes and asks, "How well do you know Margaret O'Connor?"

"Margaret has never exhibited the depth of faith or the interest in church activities that her sister did. Other than Christmas and Easter, she rarely attends Mass. I like the woman; I just don't know her very well. I have no idea what happened to her faith. I guess she's just one of those who have gradually fallen away. Like so many."

"Like me. I fell away too, Matt," Manning tells him with a directness appropriate to the confessional.

"I wondered. Professional curiosity. But I'd never have asked."

"I know you wouldn't have. And I guessed that you were wondering. I wanted you to know."

"Why?" asks the priest, leaning close. His knee touches Manning's.

"So you would *know*," Manning says softly. "So you would have a clear picture of the person you're dealing with. I don't expect you to sanction my views. I don't even *want* you to—that would imply a belief that I long ago abandoned."

The priest leans closer still, his leg pressing against Manning's.

"What is it, Mark, that you don't believe in—the pope, the Immaculate Conception, heaven, hell, Christ, the Trinity, God?"

Father Matthew Carey may be testing waters that are not entirely theological—Manning isn't sure. His mind reels with a mix of conflicting emotions. Both attracted and repelled, he answers, "God."

"That's the one I can't touch," says the priest with a vanquished smile. His leg no longer presses against Manning's, but there is still a point between their knees where fibers of their trousers kiss, like microscopic diodes, arcing hot energy. "Any of the others, I might have offered logical arguments, or I might have slyly advised you to dismiss the smaller issue in favor of the larger. But you've already hit theological bedrock, so to speak, and I won't question your intelligence by asking how you've drawn your conclusion. So we disagree. Let's just say that what's 'right for me' may not be 'right for you.'"

"Sorry, let's not. When it comes to a question of existence—*does God exist?*—there can be only one answer. Yes or no. Something either is or it isn't—that's irreducible. If you say there is a God and I say there isn't, one of us is *wrong;* it's not an issue that we can have both ways. By your own definition, belief in God is a matter of faith, a faith that cannot demand proof and that condemns rational scrutiny. I hate to draw flat statements, but you're wrong, Matt, and I'm right."

They sit in the front pew before the sanctuary, eyeing each other with an unwavering gaze. The church is silent except for the low rumble of a blower fan churning in distant ductwork. The banners waft lazily overhead. At last the priest blinks and, almost imperceptibly, shifts his weight away from Manning. Their knees no longer touch.

"Seems we got sidetracked," says Manning with a quiet chuckle that further breaks the tension. "We were talking about Margaret O'Connor. I saw her at the estate on Monday, as you know, and afterward I spent some time with Arthur Mendel, the houseman. He mentioned that Margaret once caused an uproar with her 'loose ways.' I can't imagine what he meant. Can you?"

The priest stands, pressing his hands together, forming a little steeple. He touches his fingertips to his lips, paces a few steps away from Manning, then turns back to him. "I want to help you get to the bottom of things," he says, "but this isn't a subject for print. I wouldn't want to be quoted."

"All right." Manning caps his pen. "Background only. What happened?"

"Margaret O'Connor had a brief affair with Ridgely Carter, her sister's husband, right there at the estate."

"Jesus!" says Manning, instantly wishing he could retract the expletive. "Right under Helena's nose?"

"No. Helena frequently traveled to cat shows, so Margaret and Ridgely had ample time to themselves. I get the impression that poor Margaret was ... well, desperate, and Ridgely sort of took pity on her. Somehow, Helena got wind of it after Ridgely died. Understandably, she was plenty pissed."

Surprised by the priest's candor, Manning asks, "What did she do?"

Father Carey sits next to Manning again. "She threatened Margaret—talked about throwing her out of the house, cutting her out of the will. Helena told me all these things, and I counseled her at length, urging her not to let anger, which was justified, fester into spite. Later, after she disappeared and her will was opened, it was gratifying to learn that Margaret would be generously cared for through a separate trust. Knowing Helena as well as I did, I should have known that her good nature would be predictably constant."

"On the other hand," says Manning, "Margaret is *full* of surprises. When I spoke with her Monday, she said something that really threw me. She mentioned that when she and Helen were very young, there were twins growing up at home with them. It was the first I'd ever heard of them."

Shaking his head in bemused disbelief, Father Carey says, "Margaret is a sweet thing. Her sister's disappearance has been a source of profound stress, and—I hate to say it—sometimes I wonder if she's entirely lucid. Helena and I had many long conversations about her childhood, and she never said anything about having brothers. She surely would have mentioned it."

She surely must have, Manning tells himself. He told the priest about "twins," yet the priest has spoken of "brothers." Manning uncaps his pen and scratches on his pad: *Father Matthew Carey lies.*

* * *

Later that morning, a bird caws and fidgets on the cross atop a very different church, a traditional little Gothic church that stands in defiance of a white desert sun. Nothing stirs in the scrubby, treeless landscape below. The town that renamed itself Assumption has taken refuge against the heat.

The bird, responding to some arbitrary synapses within its gravel-size brain, hops off the cross, swirls earthward round the spire, then glides over the roofs of several nearby houses. All the houses in Assumption are in various states of disrepair. Most are wooden, some are stucco or adobe, but only one—the rectory, the priest's house—is made of brick. The bird lands on a weathered stone finial, a pineapple, that graces a brick pier to one side of the rectory's front stairs. The opposite pier has stood unadorned for years, denuded of its pineapple by vandals or by the ravages of heat or simply by the passage of time—it's been longer than any of the current townspeople can remember.

Inside, Father James McMullen sits at a rickety dining room table spread with paperwork that has outgrown his cramped office. He signs a document, stuffs it into an envelope, then tries to decide which pile of papers to tackle next, avoiding the tallest, the unpaid bills.

It is late morning—almost lunchtime, he notes—and the house is quiet. A clock ticks on the mantel. Down the hall, in the kitchen, his housekeeper is fussing with something. He wonders what Mrs. Weaver has in mind for lunch, hoping it's not tuna salad. He's never liked those sandwiches, so quintessentially Catholic—not since he was a boy, when he had to eat them every Friday at school. Though he still observes meatless Fridays with everyone else in Assumption, Mrs. Weaver is apt to foist tuna salad on him any day of the week, describing it as "heart-healthy," at least the way *she* fixes it, without mayonnaise, which makes it even worse.

The stillness is broken by the phone, ringing once, in the kitchen. A few moments later, Mrs. Weaver appears in the doorway, wiping her hands on her apron. "Telephone, Father." She turns to walk back to the kitchen, then stops to tell him, "Lunch'll be ready whenever you are."

He rises from his chair slowly—not that it's difficult for him, but he sometimes feels dizzy if he gets up too fast—and follows her down the hall. Mrs. Weaver resumes rinsing something in the kitchen sink. It's celery. Tuna salad, alas, is inevitable.

The old black Bakelite wall phone is mounted near the doorway. Next to it, thumbtacked to the woodwork, are the last three pages of a church calendar. Little paper shreds, remnants of the past nine months, sprout from its wire spiral. The priest picks up the receiver. "Good morning. This is Jim McMullen."

Smiling, he listens to the caller, but has trouble hearing over the water gurgling in the sink. "Yes, Mr. Manning? *Where* are you from?"

"I'm a reporter for the *Chicago Journal*," says the voice over the phone, "and I'm working on a story about Helena Carter, the heiress who disappeared about seven years ago. Perhaps you've heard of her?"

The priest's smile fades. "I'm aware of the incident, yes. In fact, I had some correspondence with the woman's home pastor shortly after her disappearance."

Manning says, "I spoke with Father Carey just this morning, and he told me about that."

"Then he must have also told you that I know nothing of her fate."

"He did," confirms Manning, "but that was quite a while ago, and I couldn't help wondering if there had been any further developments in the intervening years."

Father McMullen turns away from the housekeeper and huddles the phone into his shoulder. With anger mounting in his voice, he asks Manning, "Why would I conceal any knowledge of this woman's whereabouts? The terms of her will are well known. Her fortune will go to the mainstream Church. What would be *my* motive for deception?"

Mrs. Weaver turns off the water and is poised to begin chopping celery. Listening, she doesn't move. The dried-out linoleum pops under the shifting weight of her feet.

Friday, October 9

84 days till deadline

Dressed to run, Manning stands on the sidewalk looking down the street. Though he has never been here, the place seems familiar, pieced together from countless recollections. It is midday, warm, and perfectly clear. Birdsong drifts from colossal elms that arch over the street to form an endless fluttering tunnel of green, dappled blue. There are no people, no cars. Except for the shifting light in the trees above, all is still.

Neat white houses line both sides of the street—big clapboard houses with pitched roofs and open porches. Raised windows frame the soft folds of lace curtains, brilliant in the sun against the void of dark rooms within. Lawns are sheared smooth as carpets, yet no one mows them this fine day, no one trims their chalk-snapped borders with little silver scissors.

Manning turns to glance behind him, hearing the scrape of his soles on the pavement. The rows of houses and trees look identical to those ahead, as though he stood within the plane of a mirror bisecting the planet. He steps off the sidewalk and into the center of the street. A white line divides it, unsmudged by tires, freshly painted with laser-crisp edges that have not dripped into the little valleys formed by pebbles poking through the asphalt.

He wears new white leather running shoes with still-clean laces. Won't get them dirty on *this* street, he assures himself. The shoes are worn over rumpled white socks that bunch beneath the muscles of his calves. His shorts are old and comfortable, of bleached white cotton. They balloon a bit, hanging loosely from the elastic band that circles his waist. A tight black T-shirt pinches under his arms. In the sunlight, it makes him feel sticky and hot, so he peels the shirt over his head and lets it drop to the street.

It floats too slowly, he notes, landing like inky mire on the virginal white line. He rakes ten fingers through his mussed hair, which is longer than he has worn it in years.

Manning stands on the stripe and decides he will run directly down the center of the street, setting the impossible goal of reaching the point where stripe and sky converge. His mind rushes with confidence and doubt, determination and resignation, exhilaration and fatigue—the emotional jumble known to any runner who summons the will to begin. He sets off with those first awkward steps that precede a running stride.

His feet tangle. He trips. And though he feels the forward pitch of his body, *he does not fall.* Glancing down, he finds the T-shirt wrapped around the tips of both shoes. What's more, the shirt has somehow worked its way beneath the stripe.

He squats to untangle the shirt. Examining the stripe, he finds that it is not paint at all, but a rubbery ribbon, a tape of fine elastic film that stretches tightly to both horizons. He straddles the stripe and grasps it with both hands, yanking it up between his legs. He lets go. It slaps the ground with a resounding whack that silences the birds. Manning grabs the shirt, tosses it aside, and watches it drift like a leaf, undulating through sinuous, contorted shapes. With his weight thrust to one leg, hand on hip, he stands akimbo like a Greek athlete cut from marble. Birdsong swells again. Eyeing the point where the stripe vanishes, he musters the will to run.

He raises one leg and begins at a trot, trying to find his stride, unable to goad the mechanism of his body into a full run. His shorts no longer drape loosely, but pinch his waist and thwart his movement. He is running in place without moving from the spot. Closing his eyes and lowering his head, he redoubles the pumping efforts of his legs.

He trips—feels the ground pull out from under him—spreads his arms before him to break the fall, to cushion the grinding of pavement against flesh. But the blow is not delivered; he feels nothing. Opening his eyes, he is amazed to see the street floating beneath him, inches away. He hovers above the line, suspended. With the tips of his fingers, he nudges the ground, propelling his body upright.

The futile run has left him confused and breathless. His groin burns. His shorts bind his hips in a clammy grasp. Without hesitation, he slides his thumbs inside the waistband, pushes downward, and lifts each foot to freedom, kicking the shorts to the side of the street.

Manning stands broadly, both hands on hips, naked except for his immaculate running shoes. He feels the play of fresh air on his genitals and savors the sensation with face skyward, eyes closed, mouth open. Once more he summons the will to run, and this time his head fills only with emotions that will push him onward—no dread, no fear, no doubts. His brain sends the message to his feet with an electric shock that bolts him forward. Each foot pounds in front of the other; the street's pebbles streak backward. Each impact pulls harder on his swaying genitals, and he feels his penis harden, hears it slap against his legs. He fixes his eyes on the point that lies forever ahead. His peripheral vision blurs with racing houses and trees; only the stripe appears stationary in the world rushing past.

Manning quickens his pace, lengthens his stride. The muscles in his chest stretch to their limit. He no longer hears the birds, their song drowned out by the bellows in his lungs, by the heart that pumps in his ears, by the sound of feet gripping ground like the claws of an animal fleeing a predator.

And now it happens. Manning trips again, flying forward with the full force of his sprint. In one moment, he cringes at the prospect of his naked body scraping the street—in the next, *he is aloft*. His feet stop treading, for they can no longer touch ground. His breathing slows. He keeps a cautious gaze fixed on the white line.

While Manning drifts at a walking speed only a yard above ground, his uneasy thoughts flood with the mystery and awe of the phenomenon. He holds his body straight, with his head somewhat higher than his feet. His height above the street gradually lessens. He can just touch the ground with his toes and, kicking, can gain speed momentarily, but can rise no higher. He finally drifts so low that he reaches down with both hands and pushes backward; his body rights itself, and he stands motionless on the line.

Looking over his shoulder, not seeing his clothes near the curb, he confirms that he has floated a considerable distance.

Could it happen again? Can he summon this strange faculty at will—like running—or is it some outside force that acts *upon* him? Does he even *want* it to happen again? He decides that his anxiety was merely a reaction to the unknown; the experience itself, he admits, was enjoyable. He wants to repeat it, but he doesn't know how.

Manning tries jumping—and lands firmly on his feet on the same spot, feeling foolish. He jumps again, higher, this time flapping his arms once or twice—and lands as before, now feeling *very* foolish. He recalls that when he floated before, he had tripped first. So he runs a short distance, waiting to trip—or to fake a trip—but nothing happens. Perhaps if he just stands still and tips forward, as if to fall on his face . . .

Dropping his hands to his sides, he consciously relaxes and rocks forward onto his toes as if falling, not diving, off the edge of a precipice. At the moment when he loses equilibrium, he is aloft.

Just as before, he drifts silently above the line down the center of the street. Exhilarated by his ability to summon this new power, Manning itches to explore its limits. Can he move faster? Higher? He tries kicking and pushing as before. He even wriggles in midair like a fish in water, but without success. He floats along, gradually losing altitude, when the answer occurs to him, seeming so obvious—he simply *decides* to fly higher, and his distance from the ground begins to increase. He wants to fly faster too, so he *wills* his speed to increase.

Manning now flies at a height midway between the street and the canopy of trees, at the level of the houses' second-story windows. He can tell by the progress of his broken shadow on the street that he is moving faster than he could run. The birds are louder up here—he's practically in the trees with them—but their chatter is muffled by the rush of air past his ears.

He amuses himself flying higher and lower, faster and slower, as if trying out the controls of a machine. Wondering if the white line limits his pattern of flight, he focuses his efforts upon cruising to the left of it, at the same time leaning slightly in that direction. He effortlessly glides to the left of the line. Then to the right. Satisfied that the direction of his flight is indeed within his control, he returns to the center to fly straight above the stripe, enjoying the symmetry of the view.

He's having fun. And before long, he's faced with the inevitable question: How high, how fast, can I go?

Manning rises above the roofs of the houses and feels his pulse quicken. He tests his skill by boosting his speed and darting just below the branches of the huge trees. Protruding leaves brush through his hair, down his back, and over his buttocks. His groin tingles. His penis stiffens in the rush of air passing under his body. He slows his flight and rises higher into the trees. Can he pass through them and soar higher still? Ahead he sees a clearing in the foliage and a patch of sky beyond, so he flies upward through the branches toward the blue. Leaves skim the length of his body, gliding over his chest, rustling between his legs, bombarding his mind with frenzied, erotic signals. Twigs snap. Birds cackle at the intrusion.

And now it is all beneath him. Treetops glide below, clouds above. He flies faster, higher still, as the trees recede farther and the panorama of earth itself arcs before him. Thrilled yet frightened by the height at which he travels, he dares not think of what might happen if he suddenly lost his newfound power.

Power. This power overwhelms him with a freedom and virility he has never known. His erect penis drives forward, slicing two broad sheets of air, a wake in the atmosphere that fans out invisibly behind him. Pricking sensations rise from between his legs and into his chest. His genitals clench. His limbs thrust outward, making a giant X of his body like a sky diver in free-fall. The coming surge in his groin convulses his hips and at last pumps long glistening strands of semen into the air beneath him. He watches through a euphoric haze as the crystal beads glitter in the sun and plummet toward the trees. Hearing the smack of the drops as they hit the upper leaves, he wonders if they will stick there or drip like milky taffy to the street.

"Good morning," says a familiar voice—as if from the clouds, as if in his ear. "It's seven o'clock in Chicago, the ninth of October. Current O'Hare temperature is fifty-eight degrees, and we're due for more rain. Friends and neighbors, this is Bud Stirkham. Later we'll talk with a number of guests who will share their outrage over the Helena Carter murder case, and then we'll open the phone lines—because *your* views are important! But first, let's try waking up with a bit of Saint-Saëns, whose birthday we celebrate today."

Manning groans. He rolls over and squints at the clock radio, which now fairly bubbles with the strains of a bouncy tarantella. He imagines the plastic box prancing, Disney-style, on its stubby feet. The music is pleasant enough, especially after the rude awakening by Stirkham's nasal twang. Manning would like to lie in bed listening, easing gracefully into the day, but he can't afford to linger. It's Friday, and his calendar is crammed with extra deadlines for the weekend. He reminds himself, though, that the day will have its reward—Roxanne's party that night.

"**G**ood evening, sir," the doorman tells Manning, swinging the door to his side with a well-trained arm. "Whom did you wish to see?"

"Miss Exner, please. My name is Manning."

"Ah, the party. Miss Exner said you might be early. Do go on up—just press thirty."

Stepping into an elevator and pressing the button, Manning wonders, Am I *that* predictable? Why did she think I'd be anxious to get here?

He realizes that he had in fact felt rushed. He was kept at the office till well after six, and he had to go home to shower and change. It drizzled all day, and thunderstorms threatened the evening, so he planned to take a cab to Roxanne's apartment, even though it is only ten or twelve blocks up the lake from his loft. There was a break in the rain, though, so he walked, taking it at a fast clip in order not to get wet. He barely made it.

He is panting now, feeling less than shower-fresh. Rising nonstop to the thirtieth floor, his ears begin to plug, clearing when he swallows. The elevator halts and deposits him into a short hall that leads to either of two doors, the only two condominiums on the floor. He steps to Roxanne's and raps once with the chromed knocker.

Alerted by the doorman, Roxanne has been waiting on the other side of the door, which opens the moment Manning knocks. "Mark!" she gushes with a delight more typically prompted by someone unexpected. "So glad you could make it," she tells him, all but pulling him through the doorway while offering her cheek for his kiss.

"Wouldn't miss one of *your* parties," he tells her.

"Really?" She asks the question wryly while closing the door, catching him in a half-truth. Manning has been here only once—she moved to these sleek quarters sometime after their fling, around the time of her promotion—and he has turned down several invitations since. Letting him off the hook, she tells him, "The important thing is that you're here *now*. Matter of fact, you're first to arrive. Vodka on the rocks?"

"You're too good, Roxanne," he says with a sigh, needing a drink, again surprised that she finds him so predictable.

She ushers him from the apartment's entry hall into the sprawling living room. Its colors are dark and neutral, its lighting dim, its furnishings starkly modern. A bare wall of glass looks out upon a skyline aglow with a million sodium-vapor lamps, like a golden rococo fantasy flickering through the distance and the rain. Soft, bouncy jazz—party music—has been playing, and the recording now ends.

A man emerges from the kitchen to tend the music, wiping his hands on a dish towel. This must be Roxanne's houseguest, her college friend, so Manning deduces that he can be no younger than thirty-one, though he looks it. "How rude of me," Roxanne scolds herself. "First introductions, *then* drinks."

The younger man strides toward them with a broad smile. He is undeniably handsome and exudes a self-confident charm. His dress is studied though casual, with attention to every detail—well-tailored beige slacks, a gray T-shirt, and a slate-colored cashmere cardigan with its sleeves shoved halfway up his forearms. The heels of his Italian loafers clack on the teak parquet as he approaches. His overall look and bearing are not what Manning expected of the "artist friend."

"Mark," says Roxanne, "this is Neil Waite, my friend from Phoenix. Neil, I'd like you to meet Mark Manning of the *Journal*."

"The renowned reporter," says Neil, extending his hand and shaking Manning's firmly. "It's a pleasure."

"Thanks, Neil. The pleasure's mine. Reporter, yes—but 'renowned,' I'm not so sure."

"Nonsense," Roxanne insists, "you're far too modest. Your reporting of the Helena Carter case is utterly authoritative."

"I'll have to side with Roxanne," Neil adds. "The Carter case isn't exactly front-page news in Phoenix, but it does get reported there, and everything I've read has carried your byline. I'm impressed, Mark."

"What can I say?" says Manning, acceding to the flattery. Ready to change the topic, he asks, "How about you, Neil—what do you do?"

"I'm an architect. I'm here for a couple of weeks working on a project with our firm's Chicago office. That happens from time to time, and Rox is always kind enough to put me up—"

"In the den, alas," Roxanne interjects with a low chortle. Her suggestive tone strikes Manning as more inappropriate than amusing. He wants to hear more about Neil's work, but before he can ask, Roxanne continues, "Now, Mark, how about that drink? Neil, can you take care of it in the kitchen? I need to finish dressing. And I'll put the CDs in order—I like to have the evening fully programmed."

"No kidding," says Neil under his breath. With a jerk of his head, he beckons Manning to follow him to the kitchen. It is a bright, spacious room—no mere apartment-style galley. Neil has taken charge of the duties here, and all seems ready. Trays of hors d'oeuvres are arranged on the counter, something's in the oven, and the cocktail cart is freshly stocked, ready to roll. Neil offers, "What can I get you?"

"Just vodka on the rocks."

"Nice clean drink," says Neil with a tone of approval. "I'll join you." He plunks ice cubes into two squatty crystal glasses, then grabs a bottle of Japanese vodka, a brand unknown to Manning. He pours without measuring until the ice is just covered. "Let me garnish this with something I think you'll like," says Neil as he picks up an orange. He deftly strips off a long sliver of peel, then twists it over both drinks, dropping half of the peel into each. Invisible droplets of citric oil fill the space with their fragrance. Neil hands one glass to Manning and lifts his own, saying, "I've never known what to call this concoction, but I just had an inspiration. Henceforth, this is a 'Mark Manning.' So, a toast to its illustrious namesake. Cheers, Mark."

Touched by the gesture, Manning says, "I'm at a loss for words, and *I'm* the writer."

Neil tells him softly, "Just drink it."

They touch glasses and share a smile, a gaze that lingers, suddenly blocking other senses, suspending reality for a long, long instant. A wave of breathlessness passes through Manning like a roll of timpani that is felt but not heard. His jaw droops.

"*Drink* it," Neil repeats, this time through a laugh.

Manning blinks. He sips. As the icy alcohol assaults his tongue, the reality of the moment snaps back into focus. He pauses to taste what's in his mouth, swallows, and says, "Neil, this is great— the orange gives it a whole new character."

"I thought you might be ready for something different." The curl of Neil's lip confirms the double entendre.

"Never can tell," Manning admits. Then, defusing their innuendo, he asks, "Who's coming tonight—do you know?"

"Rox said we'd be ten or twelve. There's someone she works with, she mentioned 'several writers'—spouses, I imagine—and she invited someone I met here before, someone I'd rather forget."

"Blind date?"

"Not exactly." Neil snorts a loud laugh and takes a swallow from his glass.

"What's going on in here?" calls Roxanne, her tone playfully accusing, as she appears through the swinging door. She has the music going again, more upbeat than before.

"Nothing, Rox," Neil tells her. "Just swapping filthy stories— man-talk, you know." He winks at Manning.

She lets the comment pass, not believing a word. Instead, she strikes a pose and asks, "Well, what do you think?"

She has chosen a cream-colored suit of soft merino wool. Under the jacket she wears a tight black sweater and a fine gold chain that hangs in a single loop, narrowing as it descends between her breasts. The only other jewelry is a similar gold chain looped many times around one wrist as a bracelet. Her hair flows over her shoulders, framing her head like a veil. Her feet are virtually bare, guiding a pair of thin-strapped sandals with short spiked heels that would never be worn on the street.

Neil simply eyes her and nods his approval. Manning attempts—with only partial success—a wolf whistle.

"You guys are impossible," she says, dismissing the fished-for compliments.

In that instant, Manning recognizes that Roxanne, who is one of the most seductive women he has ever known, is at the same time the least flirtatious. She is unquestionably attractive, poised, and worldly, yet she dampens her glamour with a wearied indifference to her own physicality. What, Manning wonders, does that signal—confidence, or insecurity?

"Hey," says Manning, "here's an idea. Let me repay your hospitality and invite you two over to my loft—you've never seen it, Roxanne, and I've been there almost a year. How about dinner next Friday, a week from tonight?"

"Great!" says Neil.

"I'll have to check my calendar," says Roxanne, hesitating. She pours herself a drink. "I think I'm clear. I'll let you know."

The door knocker sounds from the other room. As Roxanne turns to leave the kitchen, she tells them, "Curtain going up, gents. Take charge of the booze, please—I'll meet and greet."

As Manning and Neil refill their glasses and do some last-minute arranging of the cocktail cart, they hear voices raised in greeting. Manning swings the door open and follows Neil, who wheels the cart into the living room. Roxanne has escorted her guests to the window, where they marvel at the view. Lightning flares in the clouds beyond the horizon.

Roxanne waves Manning and Neil forward to meet the new arrivals—a couple, apparently married, sixty or so, both comfortably overweight.

He wears a nubby tweed jacket with leather buttons and elbow patches, a wrinkled white shirt, and a bulky knit necktie with a knot that is far too big for the day's fashion. The overall impression is decidedly academic, though the unpolished image is flawed by his dashing silver hair, professionally styled, swept back, blow-dried, and lacquered.

The woman at his side wears a serviceable, matronly suit, also tweed. Beneath the jacket is a brown turtleneck sweater with a collar that rises in many folds, mimicking the layers of her chin. From the ripples of the collar hangs an oversize primitive necklace composed of beads, feathers, and what appear to be painted bones.

Her hair—once black, now dull gray—is braided and coiled atop her head in a style that befits the necklace.

Manning vaguely recognizes the man—his crackly voice is familiar too. Then Roxanne introduces the couple as Bud Stirkham, the author and radio commentator, and his wife, Clarice. The Stirkhams exchange handshakes with Manning and Neil. Offering drinks, Neil is asked to pour straight bourbon for both. Still pumping Manning's hand, Bud Stirkham puts aside the opinions he expressed on the air earlier in the week, telling Manning, "Mighty fine job you fellas are doing with the Carter caper over at the *Journal.* You're one hell of a reporter, sir."

Manning says, "Thanks, Bud. I'm glad to tell you how well acquainted I am with your books." He doesn't mention that he finds their underlying philosophy reprehensible. "And I hear your program all the time." He doesn't mention that he usually switches it off the moment he hears Stirkham's voice. Stirkham beams in response to the presumed flattery.

"Perhaps, Mr. Manning," suggests Clarice Stirkham, "you could appear on my husband's program. I'm sure the public would be keen to hear your thoughts on the Carter case."

"I'm sorry," says Manning, "but the public has already read everything I have to say about the case."

"No, Mr. Manning, you misunderstand me," she persists. "I'm not talking about the *facts* you've reported—that's all so dry and tedious. Many people would like to know how you *feel* about what's happened."

"I'm sorry," he repeats, "but that wouldn't be appropriate to my role at the *Journal.* My speculation as to Helena Carter's fate would do nothing to solve the mystery. I'm a reporter, Mrs. Stirkham, not a detective or a mystic. Thank you for your offer, but I must decline."

"Now, Clarice . . ." says Stirkham through a soothing chuckle, trying to unruffle his wife, who is visibly irritated by the lack of enthusiasm for her proposal. Then to Manning, "I'm sure you know your business better than we do, but if you ever change your mind . . ." he trails off suggestively.

"Mark," says Neil, bouncing to the rescue, "can you give me a hand with something?"

Manning nods a temporary farewell to the Stirkhams and

follows Neil to the kitchen. "Thank you," he says as Neil begins garnishing a tray of appetizers, "I was getting annoyed." He gives Neil's shoulder a squeeze that says, But I'm better now.

"God, they're awful—and did you catch that neck-piece? Who *are* they?"

Manning sips his vodka and lets himself relax. "Bud Stirkham," he explains, "is the most overrated and—I feel—misunderstood writer in this city." He doesn't bother to hush his words, for the music from the other room covers their conversation, and the rain now beats loudly against the big windows. "He's written a half-dozen books and a couple of plays that have received respectable critical acclaim and—for reasons that escape me—tremendous public success. He identifies himself with workers, union movements, the common man, *that* whole bit. In short, he's a knee-jerk egalitarian of the most senseless and rabid variety."

Manning stops talking and drinks. He stares over his glass at Neil, who looks back at him. Manning's words have revealed opinions not often expressed, and he finds it unexpectedly important that this young man should grasp and share his thinking.

"You handled yourself beautifully," says Neil. He hands Manning a tray of crudités and picks up a second platter, heaped with cheese. As they return to the living room with their bounty, the knocker raps.

Roxanne takes leave of the Stirkhams, crossing the room to fling open the door, revealing a short middle-aged couple who stow their dripping umbrellas in a stand near the elevator. The man wears a business suit, proper but blah, and carries a bottle of wine with a ribbon around its neck. The woman beside him wears a simple evening dress of deep blue, embellished with a strand of pearls. She has clearly spent the afternoon with her hairdresser, as her meticulous coif is done up with a tiny velvet bow that matches her dress. She smiles eagerly, suggesting she does not spend as many evenings out of the house as she would like.

"Jerry!" says Roxanne warmly. It is Jerry Klein, chief operating officer of CarterAir, and his wife. Roxanne feels the onset of panic as she struggles to remember the wife's name; this lapse has plagued her before.

As the Kleins cross the threshold, Jerry thrusts the bottle toward Roxanne, telling her, "Oh, Roxy, it's such a pleasure to see you outside the office for a change."

"Jerry and I were thrilled to be invited to your party, Roxanne," says the wife with obvious sincerity, a twinkle in her eye.

My God, *what's that damned woman's NAME!* screams Roxanne's inner voice. She says calmly, "It wouldn't be the same without *you*, my dear." The women lean toward each other, clasp hands, and peck cheeks.

"Mary's been talking about this party for a week," says Klein.

Roxanne asks herself, *Mary?* Why the hell can't I remember a name like Mary? Jerry and Mary—what could be simpler? "I hope the evening lives up to your expectations, Mary," says Roxanne while leading the woman by the arm into the living room. "Now, you two, *do* meet our little crowd."

Just as Roxanne completes the round of introductions, there is another knock at the door, requiring another round. These guests are a senior partner in Roxanne's law firm and his wife. The new arrivals know the Kleins well, and Manning speculates that they have been invited to keep Jerry and Mary company. Roxanne crosses the room to boost the volume of the music, asking over her shoulder if Neil could get drinks for the four newcomers. "But you'll have to mix your own refills," she cautions them with a wink.

The guests cluster near the window to chatter an awed commentary on the view while Neil begins pouring their drinks. As he distributes the glasses, the law partner says, "Tell me, Neil—just what is it that you *do?* Roxanne says you're involved with the arts."

"The arts?" asks Neil. "That's stretching things a bit. Roxanne!" he calls across the room. She looks over from the bookcases that house the sound system, where she shuffles CDs in search of her next sonic barrage. He asks her, "What have you been telling these people?" She breaks into a wide grin, then resumes her search.

Neil explains to the circle of faces around him, "Roxanne finds it fashionable to have artsy friends, but *I'm* no artist—at least I don't try to pass myself off as one. I'm an architect. The purest aesthetic 'calling' within my profession is residential work, and I do as much of it as I can. But the truth is, like most architects, I spend the bulk of my time on mundane, artless buildings—

anything from factories to shopping centers—because they're the projects that pay the bills."

One by one, his listeners cast disappointed glances across the room toward Roxanne. The women seem especially deflated; their image of Roxanne's exotic friend has been dashed. Manning, however, is not the least disappointed, crediting Neil for his practical attitude. He has a string of questions he would eagerly ask about Neil's work, but another rap at the door signals an abrupt end to the topic.

Roxanne excuses herself and soon reappears with the next guest. In the singsong tone of giving a cookie to a child, she announces, "Look who's here, Neil." At her side stands a young man, tall and thin, with long fingers and pointed features. His hair is cropped close to his scalp, bleached to nothing of a color. The bib of his white painter's overalls, perfectly clean, covers the front of a red silk shirt. He wears too much jewelry—a necklace not unlike Clarice Stirkham's, a bracelet not unlike Roxanne's.

With a shrug of his shoulders, Neil asks the ladies, "You wanted an artist?" Turning to the man in overalls, he says flatly, "Hello, Howard."

"*Neil!* You look *fabulous!*" says Howard, rushing across the room, necklace rattling. "I can't believe it's been a *full year.*" He grabs one of Neil's hands with both of his own and leans forward, kissing him squarely on the lips. Mary Klein gasps. The others aren't sure how to react. Roxanne flashes a satisfied smile, then steps forward to help acquaint everyone, introducing the lanky arrival as Howard Q, a noted Chicago illustrator.

"Q?" repeats Manning, making sure he heard the name correctly.

"That's right," says Howard with a laugh that suggests he is asked the question continually. "In the art game, a gimmick goes a long way to help you stand out from the crowd. So I changed my name. It's official. Just Q."

"I see you need a drink, Howard," says Neil. "Rum and Coke, right?"

"You're a *dear* to remember."

Howard turns to the Stirkhams and dives into an animated conversation with Clarice, who displays an adventurous, cosmopolitan interest in the illustrator. Roxanne, feeling her liquor by now, searches for still more raucous music, as if to signal that the "color" of the party has arrived. Neil, passing Manning on his way to the kitchen for the cola, says, "Could you come here, Mark?"

Arriving at the refrigerator, Neil says, "I'm sorry, Mark." The swift, careless manner in which he mixes Howard's drink reveals anger not apparent in his voice.

"There's no need to apologize," Manning assures him. "That guy is no reflection on you. There must be quite a few like that in the 'art game.'"

"Howard *is* a reflection on me," Neil tells Manning, looking him in the eye. "I think his whole act is tasteless, and I would never carry on like that, but we've slept together—once. He and I may seem like very different people, but we're both gay. Lots of folks can't handle that."

The words have caught Manning off guard. "Neil," he begins cautiously, "I'm not sure why you're telling me this, and I don't know what you expect me to say. If you're afraid I'll think less of you because of Howard or because of your sex life—don't. This is a big town"—Manning allows himself a little laugh—"and I've been around it awhile. I hate to sound jaded, but I'm not easily shocked."

Neil smiles with the confidence that a potential crisis has passed. "Thank you, Mark. Guess I'm not 'conditioned' to presume open-mindedness in others." Then, dropping the serious tone, he asks, "I gave quite a performance, though, didn't I?"

After a moment's reflection, they share a loud laugh.

Roxanne pokes her head through the door to tell them, "If you two could break up your private party, there *are* other guests who might enjoy your company." And she is gone—her testy tone suggesting that Neil and Manning have hit it off better than she planned.

"Oops," says Neil. "We'd better get back. Howard Q must be getting thirsty." He finishes mixing the drink and plops a wedge of lime into it.

They rejoin the group in the living room, where the babble has grown louder to compete with the music. Rising above it all are Howard Q's sporadic shrill outbursts. Neil delivers the rum and Coke, letting the glass hang from two fingers as if it held something rancid. Handing it over, he says, "I don't know how anyone over twelve can drink this craw rot."

"You're just too *proper* to be seen drinking something you *like*," counters Howard. "But thanks anyway, love." He purses his lips and blows Neil a kiss.

The group is engrossed in a conversation dealing with the need for increased public funding of the arts—because "beauty belongs to everyone" and "artistic expression is an inalienable right." Clarice Stirkham proposes a constitutional amendment to that effect. Her husband nods gravely, agreeing in principle, but he points out that mounting support for it among the labor bloc might be difficult. He hastens to add that the working man is not intrinsically insensitive to the arts, but has simply never had the opportunity to taste life's finer fruits.

Manning listens quietly and lights a cigarette, annoyed. Neil eyes him with concern, detecting his distaste for the conversation. Howard Q greets Clarice Stirkham's proposal with enthusiasm, pouting that lack of opportunity in the *real* arts has forced him to prostitute his talents and "go commercial." Roxanne surveys the cross dynamics of the room and glows with the satisfaction of a contented hostess.

"Let's talk about something else," Neil finally says, feigning boredom with the conversation.

"Like what?" asks Howard, mildly indignant.

"Well, how about the Carter case? After all, we've got an *expert*," says Neil, deferring to Manning.

"What would you like to know?" Manning asks him. "Not that there's much to tell. I hit another dead end on the phone this week."

"*I* have a question, Mr. Manning," says Mary Klein, her timidity overcome by curiosity. "I read something last week about *psychics* being brought in to help on the case. That sounds *terribly* exciting. What have you learned from them?"

"That wasn't my story, Mrs. Klein; it was in the *Post*. I think it's nonsense. I've dealt with many of these mystics, and I've yet to see evidence of any 'powers' whatever."

"Oh, *evidence*," says Howard with a smirk. "What's 'evidence'?"

"Mr. Q is quite right," Clarice Stirkham butts in. "Things aren't always so cut-and-dried as we might like. Some things are simply beyond human comprehension and will forever remain so. There are forces—there are powers—that cannot be subjugated to the evidence of our five feeble senses."

"Really?" asks Manning. "Like what?"

"Come now," she sniffs. "Surely you don't possess a *complete* understanding of the world around you. Does life hold no mysteries at all?"

"Many, indeed," he answers, "but I look upon any mystery as a question that man has simply not yet been able to answer. I do *not* think that the unknown should be revered as unknowable."

"Do you mean to tell us, Mr. Manning, that you acknowledge no force in the universe beyond the perceptions of your own mind?"

"That is precisely what I am telling you. To deliberately cloud, to *negate* the working of your mind, which is your ultimate weapon for survival, is both irrational and self-destructive. Submission to forces that display their power is only that—submission. And submission to *imagined* powers is worse yet—it is folly. What 'force' are you speaking of, Mrs. Stirkham? Is it God?"

"Not exactly," she says warily, guessing the direction of his logic. "Some may wish to think of a spiritual power as 'God.' It's a handy label. But no, I am simply referring to any manifestation of the unknown or the unknowable—clairvoyance, death, dreams, and such."

The conversation stops. The listeners have been engrossed in the volley of dialogue, and they now wag their heads indecisively, waiting for someone to clinch the last word.

No longer argumentative, but genuinely inquisitive, Manning says, "Mrs. Stirkham, you mention dreams. Do you know anything about their interpretation?"

"A bit." Her tone is guarded.

"I had a dream last night," Manning continues, "totally unlike any I've had before. It's been on my mind all day."

Neil's gaze is fixed upon Manning's green eyes. He commands gently, "Tell us about it."

"This may sound a little crazy," Manning says with an apologetic laugh, "but I dreamed that I *flew.*"

"I've often had such dreams," Clarice Stirkham assures him.

"How awful!" says Howard Q.

"I once had a dream like that myself," Neil says quietly.

"Not me," says Roxanne. "It must be quite an experience."

"It certainly was," Manning tells the group. "I've never paid much attention to my dreams, but this one was so different, so vivid, I wonder if it has a particular meaning."

"Dreams can often be interpreted in different ways," Clarice Stirkham explains. "It depends from which school of thought you derive your analysis. Dreams of flight are a classic example. Some people maintain that the flight represents exactly that—a flight or escape from something, a warning from your sleeping mind that you are in danger or that you need to alter your life in some fundamental way. Others view flight dreams as a kind of psychological overflow valve, releasing the accumulated pressures of waking life through the rapture of self-propelled flight. And then there's Freud . . ."

"Sex, sex, sex," the law partner interrupts, grinning. "I suppose Freud would say that flight dreams signal sexual repression." He laughs, and the group chortles with him.

"Oh, that couldn't be *Mark's* problem," says Roxanne with a suggestive wink, laughing a low, convulsive sound.

Manning recognizes the sound—Roxanne has been pounding her cocktails. He lights another cigarette. Having unwittingly put himself "on the couch," he shifts the course of the discussion. "Mrs. Stirkham," he asks, "in your dreams, how do you actually go about flying? That is, do you fly . . . like a bird, flapping your 'wings'?"

She blinks, considering his question, and answers, "Well, yes. I wear a long white robe with flowing sleeves—something like a choirgirl might wear. I step to the edge of a cliff and, without hesitation, spread my arms like wings and jump out over the canyon before me. I glide peacefully till I awaken. But then"— her tone turns condescending as she asks the group—"how else *would* one fly, if not like a bird?"

"I tried that," says Manning, deadpan. "It didn't work."

"Right," says Neil, suddenly animated. "In my dream, I didn't fly like a bird at all. It was more like Superman—I could leap and soar at will. And I'd be leaving out an important detail if I didn't mention that the dream was essentially erotic. Not to offend anyone, but it was the only 'wet dream' I've had since puberty."

Clarice Stirkham eyes Neil with the affronted air of having been upstaged. Mary Klein blushes but remains stoically composed. The law partner laughs gustily while muttering, "I knew it, I just *knew* it." Roxanne tongues an ice cube from her empty glass, sucks it into her mouth, and cracks it between her molars.

The group now turns to Manning for his reaction, since it was his own dream that triggered the discussion. He smiles awkwardly, searching for words. "I'd have to say that Neil's experience sounds similar to my own."

"Good *heavens*," says Howard Q with a rumbling purr and a toss of his shoulder. "I'll have to start paying more attention to my dreams. Sounds like *you* guys have been having a ball up there in the clouds."

There is general laughter among the group, though Clarice Stirkham skewers Howard with the betrayed glance of one who has lost an ally.

A sharp knocking of the door silences the banter, but not the atonal wailing of Roxanne's progressive jazz, which blares through the apartment. She excuses herself and crosses the room to greet her next guest; there is a wobble to her gait.

She opens the door. Her eyes meet the smiling features of a rotund middle-aged man who is dressed like a character from a period French farce, complete with cape and walking stick. She's not certain if the attire is simply in poor taste or if it is meant as a costume, a joke.

"Yes?" she asks, suppressing a laugh.

"Miss Exner, I presume? I am Humphrey Hasting."

"Oh!" It takes her a split second to connect the name with the *Post* and its shoddy reporting of the Carter case. Ushering the man through the door, she tells him, "I'm sorry I didn't recognize you, but I must never have seen your picture."

"Ah, yes," he moans while removing his cape with a flourish, picking a stray pet-hair from its collar. "Such is the nature of a writer's fame—to be known solely for his work, his words, his service to the reading public."

"Of course, Mr. Humphrey," she tells him, still flustered, taking his cape and folding it over the back of a nearby chair.

"Hasting, Miss Exner," he corrects her with a smile, raising an index finger in mild admonishment.

"I beg your pardon?" she asks, now totally addled.

"Hasting," he repeats. "My name is Humphrey *Hasting*."

"I'm so terribly sorry," she effuses, grabbing his hand and

patting it. She asks herself, Why in hell did I invite him, anyway? She leads him toward the windows, telling him, "*Do* come meet my other guests."

The group turns to behold the new arrival. A saxophone screams from the bookshelves. Roxanne announces above the music, "I'd like you all to meet Hasty Humphries from the *Post.*"

Manning stifles a laugh. Neil gapes open-mouthed. Bud Stirkham roars at his old pal, "Howdy, Hump!"

Hasting stands rigid and trembling while Roxanne makes an awkward attempt to undo her gaffe. A clarinet stutters wildly over her apologies.

At last a correct round of introductions has been made. Clarice Stirkham latches on to Hasting, and they are instantly in sync, immersed in a dialogue assessing the social role of news writing. Neil leaves for the kitchen to mix Hasting a drink. Manning escapes with him.

They arrive to find Roxanne downing a quick, stiff refill. She turns as they enter and, anticipating an attack, spits at them, "All *right*, I'm *sorry.*"

"It's *your* party," Manning tells her. "Far be it from me to question your guest list."

"Christ, Rox," says Neil, "how could you invite that . . . fruit-cake? My God, he looks like a wine steward!" He breaks into laughter.

"I've never *seen* him before." She's defensive. "We've never met."

Neil stops laughing. "Then why'd you invite him?" His voice carries a tone of indictment. "To embarrass Mark?"

"*Why would I do that?*" she yells at them, at herself, then takes a deep breath, regaining just enough composure to march out of the kitchen and join her other guests.

Neil tells Manning, "Guess I'd better get Humpty Dumpty a drink." His hard features melt into a smirk as he mixes a sweet potion of syrupy red glop and dresses it up with orange slices, cherries, a straw, and a little paper umbrella that he finds in the back of a drawer.

Neil and Manning rejoin the crowd in the living room. The music convulses hysterically while bursts of laughter punctuate the beat. Clarice Stirkham's head bobs with enthusiasm as she listens to Humphrey Hasting, who tells her, "I was at a party last weekend with my sister, and we had a little chat with Nathan Cain. He agrees entirely."

She responds, "It's so refreshing—"

Neil interrupts her briefly as he hands Hasting the drink.

"My, how *pretty*," says Hasting, holding the glass before him as if it contained a rare wine.

Clarice Stirkham says to Manning, "I was just remarking to your distinguished colleague," referring to Hasting with a courtly bow of her head, "how refreshing it is to find a journalist with a true and proper sense of social mission."

Hasting giggles modestly, his free hand fluttering to straighten a pouffy red velvet bow tie. "I'm not all *that* progressive, Clarice. I've *yet* to master those damned computers at the office—I still write my stories on an ancient newsroom Underwood. It's a bit banged-up, but it gets the job done."

"Really?" Manning asks him, amused. "Every writer seems to have his quirks. I myself take notes with a fountain pen. I can't stand using a ballpoint—it's like writing with a nail."

"Even so," Clarice continues, "a great many of the ills facing our woe-ridden masses would be brought quickly into perspective if more journalists could fathom—as our dear Mr. Hasting does— the vast potential of the role they play in our complex social fabric. I *shudder* to think," she says, forcing her torso to quiver while the bones of her necklace clatter menacingly, "I shudder to think of the sorry situation that would face us if *all* reporters limited their practice to . . . *reporting*."

The music shrieks violently. Then a stunning shard of light- ning explodes just beyond the windows. Someone drops a glass. Mary Klein screams. The lights flicker—a momentary outage sufficient to cause the CD player to mistrack, plunging the room into silence.

As the partygoers exchange disoriented glances, Humphrey Hasting finishes his drink with a burst of suction noises from his straw.

Friday, October 16

Jerry Klein, chief operating officer of CarterAir, sits behind the big mahogany desk in front of a big window in his big office. The little man rises, curling his lips into a little smile as Manning is escorted into the room.

The reporter tells him as they shake hands, "I enjoyed getting to know you at Roxanne's party last week. Thanks, Jerry, for taking time to see me."

"My pleasure." Klein gestures that they should sit. "I'm totally at your service. Anything to help solve this mystery." Two ornately framed photos—one of the heiress, the other of company founder Ridgely Carter—are conspicuous among the few articles atop Klein's clean desk.

Manning settles into his chair, flips open his note pad, and uncaps his pen. He's had a few days to look into Klein's background. The *Journal*'s business editor, as well as Roxanne, confirmed Manning's impression of the timid man who was a protégé of Ridgely Carter and a close friend to Helena after she was widowed. Klein is regarded as a crack accountant, intellectually well qualified for the position that was thrust upon him, but only awkwardly suited to its trappings. During his seven years at the airline's helm, he has grown to be an able administrator, but has never donned the mantle of leadership worn so naturally by his charismatic mentor.

Klein says, "Most folks assume Helena is dead, but *you* have doubts. I share those doubts, and I'm grateful for your persistence. I'm also sorry that your convictions have put you in such a fix with Nathan Cain." Klein sees that Manning is surprised that he knows of the ultimatum, so he explains, "Nathan phoned to explain what had happened—he thought I'd be interested."

Manning asks, "Do you know him well?"

"Only through the Carters, and they're gone, of course. When Ridgely was alive, Nathan was a frequent guest at the estate, as I was, so we became well acquainted. But he's always struck me as an odd duck, rather cold—not someone I'd choose to spend time with on my own, so we haven't." Klein pauses while Manning finishes making a note, then tells him, "Enough of unsavory subjects. We were talking about Helena. Have you learned anything at all that convinces you she's alive?"

Manning breathes an exasperated sigh. "I got a fresh lead last week from Father Matthew Carey at Saint Jerome's in Bluff Shores, but it didn't pan out. Even though Carey wasn't entirely forthright with me, I was intrigued by his story of a community of reactionary Catholics—it's a little desert town called Assumption. Apparently Helena had an interest in this movement, so I did some checking of my own, to see if maybe she had gone there. I phoned Father James McMullen, who runs the town and reports to some cardinal in Belgium."

"Cardinal L'Évêque," says Klein.

"Right," says Manning, surprised that Klein would know such a detail. "McMullen seemed flustered by my call, which heightened my suspicions. But when I suggested that he might have some knowledge of Helena Carter's whereabouts, he got miffed and pointed out that the terms of Helena's will are well known. 'Her fortune will go to the mainstream Church,' he told me. 'What would be *my* motive for deception?'"

"What, indeed . . ." says Klein, deep in thought.

"I have to admit, he had me," says Manning. "His logic was simple and airtight, so I apologized, hung up, and lost the only decent lead I had." Refocusing their talk, he asks Klein, "How do *you* feel about the will?"

"It's Helena's money," he answers with candor. "Personally, I don't begrudge the Church—or the Federated Cat Clubs—her fortune. As COO of CarterAir, though, I don't relish the intrusion of new partners in the business. They'll most likely want to liquidate their assets, which means a public stock offering—and the inevitable complications that go with it."

"It's amazing that CarterAir has managed to remain private this long," notes Manning. "The company has a long history of innovation and progressive management. I can appreciate your pride in it."

"That was all Ridgely's doing," says Klein. "He built the company like a loving father. As a result, we've always enjoyed harmonious relations with our unions and have rarely been affected by strikes. He was constantly looking for new ways, little ways, to be better; during his last year with us, for example, CarterAir became the first airline to offer public phone service on every flight. Since then, the company has continued to thrive during a period when many other airlines have folded or been forced to merge. I recognize that my role here is essentially a caretaker's, but I think I can take a measure of pride in knowing I've preserved what Ridgely worked so hard to build."

"You certainly can," Manning assures him. Then he asks, "As long as we're on the topic of the company's finances, would you be willing to get more specific on a few matters?"

Klein grins. "I'm sure you can appreciate that I wouldn't normally be inclined to share a private company's financial figures with the press. But these *are* unusual circumstances, and there's nothing to hide. Even Hank Ferret, a damned tough lawyer appointed by the court to serve as Helena's guardian *ad litem*, has been completely satisfied with our accounting. Besides, it seems only fair to supply you with the same information I gave the *Post.*"

"What?"

"Humphrey Hasting was here yesterday," explains Klein while pulling several bulging files from a drawer and presenting them to Manning for his perusal. Klein guides Manning through the material, pointing out significant documents, answering questions, ordering copies of spreadsheets from one of his secretaries.

Manning dutifully takes notes and arranges his own file of the copies he is given, but after a half hour of this number-crunching, he needs to come up for air. "I'm sorry to interrupt, Jerry, but I'm finding it hard to concentrate on all this. Something is troubling me. Humphrey Hasting—I can't quite believe that he was actually here doing the grunt work of reporting. Either he's turned over a new leaf, or I've badly misjudged him."

Klein laughs, having wondered how long Manning would wait before questioning him about the other reporter's visit. "The truth is, Mark, that Hasting didn't give a damn about the financials. He rushed me through my report and shoved the spreadsheets into his briefcase like so much . . . *trash.*" Indignation colors Klein's voice as he taps the folders on the desk. "These numbers represent the labors of thousands of people, spanning two generations, and he showed no interest whatever in the privileged information I offered him." With uncharacteristic fire, he concludes, "The fat bastard!"

Relieved and amused, Manning asks, "What *was* he interested in?"

"Arthur Mendel, the houseman at the Carter estate."

"Ahh . . ."

"Hasting kept pumping me for information about the man, regardless of where I steered the conversation. It was clear from his questions that he sees Arthur as a convenient scapegoat—a scheming, demented psychopath."

"That sweet old guy?" Manning smirks at the notion, but recognizes that his attitude toward Mendel has been colored by knowledge of the gambling incident.

"It's ridiculous, of course. Arthur has been with the Carters longer than I can remember. His loyalty is transparent to anyone who talks to him."

"Hump wouldn't think of *that* tactic, so I'd better drive up to Bluff Shores next week and talk to Arthur again myself." Manning notes it on his pad, then tells Klein, "Hasting may have no appetite for your financials, Jerry, but I do. Shall we get back to them?"

"With pleasure." Another half hour of amortizations and accruals, profits and losses, returns on investments—and Manning is fully satisfied with the sound management of both the airline and the Carter estate.

The secretary enters Klein's office to deliver one last set of photocopies. "Mr. Manning," she says, "Roxanne Exner just phoned and asked me to give you a message. She and a friend are scheduled for a social engagement at your apartment this evening, but she has a conflict and must cancel. She's terribly sorry—and wonders if it's all right for her friend to come alone."

Manning coughs and covers his mouth—to conceal a grin—while saying to the woman, "Could you return a message for me, please? Ask Miss Exner to have Mr. Waite come over around eight."

Why in hell didn't I take care of this earlier? wonders Manning as he struggles to hang a painting that has leaned for months against a bare wall in his loft. It's an oil—or is it acrylic? Such details are beyond him. In either case, it's five feet square, and hanging it is not a one-man job, even with a good stepladder. He manages at last to slip the wire over the hook, checks the top edge with a level, then climbs down the ladder and steps back to pass judgment. He's pleased. The windowless wall is at least twenty feet high. It needed *something*.

Manning first noticed the painting in one of the little galleries off Michigan Avenue. Richly detailed, but with a restrained palette, it appealed to him at once. The dealer assured him that the artist was "significant" and that the painting, which would surely appreciate in value, was a wise investment. Now it hangs in its intended spot, lending a note of refinement to its sparse surroundings. "Nice," says Manning aloud. Glad you like it, he reminds himself—it cost as much as a good used car.

He glances at his watch and confirms that he's running late. It's twenty to eight, and he suspects that Neil will be punctual. He stashes the ladder and tools in a closet, clears up some kitchen debris, and takes off his shirt as he heads toward the shower.

At one minute past eight, while Manning inspects the results of his grooming in a mirror, a buzzer announces that Neil, as predicted, is prompt. Unsure of what the evening may hold— even more uncertain of what he *wants* it to hold—Manning takes a deep breath, summoning courage, before crossing the apartment to answer the door. He swings it open and cannot control the goofy smile that spreads across his face. "Hi, Neil."

"Hello there, yourself," says Neil, stepping inside. He carries a couple of shopping bags and seems winded, explaining, "I decided to walk, and halfway here, it clouded over and threatened to pour."

Manning takes one of the bags and leads Neil to the kitchen, where they unload the contents onto the counter. "You needn't have brought all this," says Manning, surveying an assortment of delicacies that includes fresh breads, pâté, chocolate truffles, and several bottles of good wine.

"We didn't know what you'd be serving," says Neil, "and Rox felt guilty about canceling, so she stocked me up with goodies to offer as amends."

"Too kind. Thanks to you both." Manning stows some of the items in the refrigerator, then extracts from the freezer a bottle of Japanese vodka, offering, "Drink?"

"You temptress," says Neil, laughing, while Manning performs the ritual of the orange peel.

As they clink their glasses, Manning says softly, *"Compai."*

Neil winks at him. They taste their drinks. Then Neil asks, "Aren't you going to show me around? What a wonderful space!"

Manning leads him away from the galley kitchen and into the main living area of the loft. Their footfalls reverberate in the big room. "The cement floor is not an urban 'design statement,'" Manning assures Neil. "Nor is it entirely the result of a cash crunch. Truth is, I can't decide how I want to finish it."

"Then you're wise to wait," Neil tells him. "Sometimes your vision of a space has to evolve over time, and *this* space has tons of potential. It's worth developing carefully, with sure steps. Meanwhile, you seem comfortable enough, and you've got plenty of room. There's no hurry." Pointedly, he adds, "It's not as if you've got kids to raise here."

"You live alone, don't you?" asks Manning. "Roxanne said you designed your own house. I'd like to hear about it."

"Whoa," says Neil, reining in the conversation, "if you get me talking about *that*, I could blather all night."

Manning reminds him, "I'm not going anywhere."

Rain begins to fall heavily outdoors, but there is no wind to drive it, and it streams down the huge panes of the window. Reflected light from within the apartment dances on the slithering fingers of water, black against the lakefront sky. After an awkward silence broken only by the sound of rain, Manning says, "It's a terrible thing to admit, but I'm glad Roxanne couldn't make it tonight. I wanted to get to know you better. I can't quite believe you're here."

Neil steps to Manning and spreads his arms to hold him in a clumsy embrace, both of them careful not to spill their drinks.

As Neil gazes over Manning's shoulder toward the opposite wall, something catches his eye. "My God, Mark. It's a Bird!"

"What?" Alarmed, Manning turns to look, jostling both drinks.

"The painting. It's a Clarence Bird," he explains, whisking vodka from his sleeve while walking over for a closer look. "Wherever did you get it?"

"A little gallery not far from here. You mean you've *heard* of this guy?"

"Of course. He's awfully significant—at least he *will* be."

"So I've been told," Manning says with a wry laugh.

Neil shoots him a knowing glance. "A shrewd investment, Mark."

"It wasn't an investment," he insists. "I bought it because I like it. I've never bought a painting before, but I see something in this one that speaks to me, that actually has something to *say*. Listen, Neil: I'm a writer, and I work with other writers, lots of 'word people,' from reporters and editors to lawyers and politicians. Most of them seem to think that the only worthwhile task for the mind is to make one word follow another. The brain feeds the mouth or the pen, yet the eye never seems to feed the brain. I haven't known many artists—painters and sculptors or even architects—but I've always assumed that they don't think very clearly, that they must be slaves to the realm of emotions. As a result, I've been skeptical of what artists try to foist upon us as their 'work.' You go to a gallery and read the little cards posted next to each artifact, or you wade through the 'statement' the artist has written for the show catalog, and the only way you can react is: My God, what garbage! Incredibly, these statements seem to be given as much weight as the art itself. It's nothing more than academic drivel intended to justify meaningless junk by making it appear profound. I'm sorry if I seem close-minded in this attitude. I've sincerely tried to understand the art of our times, but I can't. And I won't pay lip service to a sham. I wish I had the background to appreciate the art of other ages, because I sense there's something there that's simply lacking today. Don't get me wrong— I'm not so naive as to suggest that it's only valid to paint pictures that *look like* pictures. I'm sure that visual abstraction *can* be meaningful and moving—after all, the power of mental abstraction is among the most extraordinary of all human traits. But I've rarely seen an artist pull it off convincingly. Splash painting—finger painting—is a diversion of children, nothing more. It is not art. Does it all even matter? I wish I understood."

Manning falls silent. He has said far more than he intended, and he fears that Neil may be offended by views that seem ignorant or, worse, didactic.

Neil has listened carefully. His features reveal no reaction to Manning's words, and the pause in their conversation is magnified by mutual anticipation. Neil decides that it's time to share a few ideas of his own.

"You *do* understand," he assures Manning, "far more deeply than most self-proclaimed artists ever begin to grasp. I went to art school to become a designer, to *get a degree* as an architect. I attended classes side-by-side with others who were there to *get a degree* as a painter, sculptor, printmaker, what-have-you. All the degree guarantees, of course, is that we've been exposed to a regimen of techniques and, one may hope, a body of aesthetic thought. That's it, kid. An art degree means nothing else. Yet art in practice has become a purely academic discipline—and the result speaks for itself. Artists go to school; they're taught to be open-minded and sensitive; they learn that method and logic and thought itself are alien to the visual arts. The only purpose left for words is to support the next artistic trend with rhetorical bullshit that replaces meaning with a skin of profundity. It *is* a hoax. It leaves me frustrated and bewildered. And the one question that gnaws at me every time I stroll through a gallery or pick up a copy of *Art News* is this: Just how seriously do these people take themselves, deep down inside when they're alone in bed at night with the lights off and no other stimulus except the churning of their own brains? Do *they* believe the things they paint? Do *they* believe the things they say to support their art? You know what scares me, Mark? I think they do believe it—*all* of it. They willingly submitted to the indoctrination, they swallowed it whole, and now they're playing the game themselves. *That*, all too often, is the art of our age."

Manning's green eyes pierce Neil's with a clarity and a directness that shoot through Neil and rest in his stomach. The penetration of one mind by the other is so complete and reciprocal that neither of them can evade its carnal overtones.

"Thank you," says Manning.

Neil doesn't ask, What for? He knows, as Manning does, that something has *happened*. He recognizes that they have achieved a level of communication that embraces words and thoughts, emotions and intellect. As if emerging from a daze, Neil asks, "Where were we?"

"I was showing you the apartment," Manning reminds him. "Not that there's much to show. Like most lofts, it's basically one big room—and as you can see, it's nearly empty." He waves an arm to encompass the whole condominium, which lacks all furniture other than a bed and a small dining table with its chairs.

"I love raw space," says Neil. "Must be the architect in me. There's so much you can *do* with this. The fixtures and built-ins are first-rate. Mind if I snoop around?"

In addition to the entrance, the apartment contains only two other doors, located on the wall behind the bed, flanking it. One leads to the bathroom. Indicating the other, Neil asks, "What's this?"

"Closet," says Manning. "It's huge. Take a look." Then he adds, "But please, no closet jokes."

Neil rolls his eyes, then opens the door, which switches on a light. Inside is a large windowless room that could easily double as a storeroom or even a study. It contains Manning's clothes, and Neil feels a tinge of excitement in stealing this intimate glimpse of his new friend's life. Manning's wardrobe is arranged, as Neil would have guessed, with neatness and precision. There is an inordinate number of khaki slacks. Shirts, all white or pastel, are grouped according to hue, and an ironing board stands ready for last-minute touch-ups. The room's sole element of clutter is the well-worn pair of Reeboks tossed in the corner with a pair of nylon shorts. "I see you're a runner," says Neil, closing the closet door.

"I wouldn't quite call myself a 'runner,'" Manning tells him, "if that implies I'm avid about it—because I'm not. Now and then, on a beautiful day, or at the end of a bad one, I like to pound off two or three miles—four or five if I'm ambitious. But I have no interest in distance and even less in speed."

"A sensible approach," Neil approves. "We should run together sometime, although it's been raining since I arrived last week. Here's a better idea: Maybe you could visit Phoenix this winter. It's *plenty* dry there, and we could run in the mountains every morning. It's wonderful—to be up early, under a warm winter sun, sweating—especially when you know that everyone back home is freezing."

"That sounds great," says Manning. "I haven't taken a winter vacation in years. We'll see."

"But," adds Neil, raising a note of caution, "there's not much *else* to do there. I suppose we could watch TV—there's our local crackpot evangelist of the airwaves, Brother Burt—*he's* always good for a laugh." Neil's playful tone now turns suggestive. "Or we could invent our *own* activities."

Manning repeats, "We'll see." He checks his watch. "Let me get you a fresh drink, then I'd better get dinner going. Care to help?"

"Natch."

Manning busies himself in the kitchen, putting Neil in charge of the table, which must first be cleared of some paperwork. Manning explains over his shoulder, "I made copies of the plans of the loft, and I've been trying to work up a few ideas—without success, I'm afraid. Just stow all that under the bed."

"Hmm." Neil finds a clean set of the plans and puts it aside, along with an extra copy of a document titled "Codes and Covenants." He slips these into one of his shopping bags before putting the rest of the material away.

While Neil fusses with the table setting, Manning asks, "Would you like to put on some music?"

"Thanks," replies Neil, "but I've had my fill of it this week. You know how carried-away Rox can get. Let's keep things quiet tonight."

"Amen."

Within a half hour, they are seated at the little table together. Manning has prepared a simple steak dinner, supplemented with brioches and a *grand cru* Bordeaux from Roxanne's CARE package. Candles are lit, flowers are arranged, and the rain beyond the windows is now driven in sheets by a gusty wind. The cozy setting is overtly romantic, but the conversation is limited to small talk about the food, the weather, the missing heiress.

Neil eats his last bite of tenderloin, sets down his fork, and dabs his lips with his napkin. Fingering the stem of his wineglass, he asks, "Why did you invite me here tonight?"

"To see the loft . . ."

"Yes?"

"There may have been other reasons. I'm not sure. Why did you *come* here tonight?"

"To see the loft. To find out why you asked me. Most important, to get to know you better." He pauses before getting to the point. "I like you, Mark, and if there's any kind of relationship that's possible between us, I'm interested. More than interested. But: I will not seduce you."

Manning grins. "Are you sure you haven't already?"

"Not actively. I'm sure of that. I've been too careful. If somehow you interpret my friendliness or my personality or even my very presence as a form of seduction—that's just *your* reaction to the way I am."

"That is exactly my reaction to the way you are."

"May I ask you something directly, Mark? Have you ever had sex with a man?"

"No."

Neil looks at him skeptically.

"Truly, Neil, I haven't—not as an adult. Sure, kids play around, and I was no different, but I've never done it in a mature, willful sense."

"You've never even been approached?" asks Neil, his voice colored with disbelief as he openly sizes up Manning.

"Yes, I have. Just once."

"Thank God," says Neil. "I'd be amazed if no one had ever *tried.*"

"A guy got suggestive at a party once. I was repulsed, so I left."

"Repulsed by the suggestion?"

"No, by the person. He was drunk and obnoxious and . . . well, not very attractive."

"Ohhh," Neil says softly, drawing out the monosyllable as he turns his head to gaze at the rain, thinking. Then he turns back to Manning, peers at him, and asks with a voice that sounds almost accusing, "Suppose this guy had been sober and pleasant and built like an Adonis. Then what?"

"I've no idea. Under the *real* circumstances, his suggestion was unthinkable. Maybe I've been kidding myself, but I never seriously weighed the possibility of sex with a man—until I met you." Manning stops short. Though he has picked his words carefully, he is stunned to hear the admission from his own mouth.

Neil asks, "What are your qualms?"

"Times have changed a lot since I was young. There's AIDS, of course, and there are still prejudices, but being gay doesn't seem to have the stigma it used to. Now they say it's in your genes, and in some circles it's out-and-out fashionable. Still, there's something about sexual identity that's deep and, yes, irrational— but it's real, almost tangible. People always want a label. They think of themselves as straight or gay or maybe somewhere in between, but they always define it. I'll soon turn forty, Neil, and I've never before dealt with the prospect of consciously labeling myself gay—or any of the other names they call you. Do I want you? Do I want to lie with you and indulge a nagging curiosity? *Yes.* I'd be a liar if I told you—or myself—otherwise. But the label scares me. Even if no one else knew, I would. I'd be waiting there with the label, and I don't know what it would do to me. This fear must strike you as silly or trivial, and I'd even understand if you found it insulting. I mean, *you* seem to have no difficulty coping with all this."

"This may come as a shock, Mark, but your label-crisis works both ways. I'd hate like hell for people to label me straight—a het, a *breeder*. That would be an identity crisis every bit as deep and real as the one you're flirting with. So I understand your concerns. I'm glad you've raised them because I would *not* want to be the person who saddles you with confusion or guilt. You mean far too much to me. That's why I won't seduce you. It would be too easy. Too easy for me to get away with and too easy for you to dismiss. When it happens—if it happens—there'll be the recognition that complete, powerful, lusty sex involves a certain responsibility and perhaps even commitment. *If* it happens."

Neil stops talking and searches Manning's face for some reaction to his words. Manning peers back, at first with a blank expression, then he smiles.

"Good," he says. "If it happens, it'll be just as you've described. There'll be no room for self-doubt, let alone guilt." Manning swallows hard, not daring to meet Neil's stare as he continues. "I hope it happens. But wanting things is a far cry from having them. There's always a price. And the price may be too high for me."

"Understood," says Neil with quiet finality. "And now that the great looming 'question mark' of the evening has been dispelled, shall we move on to frothier concerns, like dessert?"

"Great idea." Manning rises and begins to clear the table. As Neil pushes his chair back and slouches into it, getting relaxed, Manning turns to remind him, "You still haven't told me about the house you built. I want to hear everything."

Neil needs no further prompting to launch into an energetic recounting of the project, in which he has clearly staked great professional pride. Manning is fascinated by the tale, interrupting to pose thoughtful questions that in turn refuel Neil's enthusiasm. Hours pass as dessert leads to coffee, coffee to cognac. The two men have talked continuously, exhausting the topic of Neil's house, moving on to the random trifles found so revealing by those who are getting to know one another. It is well past midnight. The storm howls beyond the windows. The candles on the table have burned low.

Manning tells Neil, "Time to make a decision about something. It's raining like hell, and there are no cabs on the street—you'd get soaked trying to find one. Would you like to spend the night here?"

"No sex?" It is both a question and a stipulation.

"No," says Manning, grinning.

"I'd love to stay. But I'd better call Roxanne. She'll be wondering, I'm sure."

"I'm *sure*," echoes Manning while handing Neil the phone.

Neil dials, then waits while the other phone rings. "Hi, Rox, it's me. Yes, a wonderful evening, thanks. I hope yours wasn't too awful at the office. Roxanne, I think I'll be staying here tonight—the rain, you know. Just wanted to tell you not to wait up." He pauses, blinks, and puts back the receiver.

"What'd she say?" asks Manning.

"She hung up."

Manning whistles pensively.

Saturday, October 17

76 days till deadline

By morning the rain has stopped, but clouds still churn the dark sky. At eleven o'clock, the streets are eerily quiet as Neil walks the few blocks from Manning's loft to Roxanne's building. An elevator is waiting for him, and he soon stands outside the door to her apartment, hearing the wails of one of her more eccentric recordings within. He braces himself as he enters, setting his shopping bag on the floor.

Roxanne sits in the living room, listening to the music with the morning papers spread messily about. Her eyes are dark, her hair unkempt. The apartment smells heavily of smoke, and a hulky alabaster ashtray is filled with butts. She has been drinking—last night or this morning or both—Neil is not sure.

"Well, good morning, Rox," he says with an uncertain cheeriness.

"Did you fuck?" she asks flatly, sternly, in a voice he barely recognizes.

Neil is tempted to stretch the truth and confirm her suspicions, but his momentary triumph would quickly be quelled by her rage. On the other hand, if he answers truthfully, his denials would surely be met by her scorn and disbelief. It's a no-win situation, so he decides not to dignify her question with a response.

He tells her, "I've got some work to do on a new project." He picks up the shopping bag, crosses the room, and disappears down a hallway to the den, where he closes the door behind him.

Roxanne remembers younger years when even the worst bitch of a hangover lasted only twenty-four hours. Now the doozies last forty-eight. Her Friday-night binge, which flowed nonstop into Saturday morning, left her vomiting in bed by that afternoon. Sunday she could barely move. Dehydrated, wracked by both fever and migraine, she finally managed to eat something solid by evening while exchanging a few heated words with Neil. She was tempted to call in sick today, but there was far too much work needing her attention—besides, she *deserved* to suffer through a Monday's penance at the office. So here she sits, propped by her forearms at her desk. Though the worst symptoms of her bout of intemperance have mercifully passed, she feels shaky and depressed in its aftermath.

The latest edition of the *Post* lies before her. Its headline proclaims, WAITING GAME MAY BE OVER: INVESTIGATORS TO GET TOUGH ON HEIRESS MURDER SUSPECT. In the bylined story on page one, Humphrey Hasting has written, "The public may soon be offered a modicum of enlightenment into the mysterious circumstances surrounding the disappearance of airline heiress Helena Carter. Deputy Chicago police superintendent Earl Murphy revealed to the *Post* late last night that intensive administrative efforts are under way to bring a prime suspect to justice."

The article explains that Carter's houseman, Arthur Mendel, will soon be the subject of an inquest. "The hearing is not technically a trial, as no formal charges have yet been filed. However, Murphy conceded that the inquest will in fact be held in a courtroom before a judge. No date has been set."

With a disgusted flick of her wrist, Roxanne tosses the *Post* to the floor, where it mingles with sections of the morning *Journal*, which she has skimmed for a similar story. There is none.

Rising from her desk, she begins to pace the office, stopping at the window to bite her lip, looking out across the city without seeing it. She glances toward her feet and at the *Post*'s headline, reading it upside down. Things are heating up, getting messy. She really ought to phone Manning and discuss all this. But *can* she? She was justifiably pissed at him—as well as Neil—and she's nursing the hangover to prove it. God, what made her do it? The reason has gnawed at her all weekend, but it has not, till now, congealed into thoughts formed in words.

Jealousy? she asks herself. Yes, airhead, it's got something to do with jealousy. Plenty. You needn't be so analytical. This is no great mystery. You want to be screwed, right? A perfectly natural drive. Is that so hard to admit? You haven't betrayed your career— or compromised your feminist instincts—by owning up to your desires.

They're the two men you've wanted most and apparently have the least chance of getting. Neil is the best-looking man you've ever met, and you've known from the start that he's not available. Yet you've tortured yourself through more than ten years of "friendship," hanging on to the dim hope that maybe someday he'll lay you. And then there's Mark—intelligent, sensitive, *eligible*—a perfect match, or at least a good candidate for a long, comfortable affair. You've had him exactly once, but it was years ago, and you sensed even then that his heart wasn't in it.

Face it: You've wanted each of them, *both* of them, to splay you like some damned animal. And what did you get instead? An evening home alone, guest of honor at a party for one, while the two of them spent the night together. God only knows what went on over there—you may have lost them both for good. And who's to blame? Who brought them together? Wouldn't it be a scream, the very height of perverse justice, if you ended up losing them *to each other?*

Roxanne licks her lower lip, now puffy and raw, grated by her teeth. Squatting clumsily in skirt and heels, she snatches up the *Post* and shoves the tabloid into the wastebasket by her desk. Then she kicks at a section of the *Journal* that lies near her feet. The broadsheets of newsprint respond with a dull, unsatisfying slap against her shoe, so she kicks at Manning's paper again, breaking a heel. She drops to her knees, pounding the scattered pages into wads that crinkle between her hands, gathering the shreds into her arms, pressing them to her chest and face, finally stuffing the mess into the wastebasket. Tears stream down her cheeks. Her shoulders heave with convulsive sobs.

When she has regained control, she hobbles to the desk and wipes her eyes, as a child might, with swipes of her palms. She takes a mirror from her purse and checks her face, only to find it smeared with streaks of black from her hands, filthy from the *Journal*'s ink. She stares at herself in disbelief for a long silent moment, then erupts into laughter.

Several blocks away, at his desk in the *Journal* newsroom, Manning has also trashed a copy of the *Post*, though without the theatrics indulged in by others that morning.

"Mail call!" intones Daryl as he sidles into Manning's cubicle. He examines a note-sized envelope. "Looks like a love letter," he coos. With a single silky movement, he hands over the letter and disappears down the aisle with his cart.

Manning turns the envelope in his fingers and finds no return address on either side. There is the imprint of a generic postage meter, but no postmark. His curiosity stirred, Manning slits the envelope and removes a single sheet of plain white bond. He unfolds it and reads the message, carelessly typewritten:

```
Mark Manning,

    AnyonE with ~~thE slightEst~~ a modicum of
imagination could figurE out that thE
housEman did it. I sEE thEsE things. I
know. Now you do too.
    PEoplE in your position should takE
thEir social rEsponsibility morE sEriously.
An untimEly End facEs thosE who bEtray thE
public trust.
    You arE warnEd by
    —A FriEnd
```

Manning holds the letter up to the fluorescent ceiling lights to see if the paper has a watermark. His suspicion confirmed, he laughs openly. Setting the letter on his desk, he reaches for the phone and dials.

Daryl cruises by again with his cart, breaking stride long enough to ask, "A secret love?"

"Nah," says Manning, bored with it all. "Death threat."

"*I'm* impressed," Daryl says over his shoulder as he trundles off in the opposite direction.

Manning's attention returns to the phone. "May I speak to Roxanne Exner, please? This is Mark Manning."

After several tinny measures of "Tea for Two," the Muzak cha-cha is cut off by Roxanne's voice. "Mark!" she says with a strange combination of surprise and restraint. "I was about to call you. You've seen the *Post?*"

"Sure," he tells her. "I've also just read one of Humphrey Hasting's less *predictable* literary efforts."

"Whatever do you mean?" she asks with confused inflections, straining to establish a chatty tone.

"I got something from him in this morning's mail. Listen to this." He reads her the note.

"How perfectly dreadful," she tells him, her concern now genuine. "But what makes you think it's from Hasting?"

"Even though it's not signed, his style is unmistakable. What's more, the stationery carries the *Post*'s watermark. The clincher, though, is the typing. Hasting mentioned at your party that he still uses an old newsroom typewriter. In the days before electronic typesetting, reporters wrote their copy using multiple carbons, and newsroom typewriters usually had their type modified, replacing the lowercase 'e' with a block-style capital so that it would remain distinct on fuzzy copies. The letter I got was typed on just such a machine. It *has* to be from Hasting."

"Good Lord," she says, convinced of the letter's authorship. "Do you think he's actually capable of harming you—physically?"

"I doubt it. More likely, he's simply trying to lend credibility to his houseman accusations, hoping I'll jump on the bandwagon, which would enhance his *Post* campaign with the *Journal*'s stamp of legitimacy. I'd actually admire the man's cunning if he weren't so inept."

"Even so," Roxanne tells him, "it's frightening to think that he would make a scapegoat of Arthur Mendel, that he'd be willing to sacrifice that dear old man for the sake of concocting a few headlines."

"He may talk a good line about the 'public trust,'" Manning tells her, "but his personal ethics are nil. I'm driving up to the Carter estate tomorrow to interview Mendel and see if I can make any sense of this."

"Good luck," she tells him.

"Thanks. I'll let you know if I learn anything. But actually, Roxanne"—his tone is now distinctly less serious—"I didn't phone you to talk about conspiracies or death threats. I was wondering what you and Neil have planned for Saturday afternoon."

The mention of Neil's name hits Roxanne like a slap, reminding her that she's miffed. She tenses at her desk and grips the receiver with blanched fingers, her nails digging into the fleshy base of her palm. She exhales an indignant puff of breath into the phone before responding tersely, "We have no plans. Why do you ask?"

Manning's voice buzzes from the earpiece, "There's a cat show in the suburbs this weekend, one of the largest in the Midwest. I'd like to check it out—to get a bit of background—since Helena Carter was a big-time breeder. As long as you and Neil aren't doing anything, maybe you'd like to join me. Who knows? Might be interesting."

Roxanne doesn't mention that she is allergic to cats. If she declines the invitation, Manning will surely extend it to Neil anyway, and she's damned not going to hand them *another* opportunity to frolic as a twosome. Thank God for antihistamines—they were invented for just such predicaments. "Sounds like fun," she tells Manning with feigned enthusiasm. "Are you driving?"

After detailing the logistics of their excursion, Manning tells her, "I'm glad we could work this out. I've really enjoyed getting to know Neil. Thanks for introducing us."

She tells him flatly, "My pleasure." After a moment's hesitation, she adds, "It's too bad that Saturday's outing will be dampened by the farewells—Neil is leaving Sunday, returning to Phoenix. You knew, didn't you?"

"No, I didn't."

Roxanne could have predicted Manning's answer. Neil's decision to cut his visit short was arrived at only last night after her testy confrontation with him. She made it clear to Neil that he had worn out his welcome.

"I'm so sorry," Roxanne tells Manning. The news has clearly hurt him, and she has summoned with difficulty a facade of sympathy to mask her pleasure in delivering it.

Tuesday, October 20
73 days till deadline

Next morning, as Manning drives north again from the city to Bluff Shores, he listens to Bud Stirkham interviewing Humphrey Hasting on his radio program. The author and the reporter are trading platitudes about "the capitalist agenda" and "the common man," bucking up each other's zeal with the giddy enthusiasm of two soul mates, long lost, now found. Just at the point when Manning decides he's heard enough of them, their conversation captures his interest.

"The mystery of Helena Carter's disappearance," Stirkham intones gravely, "may soon begin to unravel, thanks largely to the selfless, untiring efforts of this dedicated journalist. Tell me, Humphrey Hasting, how did you come to focus your investigation on Carter's houseman, Arthur Mendel?"

"The conclusion was obvious, Bud, a real no-brainer! I've received numerous calls from certifiable clairvoyants, all delivering the same message: The butler did it. Their word is good enough for me, and apparently it's good enough for the state's attorney too. As you may have read in yesterday's *Post*, the mechanisms are at last in place to bring this rogue to justice."

"Ah, yes. Clairvoyants," says Stirkham. "I had the pleasure to attend a cocktail party not long ago at the home of attorney Roxanne Exner. In fact, you were there too, Hump, but before you arrived, the rest of us had a chance to engage Mark Manning, reporter for the *Journal*, in an energetic discussion covering everything from psychics to erotic dreams."

"Really?" asks Hasting, intrigued. "Did Mr. Manning offer any opinions of the paranormal?"

"He said that he's dealt with many mystics, and he feels they have no powers at all. He went so far as to say that he acknowledges no force in the universe beyond the perceptions of his own mind."

With a cynical laugh, Hasting asks, "Now *why* doesn't that surprise me? While it's only fair to acknowledge that Mr. Manning has steadfastly reported on the Carter mystery since day one, the public has understandably grown weary of his foot-dragging, his refusal to draw self-evident deductions that could prompt official action on the case. It is, after all, a reporter's sacred duty to shape public consensus and to orchestrate the cry for justice. Mr. Manning's flagrant disregard for his social mandate can only lead one to suspect the motives for his unconscionable silence."

Hasting pauses a moment, allowing his innuendo to register fully, then leans close to the microphone as if to share a secret: "I am not alone in this suspicion. During my discussions with deputy police superintendent Murphy on Sunday night, we speculated at length on this issue. I am now in a position to reveal that the state's attorney is prepared to summon Mark Manning to testify at Arthur Mendel's inquest. Manning's waffling stance on this story has clearly hurt his credibility, suggesting that his role in the mystery may be other than that of an objective observer . . ."

Hasting's speech is aborted when Manning turns off the engine of his car, now parked in the courtyard of the Carter estate.

Manning mindlessly checks his pockets for notebook and pen while stepping up to the front of the house and ringing the bell. When the door opens before him, he is surprised to be greeted not by Arthur Mendel, but by Margaret O'Connor.

She smiles and says, "Good morning, Mark." Her tone has an air of business to it, a hint of urgency that precludes small talk. "Arthur's just a *wreck* over all this," she tells Manning, ushering him into the hall. "He's in the kitchen—he's been anxious to talk to you." She strides off toward the back of the house. Manning follows without speaking.

As they enter the kitchen, Arthur stands, switching off the radio that has been playing. Manning hears just enough—"a modicum of social responsibility"—to know that Arthur is fully aware of Humphrey Hasting's rantings. There is no mistaking the fear in the old houseman's eyes as he reaches to shake Manning's hand with both of his, saying, "I'm so glad you're here."

In deference to the *Journal's* reporter, he does not wear his usual work clothes, but is dressed uncomfortably in an ill-fitting tweed suit. Manning cannot help wondering if the clothes once fit better, if the suit remained constant over the years while Arthur's body shrank.

Margaret excuses herself from the kitchen, letting the door swing closed behind her. The two men sit across from each other in a breakfast nook, where a bay window overlooks the lake. With an unsteady hand, Arthur pours them both coffee from a glass pot, already half empty.

Manning tells him, "Don't take Humphrey Hasting too seriously." He laughs before adding, "No one else does."

Pointedly, Arthur observes, "The police seem to. It's just unbelievable—it's *depressing*—to hear that guy suggest I had anything to do with Mrs. Carter's disappearance. Good Lord, she was all we had. Aside from the fact that I thought of her as more of a sister than a boss, I'd be crazy to do anything to harm her. It'd be like bitin' the hand that feeds you."

Charmed by Arthur's candor, Manning hopes that the old man will not feel intimidated by the appearance of his steno pad. He uncaps his fountain pen and begins scratching a few notes. The reporter wants to explore two topics regarding the heiress—cats and religion—and he finds that Arthur knows a great deal about the cats, but almost nothing about Carter's religious life, except that she seemed devout.

Their conversation stretches on for nearly an hour, detailing Arthur's history of service to the Carters, which spans more than thirty years, back to the days when there was a full stable of horses to tend. Manning asks him, "When your gambling debts caught up with you, and Ridgely Carter paid them off, was the incident widely known—that is, was it known beyond the household? Were there any news accounts of it?"

"Heavens, no," Arthur answers, aghast at the thought. "After Mr. Carter helped me out, he never spoke of it again. *Mrs.* Carter knew about it, of course, and she was the type who got a kick out of needling me now and then, but that was just her way of trying to lighten the situation and make me feel better. As for Miss O'Connor, well . . . it was pretty clear that she disapproved of my gambling, and it was just as clear that she sort of resented

Mr. Carter helping me out. But like I said"—he lowers his voice and leans across the table toward Manning—"she'd made a few problems of her own."

Manning has stopped taking notes. In truth, he has been digging for nothing specific. He has conducted this rambling interview simply to get better acquainted with Arthur, to assure himself that Humphrey Hasting's accusations are unfounded before proceeding with the investigation in his own direction. He caps his pen.

Arthur tells him, "Before you go, you might want to take a look at something. I got the strangest piece of mail yesterday." Arthur pulls a lumpy envelope from inside his jacket, which at least partly explains why the suit fits so poorly.

Manning examines the envelope, which carries a Chicago postmark, but no sender's address. He looks inside and finds it stuffed with cash, thousands of dollars in crisp bills. There is a typed note that reads, "For a good defense. More if needed." It is not signed. The typewriter's e's have not been altered. There is no watermark. Returning the envelope to Arthur, Manning asks him, "Any idea who sent this?"

"Not a clue."

Manning drums his fingers on the kitchen table, puzzling over the new development, then rises. "Would you mind walking me out to the cattery again? Something's been on my mind since you first showed it to me a couple of weeks ago."

Getting up from the table, Arthur tells him, "I'd be delighted. It's not far from the back of the house. This way, please." And he leads Manning out the kitchen door.

Crossing the lawn, Manning notes that the weather has improved considerably since his last visit. The lake is blue today, not gray, and the dry autumn air carries that nebulous sense of approaching harvest. Arriving with Arthur under the broad eaves at the juncture of the cattery building's two wings, he is struck by the manicured perfection of the surroundings, and he wonders what other secrets have fractured the tranquility of this seemingly idyllic setting.

His musing is interrupted by Margaret O'Connor, who emerges from inside the cattery. She wears a bulky sweater and a garden hat to protect her from the chilly breeze. "Oh, Mark," she says, surprised to see him, "I was just finishing my morning rounds. May I show you inside?"

"Thanks," he answers, "but right now, I'm more interested in the exterior of this building—or rather, its construction."

"Oh?" she says, closing the door behind her.

He turns to Arthur, explaining, "I'm curious about the foundations of the two wings—they're different. One is made of brick." He points to it.

Arthur nods. "Yes, the main wing of the cattery was built on the footings of the old stable. The shorter wing is entirely new construction, so it was built on a modern foundation of poured concrete—it doesn't have the charm of the old footings, but it's much more sturdy." He gives it a kick with the toe of his shoe. "Built to last."

Manning asks, "And the construction was under way at the time of Mrs. Carter's disappearance?"

Margaret answers, "Yes, indeed. It was Helen's pet project. What a shame she never saw it completed."

"Do you remember," asks Manning, "how much of the building was finished on that New Year's morning?"

"Oh, Lord," says Margaret, "I have no idea."

Arthur volunteers, "I remember." His expression has turned cold, and he continues without inflection. "The main wing was complete, and the shorter wing was just being excavated."

Manning asks him, "When was the new foundation poured?"

"Shortly after. A week, maybe two."

"*That's* right," says Margaret, remembering the details. "There was some confusion as to whether the project should even continue—because of Helen's disappearance—but we knew she wanted the cattery built, and the equipment and such was already on the property, so we decided to forge ahead. I'm glad we did. Those were fretful times, and it gave us something else to think about. But tell me, Mark: Why do you ask? What difference does it make now?"

Manning gathers his thoughts and prepares to respond, but Arthur answers for him.

"He wants to know about our decision to pour the concrete because the timing looks bad for both of us."

Saturday, October 24
69 days till deadline

"But I'll freeze my ass off," whines Roxanne.

"I don't give a damn," Manning tells her. "You're not wearing that thing inside."

"I've got to hand it to you, Rox," says Neil from the backseat. "You add a whole new dimension to the concept of 'politically incorrect.'"

It turned cold last night, the first hard freeze of the season. Manning's car started grudgingly today when he left his apartment to pick up Roxanne and Neil for their trek to the cat show in the booming western suburbs. This weather won't last, but the morning is still frosty. Even though the car is warm by now, Roxanne snuggles theatrically into the fulsome collar of a lavish lynx coat. She tells the men, "I didn't know I was keeping company with animal-rights activists."

"You're not," Manning assures her, "but it strikes me as a tad insensitive to flaunt your feline fur among a bunch of cat lovers—on their own turf, no less."

"Ooga booga!" grunts Neil in a low caveman voice. "Great white huntress gird loins with cat pelts."

Allowing herself to laugh at Neil's clowning, she accedes, "All right. The coat stays—locked in the trunk. But I get to borrow one of your jackets for the run from the car to the building. Parking lots can be so nippy."

Always the gentleman, Manning offers at once, "You can have mine." He fails to mention that the amphitheater has indoor parking, but he does mention the topic that has dominated their conversation for the last half hour: "In return for this gallantry, may I assume that you agree to represent Arthur Mendel at the inquest?"

She pauses before answering. "Very well. Let me run it past my partners—I don't think they'll find a conflict of interest. But honestly, Mark, if I'm taking on a new client, it ought to be *you.*"

He breaks his steady driver's gaze to turn and look at her wide-eyed. "*Me?*" he asks. "What'd *I* do?"

"Nothing, I assume," she tells him calmly. "But Humphrey Hasting . . ."

"Roxanne." His eyes are fixed on the road again. "It's bad enough that Hasting manipulates the media for the sake of some half-baked social agenda; now he's trying to manipulate the judicial system as well. Yes, he has a forum, but he's blowing smoke. There's no way he can turn his insinuations into substantiated charges."

Neil says, "Hasting may be a jerk, but he's a dangerous jerk, and I think you should heed Rox's advice and prepare for the worst—just to be safe."

Manning falls silent, as if intent on his driving, but in fact his mind is focused on Neil's warning, on the possibility that Hasting's contrivances could prove genuinely threatening. Manning's New Year's deadline is little more than two months away. If he's to save his job, salvage his career, he has his work cut out for him. The last thing he needs right now is the nuisance of fighting off trumped-up litigation.

Roxanne and Neil's chitchat lapses as the car banks into the curve of the exit ramp. With the amphitheater looming in the distance, Roxanne says, "You've gotten kind of quiet, Mark. Tell us something about this cat show. Neil and I are new to the game."

"So am I," Manning reminds her, "but I've done some research this week. Cat shows are held all over the country all year round. Today's show is a big one—about three hundred cats. Each show is sponsored by a specific cat club. There are many clubs in the Chicago area, and each is affiliated with one or more national organizations, of which there are seven or eight. The club sponsoring today's show is affiliated with the Federated Cat Clubs of America. The FCCA, remember, is named as one of the heirs to the Carter estate, and I wouldn't be surprised to find Margaret O'Connor here with some of her Abyssinians."

Neil asks, "Will the animals be paraded?"

"No," says Manning, "it's not at all like a dog show. The FCCA maintains standards for each breed, and they train and certify judges for the shows. The cats are appraised solely as specimens. Behavior is irrelevant, and the judges don't let an animal's 'personality' color its evaluation."

"Sounds kind of dull," Roxanne tells him. "Is there anything in particular you're hoping to learn?"

Manning thinks for a moment. "I've been trying for nearly seven years to figure out what makes Helena Carter tick. These shows were a big part of her life, and I've never been to one. It's time to correct that. Also, it's a good excuse for the three of us to get together before Neil flies home tomorrow."

A loaded silence falls over the car, and Manning wishes he had not mentioned Neil's departure. The early return to Phoenix has been prompted by a web of emotions that confuses and frustrates all three of them.

"I had my doubts," says Neil, breaking the tension, "but this whole cat-show business is starting to sound interesting. I wish I knew more about the breeds, but then, this is probably the best way to learn."

The car plunges into a dark tunnel that leads to the parking garage. Roxanne removes her big Jackie-style sunglasses. As her eyes adjust to the indoor lighting, she tells Manning, "I might have known. While I appreciate the chivalrous offer of your jacket, I *thought* it came too quickly."

It is nearly noon, and the show is well under way, so the lot is almost full. Many of the parking spaces are occupied by vans with out-of-state plates, driven there by breeders with their cats, cages, and exhibit paraphernalia. Manning finds a spot, helps Roxanne stow the lynx in the trunk, and removes his sportcoat, which she dons like a cape, its arms hanging limp.

Neil cracks, "Broad shoulders become you, Rox."

Grinning, she assumes the lead to the elevators and swaggers off *à la* Joan Crawford, heels snapping at the cement floor.

The threesome enters the hall, paying admission in the lobby. Each gets the back of one hand rubber-stamped with a paw print that allows its wearer to leave and return without paying again. Manning buys a copy of the show catalog—a daunting booklet of computer-printed lists—and gives it to Neil, asking him to try to figure it out.

Roxanne sneezes.

The exhibit hall itself is a single vast room, a utilitarian space with no pretense of décor. The main expanse of its floor is set up with row after row of numbered tabletop cages. Neil notices that these exhibit numbers are also found in the catalog, which lists each cat by lineage, owner, and breeder. The people who are showing the animals stand near the cages or sit on lawn chairs. Some listen to radios. Some drink or eat. Others groom their cats or fuss with cutesy decorations within the cages. The general confusion is compounded by the constant milling of spectators up and down the aisles. The animals make little if any noise, and the room is surprisingly odorless—for a space containing three hundred cats.

Roxanne sneezes again.

Along the far wall are five judging rings—not really "rings" at all, but called that by tradition. Each consists of a long judging table with a raised platform at its center. In back of the table are about a dozen numbered cages; in front are two rows of folding chairs to accommodate onlookers. A droning loudspeaker calls cats by breed and number to each of the rings. Each cat will eventually be seen by all judges. Owners and breeders whisk cats in their arms from the cages in the aisles to the cages in the rings, announcing, "Cat coming through," parting the crowds.

Again Roxanne sneezes, this time with a blast that makes her nose drip.

"Are you okay?" asks Manning, remembering Roxanne's history of allergies. "Do cats bother you?"

"Afraid so," she answers, fingering a blurry gum from the corner of one eye. "But I brought my pills. I'll be shipshape in a minute. Excuse me," she says, taking her leave, wandering off in search of a ladies' room.

Neil tells Manning, "Rox never mentioned that she was allergic to cats. Why on earth would she want to come *here?*"

"Because *we're* here," Manning says without comment.

Neil nods, enlightened.

The loudspeaker dryly calls the numbers of seven Abyssinians to one of the rings for judging. "Come on," says Manning, jerking his head in the direction of the ring. "I'd like to see this."

They jostle through the crowd and arrive at the judging area as the owners deposit their paged Abyssinians into the numbered cages. The two rows of chairs are already filled, so Manning and Neil stand.

The judge, Mrs. Ripley, is a buxom lady with stiff silver hair. She chats with her two assistants—a younger man and woman who sort through a pile of carbon forms that will record results of the judging. Ribbons of different colors and sizes are arrayed along the front edge of the table. Manning assumes that these ribbons will be awarded throughout the weekend's show—there are seemingly far too many for the seven cats now assembled.

"What utterly beautiful animals," Neil says *sotto voce* to Manning, beguiled by the cats.

With cats, spectators, and carbon forms assembled, the judging begins. Mrs. Ripley goes to the first cage, opens its door, and pulls out the cat. She holds it like a big sausage, one hand between its forelegs, the other grasping its hindquarters. Manning has never seen a cat held this way, but the animal doesn't mind—in fact, it seems content and docile. The matronly woman looks into the cat's eyes, coos at it, then clutches it affectionately to her chest—the way any layman would hold a cat. She places it on the little platform in the center of the table. A gooseneck lamp shines on the animal at close range. Still holding the cat with both hands, Mrs. Ripley runs her fingers through the fur, examining the quality of the coat as she parts it to reveal the vivid apricot of the undercoat near the skin. When satisfied that the animal will not bolt, the judge lets it stand freely on the platform, displaying its stance, its "conformity to type." She picks up a peacock feather and waggles it before the cat. With eyes following it alertly, the animal paws and snaps at the gaudy plume. The judge again picks up the cat in the strange sausage-hold, displaying the animal at different angles to herself and to the onlookers. She deposits the cat back into its cage and returns to the table, where she makes a few brief notes on one of the forms. Without comment, she plucks a ribbon from the table and hangs it on the cat's cage; there is no discernible reaction from those watching. Mrs. Ripley spritzes her hands and the platform with disinfectant, wipes up with paper towels, then goes to the second cage and begins again.

Manning and Neil look at each other with quizzical glances.

The judge works her way through all seven cats, exhausting the supply of ribbons while her clerks record the results. Some cats receive as many as three ribbons; two receive none. Occasionally Mrs. Ripley chuckles with her audience when one of the animals engages in some antic or another, but the whole proceeding is otherwise carried out in silence. Finally, one of the clerks announces, "The Abbies can return now," and their owners step forward to retrieve their cats and booty.

Manning and Neil are about to leave in search of Roxanne when Manning notices Margaret O'Connor rising from her seat in the front row.

"Margaret!" calls Manning. "I wondered if I'd see you here."

"Why, *Mark*," she says, bustling toward him, "I didn't think for a minute that I'd see *you* here."

After introducing Neil, Manning says, "You got me interested in Abbies, so I wanted to check out your competition. Are you showing today?"

"I've brought a pair of kittens, but I'm also here to see old friends—one in particular." She crosses her arms in a satisfied pose. "Timothy Chatman, president of the FCCA," she says in a tone intended to impress. In response to Manning's inquisitive gaze, she explains, "Timothy Chatman is one of the country's most respected authorities on Abbies. He consulted with Helen often during the early years of her breeding program, then went on to write the federation's Abyssinian standard—largely on the basis of Helen's cats. He's here to judge the finals, which is a real honor for the club. I'll introduce you later, if you like. He's over in ring five."

Manning peers across the room toward the last judging ring. Through the bobbing heads, he can see a figure who he assumes to be Chatman. He tells Margaret, "I'd like that very much, but first, why don't you show Neil and me your kittens?"

"I thought you'd never ask," she says with a playful smile, leading the two men down a nearby aisle.

As they approach the cage that houses Margaret's kittens, Manning is surprised to see Roxanne already standing there, peeping at the animals while checking details in her own copy of the show catalog, which she must have bought while returning from the rest room. He tells her, "I see you're one step ahead of us."

"Mark," says Roxanne, turning, "look who's here today." She points to the cage with one hand and holds out the open catalog with the other. "These are Carter's sister's cats."

"And *this*," says Manning, ushering Margaret forward, "is Carter's sister."

Roxanne blushes, stifling a laugh, while Manning introduces her to Margaret O'Connor.

"That-a-girl," Margaret tells her. "I'm glad to see you know how to use your catalog. Want to meet my babies?"

"Of *course*," Roxanne answers, mustering a show of enthusiasm to offset an allergy-inspired wariness. She traces her index finger down a page of the book. "Let's see," she says, all business, "one is Carter-Cat Abby Albert, and the other is Carter-Cat Abby Abbot. They're five months old."

"That's right," says Margaret, opening the cage. "But we just call them Al and Abbot. The long titles are their registered names; 'Carter-Cat Abby' is our cattery prefix. Here we go." She pulls one of the kittens from the cage and hands it to Roxanne. "This is Abbot."

Roxanne holds the kitten awkwardly at arm's length.

Margaret coaxes the other kitten from the cage and hands it to Neil. "This is brother Al."

"Hello, baby Al," Neil tells the kitten with a delighted, paternal grin that surprises Roxanne. "Ya bringin' home lots of ribbons this weekend?" The little cat looks at him with sleepy gold eyes, purring in the nest of his hands. Al's ears are enormous; his coat glistens; his body is lithe and long as a mink's. "I'd say you've got a little champion here," Neil tells Margaret while trying out Mrs. Ripley's sausage-hold on Al.

The kittens' cage already sports an impressive variety of awards. Manning says, "I'm confused, Margaret. What do all these ribbons mean? In the judging we watched, it looked like everyone won—some of them several times over."

Margaret laughs. "The ribbons always confuse newcomers. You see, of the seven Abbies you watched, six were ruddies and one was a red—the colors are judged separately. Of the ruddies, four were toms and the other two, queens—they're judged separately too. So a cat can place for best of breed, color, or sex, as a first, second, or third. But the only award that really *counts* is this one," she says, fingering a bunting-striped ribbon that hangs among the others on Al and Abbot's cage. "This is a winner's ribbon. A judge can award it to any particularly fine specimen. In the FCCA, a cat's status is determined by how many winner's ribbons the animal accumulates from show to show. Before a cat receives one of these, it's called a novice. After the cat gets its first winner's ribbon, it's known as an open. Four ribbons make it a champion, sixteen a grand champion, four-times-sixteen a quad-grand, and so on. Few cats get that far, only those that are seriously campaigned by their breeders. Abe—one of the cats that disappeared with Helen—was a champion many, many times over. Abe was the greatest Abby on record."

"Who got this winner's ribbon?" asks Manning. "Al or Abbot?"

"That one went to Abbot."

Neil says to the cat in his hands, "It must have been rigged, Al. We'd better demand a recount."

"Don't worry about Al," says Margaret. "He'll do just fine. These kids have four judgings left." She puts the kittens back into their cage, where they curl into a single ball of ruddy-colored fur. Then she suggests, "Why don't you folks make yourselves at home and take in the rest of the show? I'm going to track down some missing friends. But don't forget, Mark—I'd like for you to meet Timothy Chatman later."

"I won't forget," he assures her as she trundles off in search of old acquaintances.

Neil tells Manning and Roxanne, "Let's work our way up and down each aisle. That way we'll be sure to see everything."

As the three of them begin strolling past the first row of cages, Manning remembers Roxanne's attack of sneezes. "How are you feeling?" he asks her.

"Much better, thanks. I took a double dose for starters—my trusty antihistamines never fail me." She pats her purse.

Manning thinks it's risky to tamper with the dosage of a potent drug, but he keeps the opinion to himself, unsure of Roxanne's mood today. Besides—what's done is done.

As they round a corner and begin to plod through the crowd in another aisle, Neil stops in his tracks. "Mark, *look*," he says, pointing to the back of a rotund man leaning forward to fuss within a cage.

Manning and Roxanne stare, incredulous. Gaping back at them is a corpulent rump sheathed in burgundy polyester. Roxanne, now pointing too, squeals, "It's the Hump!"

Humphrey Hasting does not hear her over the din of the exhibit hall. He continues fussing with something in the cage.

"My God," gasps Manning, perturbed, "what the hell is *he* doing here? I wonder if he's *on* to something. Just look at him—snooping around like he owns the place."

"Relax, Mark," says Roxanne, holding forth an open page of the catalog. "Believe it or not, Hasting is here to exhibit a cat. See"—she points to an entry on the page—"he's showing a blue-point Himalayan."

"What's *that?*" Manning asks testily.

Roxanne states the obvious: "One way to find out."

Manning doesn't relish the idea, but admits, "I suppose it would be childish not to say hello."

Neil tells him, "I really dislike that man. I'll just keep my distance."

"Oh no you won't, kiddo," Manning chides him. "We're all in this together." He motions for the others to follow as he steps up behind Hasting. As if taken by surprise that very moment, he says, "Well, Humphrey Hasting! What a small world."

Hasting gapes at them, astonished. "Why, Manning . . ." he stammers, "of all people." He breaks into a sweat, wondering whether Manning heard his accusations on the radio a few days ago. Then, recognizing Roxanne, "Miss Exner, so nice to see you again. And your college friend—Mr. Waite, I believe. Do you attend these shows often?"

"No," Roxanne answers for the group, "but we see that *you* do." She gestures with the catalog toward Hasting's exhibit.

Hasting presumes he is off the hook. The color returns to his face as he waxes rapturous. "Let us leave all animosity at the door, my friends, lest we forget our sacred, fraternal bonding within the cat fancy. Yes, Fluffbudget and I have been entering all the local shows for years now." He taps the cage lovingly. "Of course, she never wins anything, but we just keep trying, and I do enjoy the fellowship of the club. In fact," he adds, squaring his shoulders with pride, "my increasing involvement with the federation has recently landed me a board position—I am national secretary of the FCCA—something of a tedious honor, I admit, but it does make good use of my note-taking skills." His voice becomes suddenly indignant. "If those damned judges had any taste at all, Fluff would be a grand champion by now." Then sliding again into sweetness, "Isn't that right, darlin'?"

The cat is aptly named—a breathing mound of off-white fur, its face and paws tipped with the cool gray known to cat fanciers as blue. It has a flat face with a punched-in snout and glistening black pellets for eyes.

Fluffbudget's cage is truly a home-sweet-home away from home, as attested to by a florid needlepoint sampler hanging on the back wall. Hasting proudly points out that they've won the award for best-decorated cage at every show they've entered. In the center of the cage is a cat-size four-poster bed of real brass. Its canopy and dust ruffle are of fine lace, its bedspread and pillows of smoky-blue velvet that accentuates Fluffbudget's "points." The front of the cage is framed by matching velvet curtains, tied back with tasseled silk cords. The cat will not go near the bed, but sits instead with a surly expression in its litter tray. Manning wonders if the cat prefers to sit among its droppings, or if Hasting has trained the shedding animal to keep off the velvet bedspread.

"Come on, darlin'," Hasting baby-talks the cat while opening the cage. "Let's come out and show off our beautiful fur coat." As Hasting yanks the disgruntled animal from its litter tray, Fluffbudget opens her mouth to meow in protest, but nothing comes out. Hasting displays the cat, holding it in his arms like a muff. "Isn't she a sweetheart?"

"My, yes," Roxanne obliges.

"That's quite an animal," says Manning, unwilling to be more specific.

"She certainly is," Hasting agrees, nuzzling Fluffbudget nose-to-nose. The cat tries to back off, seemingly embarrassed by its owner's affection. "She's due for another grooming," adds Hasting, fingering the fur with a touch that suggests it needs a bit of work. "It won't be long till her next judging." He picks up a long-toothed metal comb and sets to the task of raking out the Himalayan.

"Good luck, Hasting," says Manning as he, Neil, and Roxanne begin to wander farther down the aisle.

"We'll be rooting for Fluffbudget," adds Neil.

"Thank you, all," says Hasting. "Enjoy the show."

Remembering something, Manning halts and turns back to tell Hasting, "By the way—enjoyed your performance on Bud Stirkham's program Tuesday morning."

At the mention of the radio show, Hasting hits a snag in Fluffbudget's coat. The cat bares its teeth and hisses at Hasting, who raps the cat's head with the comb and hisses back at it, "Little bitch!"

As soon as they are out of earshot, Neil tells his friends, "I don't know how he can stand to *touch* that beast. Did you see the awful turned-up expression on its face? It looks like it just smelled a fart."

"And I think I just smelled a rat," says Manning. "Hasting is on the *board* of the FCCA—his campaign to bring Arthur Mendel to justice is apparently less than altruistic."

Roxanne laughs. "I've no idea what *any* of you smelled, but after all that combing, *I* smell cat dander—which can be lethal." She snaps open her purse, extracts a dose of preventive medicine, and pops the pill into her mouth, swallowing without water.

Neil warns her, "Those aren't *candy*, Rox." Then he tells Manning, "I think we should get her out of here."

"I agree," says Manning, "but I really ought to find Timothy Chatman before we go. Tell you what: You guys browse around while I go look for him. When I'm finished, we can go out for an early, leisurely supper. I know a place that makes the most incredible stuffed pizza. It's something you should try, Neil, while you're still in Chicago."

"Sounds good to me," says Neil. "We've missed lunch, and I'm starved."

Roxanne agrees to the plan as well, so Manning walks off in search of Chatman, deciding it might be quickest to ask Margaret O'Connor where to find him. Heading toward the area of Al and Abbot's cage, he sees Margaret gabbing with an aging, distinguished man who wears a tuxedo, looking absurdly out of place.

Margaret spots Manning and waves him forward. "Mark," she says, "what a coincidence. We were just going off to find you. This is Timothy Chatman, president of the FCCA."

The two men exchange pleasantries, then Manning says, "You're looking very dapper for *this* crowd, Mr. Chatman." He would not normally mention someone's being overdressed, but the sartorial excess is so blatant that it seems intended to invite comment.

Chatman chuckles. "I suppose I do overdo it, Mr. Manning. But the club gets a kick out of it, in light of my *esteemed* position," he quips. "Besides, it's about the only chance I have to get dressed up these days—not many of my friends are getting married anymore." He smiles pensively, a wistful expression that dwells for an instant on lost youth.

As they review some of the details of Chatman's relationship to Helena Carter, Manning considers that Chatman has a vested interest in the resolution of the mystery—his organization stands to inherit millions under the terms of Carter's will—which colors their conversation with new shades of meaning, with possible undertones, with motives for deception. Manning remembers his talk with Father Matthew Carey two weeks earlier. The priest was eyeing the prize, was not what he seemed, was not to be trusted. Yet *this* man, Timothy Chatman, is sincere, decides Manning. His judgment is confirmed when the old gentleman wishes Manning luck in finding the heiress, in bringing her back.

Manning observes, "You still think of her as a friend."

"Indeed I do. I knew her when she first started breeding Abbies, which I've always been partial to. Helena Carter's work advanced the breed beyond anyone's expectations."

Manning pauses a moment before asking, "Do you think of Humphrey Hasting as a friend?"

Chatman also pauses, unprepared for the question, then laughs. "Our new secretary is an avid enthusiast of the cat fancy, but he's a . . . uh, rather unusual person. No, I can't say that I count him among my friends. He's certainly proven himself a friend of the federation, however, and I believe he must have been *very* friendly with Helena Carter. It was he who convinced her to include the federation in the 'planned giving' of her will."

"Really?" The conversation has revealed more than Manning expected, so he discreetly digs his pen and notebook from a pocket.

"In fact," says Chatman, "his timing was fortuitous, at least from a mercenary standpoint. Shortly after she added the federation's codicil, she disappeared."

Trying to mask the significance he attaches to this new detail, Manning shifts the conversation, asking, "Since her disappearance, have you noticed any difference in the quality of Abbies being shown?"

"Indeed. The breed has slipped appreciably, and it's apparent to eyes less critical than mine. Good heavens, Helena Carter bred the cats against which all other Abyssinians are judged. When she disappeared—Abe and Eve with her—the only possible consequence was that future Abbies would suffer. It's so disheartening, traveling around the country as I do, judging cats that represent the finest efforts of earnest breeders, only to find that my favorite breed has actually lost ground in our quest to produce the perfect cat."

Manning glances up from his notes and sees tears beginning to well in Chatman's eyes.

The old man clears his throat and continues, "There's reason for cautious optimism, though. In the past year or two, some extremely fine specimens have been popping up in odd places all over the Southwest. Last month, for instance, I was judging a show in Albuquerque and came across a wonderful Abby kitten entered in the household-pet category, which means that the cat was neither registered nor pedigreed. A cat without a known ancestry is of no use in terms of advancing the breed, so I talked to the kitten's owner, and he knew nothing of where the cat came from—it was a gift from a friend of a friend, or whatever. And what's curious, Mr. Manning, is that every time I encounter one of these magnificent animals, I get the same story."

Chatman ponders the dilemma for a moment, then concludes, "It's horribly frustrating."

By late afternoon, Manning, Neil, and Roxanne are settling into a dimly lit booth at the Italian restaurant where Manning is a fan of the stuffed pizza. Though they parked only a block away,

Roxanne insisted on wearing her lynx coat from the car to the door. Once inside, she found no secure place to check the fur, so she asked the manager to keep it for her in his office, but her huffy manner made no points with the man, and she now struggles to roll the coat into a ball next to her in the booth. Though Manning was annoyed by the scene she created, he is pleased by the result—he and Neil are seated cozily next to each other across the table from Roxanne and her lynx.

A waiter with an accent introduces himself as Gino, but Manning has a hunch it's an act. They're all in the mood for a drink. Manning and Neil order their usual straight vodka. Roxanne, claiming the need to ward off a chill, orders grappa in a heated snifter. "I want the good stuff," she cautions the waiter, "not that Italian gasoline." Gino nods his understanding and turns to go, but Roxanne calls him back. "And a bottle of Chianti for the table—let's get this party rolling, gentlemen."

Once the drinks arrive (the wine hasn't appeared yet, presumably being held for dinner), Neil asks, "Well, Mark? Did you glean the background you wanted from the cat show?"

"More than I bargained for," says Manning. "Humphrey Hasting's history of involvement with the FCCA took me totally off guard. I'm not sure what to make of it, but it's a whole new twist I'll need to look into."

Roxanne swirls the snifter between her hands, telling Manning, "It seems you've uncovered quite a few new twists to this story. When you first told me about your predicament three weeks ago, you said that even though there was no known evidence of murder, you first had to satisfy yourself that any possible suspects had no involvement in Mrs. Carter's disappearance. You called it 'grunt work.' Has it paid off?"

"Not exactly." Manning's pensive tone is laced with understatement. "Even though there's still no hard evidence to convince me that Helena Carter was murdered, my investigation has raised more questions than it has answered."

"Such as?" asks Neil.

"First," says Manning, "why did Arthur Mendel and Margaret O'Connor order God-knows-how-many cubic yards of concrete poured on the grounds of the estate—in the middle of winter—within a week of Mrs. Carter's disappearance? That's suspicious enough in itself, but get this: Arthur once had gambling problems with the underworld of the horsey set, and Margaret had fears of being cut out of her sister's will because of a sexual dalliance she'd had with Ridgely Carter."

"Ouch," says Roxanne. She slurps a mouthful of grappa, swallowing hard.

"Ouch is right," says Manning, "but the plot—as they say— thickens. Let's say for the moment, for the sake of argument, that Mrs. Carter *was* murdered. What would be the motive? The most obvious, of course, is money. So who has the most to gain? The Archdiocese of Chicago will be the *big* winner, and to a lesser extent, the Federated Cat Clubs. So we can cast suspicious glances at Archbishop Benedict or any of his minions—Father Matthew Carey, for instance, whom I caught in a lie regarding a minor point of Helen and Margaret's family history. Or if it's the cat-folk who have blood on their hands, we should question the motives of Timothy Chatman, president of the FCCA, or even Humphrey Hasting, who's nutty enough that his involvement just might be plausible."

"Christ," says Neil, shaking his head as if to clear his thoughts, "that's a lot of loose ends. You've been led down a dozen different paths. There's nothing to tie them together."

"But there *is.*" Manning crosses his arms.

"Uh-oh," says Roxanne.

Manning tells them, "Nathan Cain, revered publisher of the *Journal*, seems to know *everyone*, and in fact he's had recent conversations with nearly everyone I've talked to. It's as if there's a network of interrelated motives at work, a conspiracy. If that's the case, it provides an explanation for Cain's bizarre ultimatum to me, which seemed fickle at best. Or maybe the ultimatum simply *was* fickle—the flexing of a powerful man's ego, no explanation required." He pauses to sip his vodka, swallows, exhales. "I'm stumped."

Roxanne starts to tell him, "You've really opened a can of . . ." but she stops short, sensing an impending sneeze. She lifts a finger to her nose, and the threat passes. "Worms," she says, finishing the thought. She raises her snifter to drink from it, and now the sneeze hits—right into the glass, spraying her face with grappa.

The guys can't help laughing. "Bless you," blurts Neil. "Sorry," says Manning, trying to compose a straight face.

Roxanne dabs with her napkin, but needs a mirror and better light. "Excuse me," she says, rising, purse in hand. Before leaving, she asks, "You'll keep an eye on kitty?"

"The lynx will be fine," Neil assures her.

And she's off to the ladies' room.

Neil turns his head to face Manning. He grins. "I thought she'd *never* leave." Under the table, he moves his leg so that his knee rests against Manning's.

The move is deliberate and unambiguous. While the situation reminds Manning of his recent encounter with Father Carey, there are no mind-games being played today. What's happening under the table is natural and appropriate, not devious or coy. Manning responds by shifting his own leg closer to Neil's; they touch from ankle to knee. Manning tells him, "I hope she's not downing more antihistamines."

"Even as we speak, I'm sure."

"Neil . . ." Manning starts a sentence without knowing its course.

"Yes?"

Manning puts his hand on Neil's knee. He tells him, "I wish you weren't going back to Phoenix tomorrow."

"I don't *want* to go," says Neil, putting his hand on Manning's, "but the tension with Rox is just too much. For now, we need some serious distance between us."

Manning is tempted to say, Why don't you stay with me? That would get you out of her hair. You could finish up your work here, as planned, and we'd have time to weigh more fully the issues we've already broached.

He wants to say all that, but the words stick in his throat. Instead, he asks, "Can I give you a ride to the airport tomorrow?"

"That's such a hassle for you, Mark. I can take a cab."

Manning places his other hand, his free hand, on top of Neil's under the table. He gives a squeeze. "It's no trouble. I'd really like to do it."

"Fine, then. Great."

Roxanne returns from her self-ministrations and sits in the booth. Without speaking, she smiles at Manning and Neil, observing the angle of their arms, which disappear beneath the table. She touches the rim of her snifter and tips it toward her, peering inside to confirm that it is empty.

"*Prego!*" she snaps at the nearest waiter, not Gino, but a waspy blond college kid named Spencer. "Where the hell's our Chianti?"

Sunday, October 25

68 days till deadline

When Manning dropped Neil and Roxanne at her apartment Saturday night, he reiterated his intention to drive Neil to the airport the next morning. Roxanne scoffed at the offer, insisting that Neil could take a cab. But Manning was adamant: "I'll be here at ten."

It's a minute or two before ten when Manning pulls into the driveway of Roxanne's building. He was almost late, dawdling at home, unsure of what to wear. His Sundays are typically laid-back, but he decided that Neil would dress smartly for travel, so Manning donned his best khaki gabardine suit.

The morning, like yesterday's, is crisp, but the autumn sun hangs low in a clear sky, brightening the day with an illusion of warmth. He can see his breath when he lowers the window to ask Roxanne's doorman, "Could you please tell Miss Exner that Neil's ride is here?"

He relaxes in the car, drumming his fingers on the steering wheel. Waiting for Neil to appear, he is vexed by a single question, which is answered when Neil emerges from the lobby, accompanied by Roxanne. Manning hoped that the drive to O'Hare would be a chance to spend some time alone with Neil, to talk freely, to confirm feelings, to be left with some sense of direction. Roxanne's presence nixes those plans—she is certainly aware of it—and he feels an unforgiving anger as he gets out of the car to put Neil's bags into the trunk.

They greet one another quietly, without enthusiasm. Roxanne is downright somber, suffering the aftereffects of an injudicious mix of antihistamines, stuffed pizza, and cheap Chianti. The lenses of her big sunglasses are a shade darker than the ones she wore yesterday. Neil is sheepish and soft-spoken, embarrassed by his inability to dissuade Roxanne from tagging along, by Manning's obvious disappointment at her intrusion.

Manning helps them into the car, announcing brightly but firmly that Neil, as the guest, will sit in front. Roxanne takes the backseat without comment, but Manning can feel her steely stare pricking his neck as he drives away from the building. Their conversation is terse and empty as they blend with the other expressway traffic leading to the airport.

"You'll write? Or call sometime?" Manning asks, as if speaking in code.

"Of course," says Neil. "You too?"

"Sure."

Roxanne offers from the backseat, "You needn't worry, Mark. Neil and I are in touch all the time. *I'll* keep you informed." Her words have a menacing ring that squelches further discussion until the car speeds down the ramp entering the airport grounds.

Deciding which way to turn, Manning says, "I guess there's no need to park. Is it okay to drop you at your terminal?"

"Sure, Mark," says Neil. "There's no point in parking. Thanks for everything." He squeezes Manning's knee.

"No point in parking," Roxanne echoes in an odd tone.

Manning turns onto the departure ramp and stops the car with its engine running at Neil's terminal. Both men jump out and walk back to the trunk. Manning puts Neil's bags on the pavement and tells him, "There's so much I haven't said to you. We'll work this out, right?"

"We will," says Neil. "One way or the other."

They reach forward, each with both hands, and interlock them in a gesture that is deeply affectionate—and openly desperate. Neil picks up his bags. Then he is gone.

Manning returns to the wheel to find Roxanne already planted on the front seat next to him. As he pulls away from the curb, she says, "I abhor long goodbyes. Was it teary?"

"Stop it, Roxanne."

"It's better that he's gone, you know. Life will be simpler. Don't you agree, Mark?"

"*Stop* it!" He spits the words, venting the hostility he has come to feel toward her.

"I understand," she says with a flat sneer, proving that she does indeed understand, which only deepens Manning's contempt. Long minutes pass in silence while Manning drives through the thickening traffic, his eyes never leaving the road, never once glancing in the direction of his passenger. Roxanne finally asks, "Mind if I smoke?"

"Of course not," says Manning, forcing a nonchalant manner as he opens the ashtray for her. He pulls his brass lighter from a pocket of his jacket and holds the dot of flame before her while she leans forward to inhale it.

She sucks a long, deep drag, then leans back to exhale with a languid toss of her head. "Mark . . ." she says cautiously, "when we get back into town, could you come up to the apartment? There's something I forgot to give you."

"Parking in your neighborhood's a bitch. Can it wait?"

"No, Mark. It's important. You won't be sorry," she assures him. Then she adds, "You'll find that a lot of things you haven't understood will suddenly fall into place."

"Okay, fine," he tells her, unwilling to pass up the possibility—however slim—that Roxanne has unearthed some new lead on his story. As they ride in silence, he wonders, What does she have for me, what scrap of paper, what tidbit of information that is suddenly so urgent? Or is it just a ruse? Is she hiding another motive? Manning knows exactly what her unspoken purpose might be.

"This better be good," he says, only half in jest, while opening the door for her to step from the car, which he has finally parked after a maddening search for a space.

When she opens the door for him to step into her apartment, Manning is overcome by the certainty that he has been duped. There is no document, no enticing clue, no tidbit, he is sure. She has brought him here to offer him her body, to prove his manhood and her womanhood, to dance, as it were, on Neil's grave. With his mind's eye he reads a neatly typed scenario of the events that will follow—predictably, mechanically, as if rehearsed—and he feels a confused rush of both revulsion and longing.

The door swings behind them and has not yet locked shut when Roxanne says, "I think we both need a drink. What'll you have?"

"The usual," says Manning, reciting his line from the imagined script, though he has no appetite for a drink.

Roxanne pours Manning's vodka, then a stiff half-glassful of straight Scotch for herself. She hands him his glass. He raises it to his lips without offering a toast, sniffing the alcohol before letting it roll over his tongue. It's the Japanese brand. He thinks of Neil.

Roxanne asks, "Mind if I play a record?"

"It's your home," he says pleasantly. But Manning does mind; when Roxanne speaks of "a record," she invariably means one of her old esoteric jazz LPs. As expected, Roxanne doesn't bother to browse through her collection. She throws a few switches and plays the album that already sits on the turntable. With an opening blast, some beat-generation combo—all of its members drugged to an early demise—lives again in Roxanne's living room. The music plays so loudly that Manning feels the ice rattle in his glass.

Roxanne strolls from the phonograph to the south wall of windows, sipping her Scotch. She basks in the October sun that angles through the plate glass in an oblique shaft, which is then refracted by the polished surface of a granite-topped coffee table. She turns to Manning, who still stands at the spot in the hall where they entered. "Well, come *in*, Mark," she says with a schoolgirl laugh.

As instructed, he steps into the living room, into the vortex of light and sound. The beat of the music pounds in his chest as he sits on the sofa and throws his feet up. Roxanne has eyed every nuance of his actions. "Make yourself at home," she says as his feet land on the granite.

Manning cannot tell whether her words are cordial or admonishing, nor does he care. He stretches his arms along the back of the sofa, a gesture announcing that he, not she, is now in control.

She studies him curiously as she crosses from the window and sits across from him on the coffee table, the soles of his shoes almost touching her thigh. Minutes pass with nothing spoken. The pause is dictated not by sexual tension, but by the dynamics of the music, which make conversation impossible. When the recording finally drifts into quieter passages, Manning says, "Okay, Roxanne. What's this important news of yours?"

She lowers the glass from her mouth and holds it with both

hands, between her knees. Her eyes drift away from him and wander about the room, then out the window, resting somewhere on the horizon. With an expressionless voice, she tells him, "There's no news, Mark. It's unfinished business."

As he hears her words, a trace of a smile turns the corners of his mouth, a smile rooted in the satisfaction of having foreknown her motives. Thinking aloud, he tells her, "You want to be fucked."

"I do." She turns to face him directly. "I want what Neil couldn't have."

"What makes you so sure he *didn't* have it?"

"He didn't," she says, aware that Manning is toying with her. "I know he didn't."

A saxophone wails obscenely at an ear-piercing level. Manning tells her, "Take off your clothes," a dull command without emotion, shouted just loudly enough to be heard over the music.

She looks at him from across the table with a quizzical smile that asks, Here? Are you serious? His humorless stare confirms his bidding, so she rises, stepping backward out of her shoes and into the broad, glaring beam of sunlight. She stands before him, before the city, hesitates, then removes her clothing piece by piece—with purpose, not teasing—dropping it to the floor.

Manning stands, revealing a lump in his slacks that stretches the gabardine. He steps over to Roxanne and grabs her wrist. She offers no resistance as he leads her, as if leashed, to her bedroom.

Entering the room, he flings her onto the bed, where she sprawls atop its tailored spread of cold-gray silk. Manning stands at her feet and removes his jacket, his tie, all of his clothes with quick, efficient jerks, till he stands naked before her, legs spread, feet planted in the hard wool carpeting. She moans at the sight of his engorged penis. The music, more feverish still, clatters in the other room. Roxanne's body ripples involuntarily to its beat.

Manning crawls onto the bed and nudges into her without foreplay. He supports himself with both arms as he grinds against her. Half audibly she mumbles, "You're not queer"—she waggles her head with abandon—"you're not queer." Manning thinks of Neil while pushing deeper within her. She begins to groan, licking her lips, craving his. But he will not kiss her. He thinks of Neil and pumps steadily harder, pumping like a machine that was designed for one purpose. Roxanne reaches an orgasm and screams an ecstatic noise as the music in the other room reaches a shrill climax of its own.

But Manning isn't through. He thinks of Neil and feels a pang of frustration that has mounted for two weeks to be released in this act, an act that carries no pretense of affection. He is servicing Roxanne, servicing himself. Basic missionary position. Nothing exotic, nothing special.

He hears the needle skipping in the last groove of the record with a dull, amplified thud and realizes that he has captured its rhythm in the pounding motion of his hips. He is fucking Roxanne at the rate of thirty-three thrusts per minute—about two seconds each, he calculates. He wonders wryly if she has guessed the basis of his technique.

Thirty-three beats per minute. He finds the frequency a bit slow. He thinks of Neil and pumps his hips faster. He thinks of Neil and feels a tingle in his groin that begins to cloud his senses. He thinks of Neil somewhere over the Great Plains at thirty-five thousand feet. He thinks of Neil without missing a beat. He thinks of Neil, and thinks of Neil, and his back arches in a spasm that drives him fully into Roxanne, releasing his frustration with a powerful surge that verges on pain. He hears a gasp, unsure if it sounded from himself or from the woman beneath him.

Their purpose is accomplished. As abruptly as he entered her, he withdraws.

He stands before her as he did before, dressing quickly, deftly. He turns to check the knot of his tie in a mirror, combs his fingers through his hair, picks up his jacket, and leaves the room.

Roxanne lies sated and speechless, grating her shoulder blades on the silk. She hears the popping of the needle stop as Manning switches off the phonograph. Then she hears the lock of the front door as it closes behind him.

PART TWO

DECEMBER

S	M	T	W	T	F	S
		1	2	3	4	5
6	7	8	9	10	11	12
13	14	15	16	17	18	19
20	21	22	23	24	25	26
27	28	29	30	31		

7-YEAR DEADLINE NEARS
Archdiocese preparing to claim Carter legacy within two weeks

By Mark Manning
Journal Investigative Reporter

DECEMBER 21, CHICAGO IL—If the mystery of Helena Carter's whereabouts is not solved within the next eleven days, the missing airline heiress will be declared legally dead on January 1, and the Roman Catholic Archdiocese of Chicago will lay claim to a fortune estimated in excess of one hundred million dollars.

Monsignor Andrew Lerner, administrative aide to Archbishop Benedict, told the *Journal* last night that the legal-affairs department at archdiocese headquarters has been working overtime to ensure that all probate mechanisms are secure by New Year's Day. He said, "We still pray for the safe return of Mrs. Carter, who was a faithful daughter of the church. Unfortunately, we now face the inescapable conclusion that Mrs. Carter has suffered an odious demise. Her memory will be best served by the expedient distribution of her estate so that the good works of the archdiocese may continue unfettered in her absence."

Helena Carter is sole heir to the late Ridgely Carter, founder of CarterAir. She disappeared from her Bluff Shores estate nearly seven years ago, along with a pair of prize Abyssinian cats, of which she was an eminent breeder. The Federated Cat Clubs of America (FCCA) is also named as heir to a substantial sum under terms of her will. The case of the missing heiress has stymied police and journalists alike, who have been unable to produce any evidence of the woman's whereabouts, whether dead or alive.

'HOUSEMAN TRIAL' SLATED

Arthur Mendel, longtime houseman to the Carter family, has been ordered to appear next week at an inquest beginning January 30 in Cook County Circuit Court before Judge Clement Ambrose. A Chicago newspaper has accused Mendel of complicity in the disappearance, and opinion polls show widespread belief in the charges against him, which have not yet been corroborated. This reporter has also been ordered to answer charges at the same hearing. ❏

Monday, December 21

11 days till deadline

Jingling bells interrupt Manning's perusal of his story in the latest edition. Daryl, wearing a Santa hat, arrives with his mail cart. Manning asks him, "Any hot tips for a needy reporter today? I could sure use *something* to jump-start this dead-end story." He tosses the newspaper aside.

" 'Fraid not," Daryl tells him, handing over a bundle of envelopes. "Just a batch of Christmas cards from the usual bunch of flacks." Shaking his bells, he strolls off down the aisle with his cart. "Ho ho ho," he intones in a low voice unnatural to him.

Manning shuffles through the envelopes and determines that Daryl is right—they are all greetings from press agents—so he places them unopened atop a stack that already teeters near the edge of his desk. Then, from the inside pocket of his jacket, he removes another envelope, not a Christmas card, that was received at home more than a month ago. He slides out the note, written in a clear, confident hand, and reads it again, hoping that this time it might say more than it did before. But it remains the same:

> *Dear Mark. Went to a cat show here in Phoenix this weekend. Wanted to relive something you and I shared. Went alone, stayed all day, came home in a funk. Saw some remarkable Abyssinians— thought you'd want to know. I think of you often (would you believe always?) and wonder if and when we'll see each other again. Hoping to hear from you—Neil.*

Manning hasn't written back. He hasn't called, though he's often reached for the phone, even dialed the area code.

I've been *busy*, he tells himself, trying to justify his reticence, but knowing better. How long would a phone call take me? Ten minutes max if it goes well, less if it doesn't. So it's not a matter of having time. It's the . . . emotional expenditure, the Pandora's box I'm not ready to open while there's so much else to deal with.

He has less than two weeks left to locate a woman who has eluded him for seven years—and only nine days to prepare for a court appearance concocted to vilify his investigation. What, then, has consumed his working hours for the past month?

Ethiopia. The crisis at long last appears to be winding down, owing largely to the efforts of an outspoken suburban woman, mother of one of the hostages, who has mounted a headline-grabbing campaign of "personal diplomacy" that has frustrated Washington and tantalized the public. Every edition of the paper now brims with Ethiopia stories—breaking news, sidebars, local-angle features—and Manning's share of these assignments has diverted his attention from the Carter case.

He has persisted, though. Every spare minute at the office, and much of his own time, has been spent searching for evidence—or even clues, threads, tidbits—that would either incriminate or exonerate the diverse characters on his dwindling list of likely suspects.

He was quickly able to eliminate Archbishop Benedict, Father Matthew Carey, and Timothy Chatman from active consideration. While each would gain from Helena Carter's demise, Manning concluded that none of these men had the direct means to perpetrate such a crime.

Still on his list are Arthur Mendel, Margaret O'Connor, and Humphrey Hasting. All three had plausible motives. Arthur and Margaret had the means. And Humphrey Hasting's unsubstantiated finger-pointing at Arthur Mendel serves only to cast darker suspicion on himself. But this is little more than circumstance, all inconclusive.

And what of Nathan Cain? His publisher hobnobs with the archbishop, engages in cocktail chat with a bombastic reporter from a rival newspaper, and orders his own star reporter to ignore the known facts of a major local story. Could Nathan Cain conceivably be *behind* it all—a mastermind of abduction and murder? If not, is he trying to influence the outcome of the story in order to help the Archdiocese hierarchy collect on the will? Or is he simply, as Gordon Smith suggested to Manning back in October, simply exercising his "perverse sense of gaming"?

Lacking hard evidence of foul play, Manning concludes, as before, that Helena Carter must still be alive, but he's no closer to proving it than he was in the beginning. And time is running out.

"Mr. Manning?"

Manning returns Neil's note to his pocket and swivels in his chair to find Gordon Smith's secretary standing behind him with a strapping young man whose owlish glasses and muscular build give him the air of a boyish Clark Kent. Manning clears his throat as he rises to greet them, wondering what mission has coaxed the woman out of the managing editor's office, since she rarely appears on the floor of the newsroom.

"Mr. Manning," she repeats, hesitates, then continues, "Mr. Smith asked me to introduce David Bosch to you. David will join us next month as an intern."

"It's a real honor, Mr. Manning," says the eager kid, squaring his broad shoulders as he crunches Manning's hand. "This is awesome. We've studied your stuff in J-school."

"Just finishing up?" asks Manning, flexing his blanched fingers.

"Yeah," says David, "one more semester at Northwestern. But the best training in the world will be right here, on the job. I was blown away to find out I got the internship—and now *this*. Who'd believe I'd actually end up working at Mark Manning's *desk?* Too cool!" The kid doesn't notice Manning's sudden pallor. "Where are they putting *you*—'upstairs' somewhere?"

As Manning mumbles, "That's sort of . . . up in the air," his phone rings.

"We can see that you're busy," says the secretary, sensing the effect of their visit. "I'd better take David down to personnel."

"Great to meet you," the rookie tells Manning as the woman leads him away. "See you in January!"

Manning musters a halfhearted smile and waves a cursory farewell as he answers the phone.

The man's voice on the line sounds nervous. "Mr. Manning? I've never telephoned a newspaper before, but I read your article this morning about the heiress, and I thought I should call. You see . . . my wife has dreams."

"Your wife," Manning repeats dryly.

"She dreams about things that might be useful to your stories."

"Really?" says Manning, feigning interest. "Tell me about them."

"I'd be delighted, Mr. Manning." The voice is now effervescent, any trace of nervousness vanishing. "This all started several weeks ago . . ." the tale begins in a gossipy tone.

Manning dangles the receiver by its cord, holding it at arm's length, and lowers it into his wastebasket. He sits back in his chair and breathes deeply, clearing his thoughts, then removes Neil's note from his pocket to read it again. He stares at the paper, but his eyes do not focus on the writing. His breathing stops, and time is suspended for a long moment. Then he blinks, inhaling, and ponders reality. The *Journal*'s management is preparing to give his desk to some upstart *kid*. They already assume he will fail at Nathan Cain's mandate.

His fists clench, crumpling the note. He wads the paper into a tight ball and flicks it into the wastebasket, where it glances off the receiver. The little voice pauses at the intrusion, then jabbers happily on.

Far from Chicago, in the rectory that stands next to a church in the desert, Father James McMullen sits at his cluttered dining room table. The piles of paperwork have grown in recent months, and he hasn't made much headway. With Christmas so near, there's a slew of administrative minutiae that must be resolved while leading his flock toward their celebration of the miracle birth. The priest turns an envelope in his hands—clearly, it isn't Christmas greetings. So he tosses it on the stack of unpaid bills.

It is midmorning, and down the hall, Mrs. Weaver clatters whatnot in the kitchen. It's too early for lunch—too early for tuna, thank the Lord. No, by the smell of it, she's baking cookies. The phone rings. Twice. Four times before she grabs it. She must have had her hands in the dough.

"Telephone, Father."

Grateful for the interruption, he hoists himself from his chair and lumbers off to the kitchen. There are indeed cookies in the works, an ovenload of Christmas treats set out to cool on the counter top. Turning in time to catch the priest eyeing them, Mrs. Weaver reminds him, "Those are for the *children*, Father," then she resumes dolloping out the next batch from a big chipped red bowl.

The priest picks up the receiver that dangles from the wall phone near the doorway. He glimpses the approaching holiday on the single page still hanging from the wire spiral of the church calendar. "Merry Christmas," he says. "This is Jim McMullen."

Listening to his caller, the priest's face blanches. He steps around the doorway and into the hall, hoping the housekeeper won't hear him. "I told you never to call me here."

The voice on the phone hisses into McMullen's ear, "This crap has been all over the news lately. We'll have to act faster than we planned."

Mrs. Weaver turns on the water to rinse her hands in the sink. The voice on the phone grows louder, spitting an obscenity. The priest inhales sharply, both shocked and angered by the invective. With hand on chest, he feels the pounding of his heart—he's sure it skipped a beat. "That's *enough*," he says into the phone. "Behave yourself. I'll talk to you later."

With attempted nonchalance, he steps back into the kitchen and hangs up the phone, but Mrs. Weaver can tell he's shaken. Wiping her hands on her apron, she asks, "Everything all right, Father?"

"Just another"—he fumbles for the words—"overanxious creditor."

"Ah." She nods. There's been a fair share of *those* calls lately. Twisting her neck to check the clock over the refrigerator, she tells him, "You'd better get a move on, Father. You'll be late for the assembly. I'll have lunch ready when you get back."

"Goodness," he says, having forgotten the town meeting, "I'm on my way." He crosses the kitchen, swings open the screen door, and steps outside.

A breath of cool air freshens the desert this morning with nature's tenuous promise that the oppressive heat of perpetual summer has indeed waned. The sky is radiantly blue—like a backdrop, the artificial handiwork of some overcaffeinated set designer—and there is no smog from the distant city to cloud the horizon beyond the mountains. Any day now, it could rain. Then the desert will bloom, and this place will seem like paradise, like a lost land found, a covenant fulfilled.

The people of Assumption sometimes forget their holy calling during the long, sweltering months that test their faith and divide them into cranky factions. But the cool morning has spruced their zeal and renewed their sense of unity. They are, after all, a people of God.

Father McMullen is thankful for the break in the weather. God's timing is good—this is the third Monday of the month, the morning when the community gathers in the shabby school hall for its regular town meeting. As both spiritual and temporal leader of Assumption, Father McMullen presides at these forums, noting with alarm lately that their tone has grown contentious. Striding down the center aisle of the packed assembly, he prays with apprehension, Dear Lord, preserve us in our mission. Let calmer heads and peaceful hearts prevail today.

He steps onto the rickety dais and turns to greet the people. Their chatter instantly ceases, and they respond like school-children with a lilting "Good morning, Father."

"Let us pray," he tells them, and they rise amid a clanging of metal folding chairs. "God, our Father," he intones mechanically, "be with us this glorious morning as we seek to find Your ways in a world that is often hostile yet forever beautiful. Make us worthy to act as servants in the home You have created for us. Make us one in mind and spirit. We ask this through Christ our Lord. Amen." He waves his hand in a loose blessing and asks the people to sit.

The only sure thing about these meetings is that they begin with a prayer; other than that, the agenda is left to the whim of the assembly. What can of worms, wonders the priest, will be opened this morning? Several hands already flutter, seeking recognition. A gangly young man, the choir director, itches to speak. "Yes, Ed?" says the priest.

Ed bolts up from his chair near the front of the hall and turns sideways to address the crowd. "Christmas is coming," he says in a loud but wavering voice. "It's only four days away, and *we* have a problem—the organ. Or I should say, the *lack* of an organ.

The one we have doesn't work and can't be fixed. Now, traditional church music—the kind of music we all expect to hear in Assumption—is almost exclusively organ music. So we are faced with two unappealing options: Either we go *a capella* again, or we substitute a piano."

"*No!*" wails an old man, rising from his chair to speak without being recognized. "We're *Catholics* here," he bellows, amazed that he should have to state something so obvious. "Catholics don't play pianos in church—not *real* Catholics. Pianos are for dance halls, not churches. Pianos are for heretics. They're for, they're for . . . *Protestants.* My God," he says in a horrified whisper, crossing himself as the thought enters his mind, "first we'd have pianos, and then—before you knew what hit you—*guitars.*" He plops in his chair, quaking at the image he himself has conjured.

An uproar swells through the hall, with a cross fire of discussions and an anxious crop of raised hands. Father McMullen recognizes a young woman who cradles a sleeping infant in her arms. As she rises, the crowd hushes itself so as not to wake the child.

In a clear, soft voice, she says, "I think we should just keep things simple. Some of us feel awful strong that we shouldn't have a piano in church, and I guess we don't have the money for a new organ, so I think we should just go on without either. The Mass is beautiful. We don't need to jazz it up. Let's keep it simple."

The room bursts into discussion as the woman sits down. The baby wakes and adds its crying to the din. Some of the crowd support the young woman, saying that she talks sense and that her solution is the only way to keep everyone happy. Others insist that they won't be happy at all if they don't get some *real* music into the church—disputing among themselves whether a piano is an acceptable substitute for an organ. Father McMullen makes no attempt to bring the meeting to order, preferring to let the assembly argue itself out. He will gladly go along with any resolution that the parish finds acceptable.

The priest notices Owen Foss sitting calmly in the crowd with his hand raised, not taking part in the discussion that roils around him. Owen is mature but not elderly, has never shown particular interest in musical matters, and the priest has always judged him levelheaded. "What's on your mind, Owen?" calls Father McMullen above the turmoil.

Startled by the priest's voice, the crowd falls silent and turns to watch Owen, who strokes his chin while rising. "I just think it's kinda funny, Father, for everyone to be frettin' over Christmas carols when there's so much other stuff—*big* stuff—that needs our attention. Just look around you, everybody. Look at this pitiful excuse for a town hall—a dirty lunchroom in a run-down old school. The whole building's a disgrace, and we need to replace it. But first, we've got to do something about health care. There's lots of kids here, and old folks too, but *no doctors*. Why, we almost lost Father McMullen when he had his attack last year. We've *got* to build a hospital, a full-blown medical center! And when we're through with that . . ."

"Now hold on, Owen," says Father McMullen through a nervous chuckle. "That's quite a wish list you've got there. Let's not allow our worthy ambitions to get in the way of earthly practicalities. We've already gotten some initial estimates, and the hospital you describe would cost almost fifty million dollars. Good Lord, that project alone would entirely deplete our expected endowment." He suddenly stops, as though he has let something slip.

Astounded, Owen asks the priest over the murmur of the crowd, "What are you talking about? That's only *half* the money—it's common knowledge."

Near the back of the hall sits the woman with a novel, which lies unopened in her lap as she watches the progress of the meeting with an icy stare. Disgusted, she rises, turns, and walks out of the room, noticed only by the priest.

As she descends the front stairs of the school and walks off toward the town square, Father McMullen rushes out of the building after her. Winded, he calls, "What's wrong?"

She stops in her tracks to look him straight in the eye. "These people make me sick," she tells him, "bickering and pouting about what they want for Christmas, carrying on like a bunch of kids. I'd call you all hypocrites if I didn't realize that I must be the biggest one of all—or the biggest fool. I have half a mind to put myself on the next plane out of here."

"If I thought you meant that . . . you know you could break

my heart." He pats his ticker woefully, reminding her of his delicate condition. With an infectious grin, he coaxes a smile out of the woman.

"I'm sorry," she tells him, unable to remain angry. "God's given us a fine cool day, and we should thank Him for it by enjoying it."

"So true. The simple pleasures of clear sky and birdsong are gifts we too often overlook." A brownish bird dives from the church steeple and caws horribly as it passes over them. A snot-like circle of birdshit lands next to Father McMullen's shoe. The woman stares at it, laughing inwardly while pretending to appreciate the priest's enraptured monologue. "The gifts of nature," he continues, "are among the sweetest of our Lord's bountiful kindnesses. He showers us with fruits of the field and the bread of heaven." The priest shifts his weight and steps on the slimy bread of heaven. The woman's eyes bulge. "But God's gifts are only one manifestation of His love for us. The trials, the *crosses* He sends us, are of course His most special blessings."

"Jamie, you're a good, holy man, and I love you like a true Christian, a brother—but I'll have none of that 'suffering is a blessing' nonsense." She beads him with a squint from beneath her sharply penciled brows, then tells him, "You'd better get back to your flock before they eat each other alive. I've got to go tend my own little herd."

Tuesday, December 22
10 days till deadline

Manning stands in the middle of the street that runs straight between two rows of white houses. This is everyone's mental picture of everyone else's hometown. Though no one ever grew up here, it is the childhood setting that everyone feels deprived for having missed.

Manning is dressed to run again. He has been lax about it lately, and guilt gnaws at the lining of his stomach. He wonders if he's fit for the task that now faces him.

The sun shines intensely from somewhere in the crystal sky, and he knows that his run will soon overheat him. He straddles the line of elastic tape in the middle of the road and removes his tight black T-shirt, his loose white shorts, and stands naked except for his running shoes. Aroused by the warmth of the sun against his body, he answers without hesitation the urge to stroke his penis to full erection. He wonders without caring if he is watched from behind the delicate lace curtains that flutter in the windows of the big clapboard houses.

He takes a deep breath. His lungs fill with the enriched and purified air that hangs over this special place. His veins course with blood that is instantly thicker, redder, more nourished for action.

Manning begins to run. His feet grate the pebbled asphalt on either side of the white line. His hair bobs rhythmically, parting into broad, tapering licks. He feels the repeated tug of gravity on the muscles of his chest and on his wobbling penis. Picking up speed, he feels no trace of pain or stress or fatigue, focusing only upon that point at the horizon where the white line ends. Houses and trees rush past him in a blur.

He trips. As though a wire has snagged his toes, he pitches

forward with a force that threatens to grind his body along the pavement, but he feels no fear, recalling in a flash that the street will not rise to scrape against him. He is aloft.

He summons with ecstatic abandon the powers that he so needlessly doubted and even feared when he first came to this place—those powers from within that erase his tensions and allow him to soar, to flee from the forces that sought to trap him, to restrict him, to anchor him, plodding forever the approved and expected pathways of a hostile earth—forces from without that he now so easily conquers from within.

Manning blasts ahead over the line that stretches endlessly toward the horizon—a horizon that curves downward at the limits of his vision as he rises steadily from the ground and approaches the canopy of trees and birds that roar above him in the gusty friction of moving air. He does not want to break through the trees—not yet—but to soar at ever greater speed just below their limbs, constantly within sight of the line. It seems as though the universe itself is ripping past him—only the hard-edged strip of white tape travels with him, fixed and unwavering, pure and straight.

Zipping through space with his eyes aimed before him, Manning now notices that there is something on the road, on top of the line, far, far ahead. Intrigued, he slows his flight as he draws nearer, approaching the unknown object with caution. A burst of anger rises within him, provoked by the discovery that *something* has encroached upon his territory, *something* has invaded a world that's been his alone.

The object moves. It's alive.

Manning freezes in midair for the slightest fraction of a second. It is not something, but *someone*, who has entered his inner world. Manning's flight slows to a crawl, high in the trees, as he stalks the alien visitor. The person is still a great distance down the road, but Manning now sees his features with sudden clarity. It is Neil.

He lies naked on the street, atop the white line, facing Manning. His legs are spread wide and his eyes are closed. He tugs comfortably, patiently on his swollen penis.

Manning's arousal grows with new intensity and fevered urgency. A single desire, a single *need*, grips all his senses. He darts from his concealed path of flight and dives toward the man lying in the street. He plummets from the trees in a state of wild excitement and at last feels the burn of flesh against his own, the stiff jab of a penis, the abrasion of hair, the tangle of legs. Manning is blind, lost in a frenzy of random thrusts when he hears the words "you're not queer, you're not queer" echoing from his partner. He looks to the head of the body he has penetrated and finds Roxanne's face thrashing in the pool of hair upon the street.

Manning awakes, terrified, gasping for each breath. His terror gives way to inexpressible confusion, and he sobs aloud. A hot tear slides from his cheek to form a cold little pool between the tendons of his neck. In the darkness, he kicks free of the sheets and tries to masturbate.

"Good morning." It is Bud Stirkham. Manning's chances for an orgasm—which were iffy at best—now wither completely. The radio drawls, "It's twenty degrees at seven o'clock in Chicago, and the weatherman says snow is coming, maybe a heap of it. In case you're keeping track, it's our darkest morning of the year, the first full day of winter. But there's news on a couple of fronts that should brighten your day and warm your heart.

"First, there are more encouraging signs from Ethiopia that the hostages there will soon be released—a lot of prayers would be answered if those heroic Americans made it home for Christmas! And locally, the state's attorney is wrapping up a Christmas gift for the people, promising rigorous interrogations when the Houseman Trial opens next week—the answer to our prayers for justice in the shocking saga of Helena Carter's disappearance.

"We'll open the phone lines later to get *your* input on all this late-breaking news, but first let's ease into the morning with a little Puccini, born this day in 1858. Let's travel back in time with him to a Christmas Eve in Paris."

Manning recognizes the festive opening of Act Two of *La Bohème*. It's a lovely recording, but he's not in the mood for it. He switches off the radio and stares into the dark silence.

He has always prided himself on his efficiency, his organization, his ability to *get things done* by rationally analyzing a situation and proceeding logically from point A to point Z. But now it's come to this: His life is a mass, a *mess* of uncertainties that threaten his job, his reputation, his very identity. Lying there in the predawn emptiness of his bed, there's not a damned thing he can do to defend his career as a reporter—not at this moment—but there is, he knows, something he can do to bolster his own self-worth through the honesty of a simple action he can no longer dodge.

Manning swings his feet to the floor and sits up. He switches on a lamp—his eyes crackle for a few seconds—then he reaches for the phone and dials a number he has never called but knows by heart. Spurts of electricity race fifteen hundred miles southwest to another time zone and enliven a bedside telephone on a mountain in the desert.

Neil picks up the receiver on the second ring. He has been roused from a deep sleep and holds the phone next to his head on the pillow, eyes still closed, unsure of what to do next.

A voice finally says, "Hello, Neil? This is Mark. In Chicago."

The words hit Neil like cold water. His eyes spring open as he bolts upright in bed, checking the time. "Is something wrong, Mark? It's six o'clock. *Are you all right?*"

Manning laughs. "Yes, Neil, everything's fine. I'm sorry to wake you, but I really need to talk. Are you angry?"

It's Neil's turn to laugh. "Hardly! I've been hoping you'd call for weeks. I'd have lost hope completely without the updates from Rox. She says you've . . . spent some time together."

Neil interprets the silence as an audible blush. The only time Manning has spent with Roxanne, other than a few awkward phone conversations at the office, was their session in her apartment after the airport.

"That was a strange day for all of us, Neil. Whatever happened—I'm still not able to make sense of it." Manning pauses, ready to change the subject, but careful to weigh his words. "You once invited me to come out and spend some time with you. I know it's short notice, but I need to see you. Soon. There's so much to talk about. There's so much that hasn't been said—or done. I can get away Thursday, day after tomorrow, if it's not inconvenient for you."

"Of *course* you're welcome. How long can you stay?"

"Just a few days, a long weekend. I've got a hell of a lot going on here right now."

"That'll be wonderful. Do you have a ticket? Thursday is Christmas Eve, so flights are bound to be booked solid."

"Oh," says Manning. He hasn't given the holidays the slightest thought. "I made up my mind about this only a few minutes ago, and I wanted to check with you first."

"Let me see what I can do," offers Neil. "I know a travel agent, and he owes me a favor."

"Please, Neil, don't bother. Truly, I forgot about Christmas. You *must* have plans. I don't want to intrude."

"Nonsense. Christmas is a *family* holiday. I have no family out here, and I have no plans that can't be broken gracefully. Besides, Mark, I'd rather be with *you*. I actually dreamed about you last night. Must've been thinking about you when I went to bed. I'd just seen you on TV . . ."

"You *what?*"

"Didn't you see it? It wasn't the *first* time, either."

Manning won't admit that he never watches television—it sounds so snobbish—yet the fact remains that he long ago lost interest in the tube.

"It was on the evening news," Neil continues. "It was just a crowd scene in some hallway, but there you were, and they flashed your name on the screen. You're becoming quite the media darling, Mr. Manning."

Thursday, December 24
8 days till deadline

O'Hare is chaos.

Bud Stirkham was right. The snow has come, and there's "a heap of it." The blanket of slop that began to cover the city yesterday—and still deepens by the hour—glistens in the delighted eyes of children who have yearned for a white Christmas. And it brings a nostalgic warmth to parents secure in their homes as they tuck in the young ones and remember the giggling excitement of bedtime that is known only on this night of the year. But to the holiday throngs milling at O'Hare tonight, the snow has brought endless delays, unexplained cancellations, growing fatigue, and flares of temper.

Manning has been at the airport since early morning and found, as Neil guessed, no open seats on any flight to Phoenix. A booking agent for one of the airlines laughed in Manning's face. So the best he could do was to buy a standby ticket and lug his bags from gate to gate in the hope that a booked passenger would fail to appear. He wishes he had let Neil pull some strings with that travel agent.

As the weather gets worse and air traffic gets more tangled, Manning finally gets lucky. A planeload of travelers from another city, scheduled to connect in Chicago with the last CarterAir flight to Phoenix, will not be arriving, and Manning is assigned a first-class seat at half the coach fare.

He has to move quickly. He'd like to phone Neil to let him know that he's at last on his way, but there's no time. Manning called earlier, because of the uncertain flights, to caution Neil not to try meeting him at the Phoenix airport. They agreed that Manning will call when, and if, he arrives.

On the plane, Manning can at last relax as he sinks into the wide leather seat and snaps the safety belt around his waist. The plane is running late and begins at once to taxi toward one of the constantly plowed runways. Manning peers through the little plastic window and watches, through the darkness and the falling snow, the spinning yellow lights that flash atop the plows that scurry around the airfield.

Once in the air, Manning orders a drink, truly needing it after his daylong ordeal. Waiting for it to arrive, he notices that there is a phone at his seat—one of Ridgely Carter's last pet projects, he remembers—so he fishes a credit card from his wallet and dials. As he listens to the ringing of the other phone, he intends to tell Neil not to wait up for him, that he will take a cab from the airport, but there is no answer.

The vodka arrives in its tiny bottle, and Manning notes, as expected, that it is not the Japanese brand. There's no point in asking for a slice of orange peel, which is surely not available, so he drinks the vodka straight over ice. It goes down quickly. Soon, Manning is asleep—sleeping so soundly that the steward decides not to rouse him for the meal.

Friday, December 25
7 days till deadline

The steward finally does awaken Manning to tell him they are landing. Manning studies his watch, dazed; he has slept nearly three hours. The captain's voice crackles that it is Christmas in Phoenix, just past midnight, fifty-five degrees under clear, starry skies. He thanks his passengers for flying CarterAir, then switches off the intercom and drops the plane silkily onto a runway that has *never* been plowed.

Manning gathers his luggage from the closet at the front of the cabin and walks the Jetway from the plane to the terminal, anxious to call Neil. He shuffles through the yattering crowd of friends and relatives who linger with arriving passengers at the gate, then emerges into a concourse and shoots off, bags in both hands, in search of a phone.

"What's the big hurry, Mark? You won't get far without me."

Manning turns. As Neil walks up behind him from the crowd at the gate, Manning puts his bags on the floor and reaches to embrace him. They hug for long moments without speaking, patting each other on the back with a silent language of tenderness that reveals the toll of their separation—the weeks they were apart that dragged into months, connected only by the thread of Neil's one awkward letter. Manning finally utters, "You're here. How'd you know I'd be on this flight?"

"I've been here since midafternoon."

Manning opens his mouth to reprimand him, but Neil continues, "I came because I couldn't get a damned thing done at work, because everyone else left early for Christmas Eve, and because I'd rather wait here to meet you than wait at home for the phone to ring. I stuck around till the last flight left Chicago, then checked with the airline. Sure enough, you were on it. And here we are.

Welcome to Phoenix, Mark." Neil produces a bouquet of delicate red flowers, like a magician yanking them from nowhere. He has made no effort to hide them, but Manning didn't notice them in the scuffle of their embrace.

"They're beautiful," says Manning as he studies the profusion of strange crimson buds. Flower names have always eluded him, but he can tell that these are some exotic species, rare if not unknown in the Midwest. "No one's ever given me flowers before."

"You're kidding," says Neil, dismayed that no one has paid so obvious a tribute to Manning's charms. "Merry Christmas, Mark."

"Merry Christmas, Neil." Then Manning adds, "It's all been so rushed—this trip, I mean—I'm afraid I didn't bring you anything."

Slyly, Neil answers, "Oh *yes* you did," and picks up the larger of his guest's bags. Manning rolls his eyes as he lifts the other bag. They walk down the concourse together and exit the terminal.

Outdoors in the parking lot, Manning is chagrined to discover that *it is not cold.* Neil wears only a light sweater. Manning's topcoat is far too warm, and he wonders why he bothered to put it on as he left the plane. He knew what temperature to expect— the captain announced it—but the words meant nothing until he felt the spring-like midnight air of December in the desert.

Once in the car and beyond the airport grounds, Neil drives swiftly through the city along boulevards that resemble express- ways more than local streets. There are few tall buildings, not by Chicago standards, but the horizon is broken instead by the hulk- ing peaks of mountains, some rising from within the city limits. Manning has always prided himself on a keen sense of direction, but he finds this environment disorienting. At home he thinks in terms of Lake Michigan—there is always water to the east. He has no such bearings here.

"So they're having a white Christmas in Chicago," Neil muses as he guides the car up a road on the side of a mountain.

"They certainly are, and they're welcome to it," says Manning, relishing his own escape. "It was a bitch of a storm."

"It's probably the same one that rolled through here on Tues- day. It *rained*, Mark. Rained hard. Now everything's washed and clean and blooming. Just wait till morning. We'll take that run together that I promised you. You'll see how spectacular Christmas Day can be."

He pulls into the driveway of a low house hidden by a wall. They emerge from the car into a parking court where soft lighting washes upward across the white stucco facade of the house—a boxy structure that blends with the wall concealing the terraced courtyard from the street. A black sky stretches overhead, pierced everywhere by stars. Manning is aware of nothing else, for the courtyard has the privacy of indoor space. Neil removes Manning's bags from the car and places them at his feet. As the bottoms of the bags scrape the terrace, their sound seems amplified in the stillness.

"Neil, where *are* we?" Manning wonders aloud. "Where's the city, what happened to the mountain, how far is your nearest neighbor?"

Neil laughs—a satisfied noise that says his efforts have succeeded. "There are houses within thirty feet of us. You're *standing* on the mountain. And the city's over there," he says, pointing through and beyond the house. He picks up the bags and motions with his head for Manning to follow.

They walk through a narrow passage that slits the front wall of the house. There's a slatted arbor overhead, a boardwalk underfoot. On both sides of the boardwalk, narrow beds sprout with leafy ground cover, cactuses, and little flowering bushes that bear the same red buds Manning still holds in one hand. At the end of the walk is a tall slab of a door, which Neil unlocks and swings open. He reaches inside to switch on a few lights, then steps aside so Manning can enter first, alone.

Manning walks into the room and is drawn to the wall of glass at its opposite end, to the panoramic display of city lights that flow down the side of the mountain then endlessly across the floor of the desert, interrupted only by the dark forms of other mountains. He crosses the room slowly, but with the confidence of having been there many times before, as though the setting were not new to him. Approaching the big windows, he finds that some of them are doors leading to another terrace, similar to the one in front except that it gives the impression not of enclosure, but of openness, like a viewing platform perched above the city below. He opens one of the doors, again as though he has done it before, and steps outdoors.

The dominant feature of the back terrace, other than its view, is a small swimming pool, perfectly square, no more than fifteen feet to a side. Its inside is tiled with black, not blue, making the water's smooth surface strikingly reflective. Interlocking rectangular decks descend toward the pool, forming ledges for sitting or lounging. The lowest of these decks, at the water's edge, is covered with long flat cushions upholstered in raw canvas. The stucco walls of the house extend outward from the sides of the building so that the terraces and pool are enclosed on three sides, hidden from the view of other homes, exposed only to the anonymous city and sky.

"Pretty, isn't it?" says Neil. He has followed Manning through the house and out to the edge of the pool.

Manning turns. He stammers, "I'm . . . overwhelmed." He waves his arm in an arc that embraces the house, the pool, the grounds. "Only you could build this. This is yours. This is *you.*" He drops the red flowers from his other hand onto the mat beside the pool and breathes a sigh of admiration for Neil's talents. "Pretty? It's sublime."

Neil tells him, "I was referring to the view, but I'm delighted that you approve of the whole package. Welcome to my home." He walks toward Manning and extends his arms.

Manning steps forward and for the first time in his life presses his lips to those of another man. He surrenders not only to another person, but to an idea, to the imagined scorn that others will hurl at him, to a drive that has been locked and buried deep within him. How long? he wonders as his tongue probes the teeth of the man whose body clings to his. Why only now? his mind asks, mocking, as he tastes the new substance of their mingled spit. It is a passionate kiss, but its physical message is one of warmth, not lust—not tonight.

Neil finally says, "It's chilly out here. Let me show you the house."

Manning obeys without protest, for he is eager to see the full product of Neil's design talents. They reenter the main room of the house, Neil closing the glass door behind them, switching on more lights. The living room, dining area, and an open kitchen are contained in the one large room, tranquil and elegant, painted a dark, nondescript color. Limestone flooring extends the depth of the house from front to back. Furnishings are sparse and expensive.

Manning's eye is drawn to an antique console table placed against an otherwise bare wall. The table is five or six feet long, barely more than a foot deep, crafted of honey-colored birch, accented with black trim. A row of shallow drawers runs beneath the mottled marble top, supported by a row of simple, classically proportioned columns that rise from the front of the wooden base. The overall style of the piece is restrained and masculine—offset by Neil's whimsical addition of bright silk tassels that hang from each of the brass keys in the drawer locks.

"Yes," Neil says, "it's real."

Lacking Neil's knowledge of such matters, Manning responds with an embarrassed shrug.

"Sorry," says Neil, leading Manning across the room to examine the console more closely. "It's Biedermeier, an early-nineteenth-century German style, sort of a workingman's version of French Empire. But the style has gotten very popular—and pricey—in recent years, so there are lots of contemporary knock-offs in production now. *This*, however"—he pats his prize piece of furniture—"is genuine. I was lucky enough to place the winning bid at an estate sale last year."

"It's stunning," Manning tells him. He gives Neil's shoulder a squeeze, as if to congratulate him on the acquisition.

"Thanks," says Neil, putting his arm around Manning's waist, "I admire your taste." Then something occurs to him. "Speaking of 'taste,' would you care for a drink?"

Manning doesn't need to answer. It's been a long, wearing day with a happy ending—of course he'd like a drink.

They cross to the other side of the room, where Neil rattles around in the kitchen. Within a minute, he hands Manning a glass. There's no need to ask—it is indeed the Japanese vodka. They raise their glasses in a toast to Manning's arrival, then drink—not quickly, as if priming themselves for glassfuls to follow, but slowly, recognizing that this is a nightcap, a moment to savor.

As Manning drinks, he studies the room again, while Neil in

turn studies his friend's wandering gaze. Manning says, "This is exactly where I would expect you to live. I couldn't quite picture it from what you and Roxanne told me about it, but now that I'm here, I can't imagine it any other way."

"But do you *like* it?" Neil asks. He's never given a second thought to other people's feelings about his house, his design work, his *taste*, so he is shaken by the fact that he now cares deeply about Manning's answer.

"Of course I do," says Manning.

Neil presses the question, "Do you like it because of your feelings toward me, or do you like it *yourself?*"

"I like it myself. I marvel at your clarity of thought and your power of vision—and your ability to translate them into something that's real and concrete, not just words or rhetoric. My God, you've taken an idea, a way of thinking, a *life*, and you've actually built a house out of it. Yes, I like it. Myself. Not because it's yours, but because of how and why you did it."

Neil kisses Manning on the cheek. "You say all the right things."

"We 'word people' deserve *something* to our credit," Manning says with an innocence that prompts them both to laugh.

Neil shows Manning through the rest of the house. It's a quick tour because it's a small house. Its plan is that of a chubby H, with the big room at its center. Each side of the H is a bedroom wing with a bath. The second bedroom is used as Neil's studio, but a comfortable-looking cushioned platform has been made up there as a bed to accommodate his guest. As Neil places the baggage near the platform, Manning stifles a yawn.

"Hey, Mark. It's getting late. It's been a hell of a day, and we're both shot. Suppose we call it quits."

"Sure," says Manning, having hoped that Neil would make the suggestion.

Before leaving the room, Neil turns to ask, "Bring your running shoes?"

"You bet." Manning waves toward one of his bags.

"It should be a beautiful morning, so let's not waste it. Mind if I wake you around eight?"

"Please do," says Manning. "But I'm bound to be up by then. I slept on the plane."

"Good night, Mark. I'm glad you're here."
"So am I."

A deathlike sleep sweeps over Manning tonight—a sleep that stops his brain, washes his mind of the accumulated tensions and doubts that have more and more muddied his waking hours. If he dreams at all, he does not know it, will not remember it.

When Neil shakes his shoulder, when he opens his eyes, he is confused by the sunlight that fills the room, certain that it cannot yet be morning, certain that he has just lain down. Yet he is totally rested, suddenly alert, aware of the powers that have somehow been rejuvenated . . . *recharged* by the silent workings of his brain and body through the night. He hears Neil tell him, "Time to get up."

Manning turns his head on the pillow to see Neil sitting on the bed next to him wearing a pair of faded gray cotton running shorts. Manning gazes openly at the other man's chest, impressed by its muscle tone, by the clearly delineated pectorals. He has felt an intense attraction to Neil since their first meeting, but he now feels his attraction redoubled with the confirmation that Neil's body is a match for his intellect—and a match for Manning's own body, his own mind.

With a still-groggy smile, Manning says, "You're beautiful," as a substitute for the more conventional good-morning.

Neil runs his fingers once, lightly through Manning's hair. "It's eight o'clock. I brought you some coffee," he tells him.

"The perfect host."

"I do try. Now—not to rush you, but if you'd like to wake up in the shower first, please do—then we can run."

Manning asks, "Will I need a shirt?"

"There's still a morning chill, but you'll work up a sweat fast enough." Neil pats Manning's head again, gets up, and leaves the room, affording his guest some privacy for his morning routine.

A few minutes later, Manning enters the living room. He wears his old yellow shorts and a new pair of white leather running shoes—he bought them weeks ago but has been "saving" them—for what, he wasn't sure.

"You're not so bad yourself," says Neil, returning Manning's earlier compliment as his eyes examine every line, every muscle of the man who stands before him, searching in vain for some evidence that Manning is nearly ten years older.

"Come on," says Manning with a laugh, jerking his head toward the front door. "Show me your mountain."

Outside in the still air, nothing moves—the rest of the world is indoors shooting videos of kids mauling presents. The sun hangs low in the winter latitudes of the desert sky, but its warm rays penetrate Manning's chest as he emerges from the shadows of the arbor in front of the house.

Without a word, Neil trots off across the terrace toward the road, pebbles grating rhythmically beneath the treaded soles of his shoes. Manning catches up with him and trots at his side. They run easily, at a comfortable gait, like animals stretching their muscles for no other reason than to limber their bodies, to test their own endurance.

They pass one of the houses that abuts Neil's property, and Manning notes the skill with which Neil has secluded his own house from it. Other houses flash by, confirming Manning's hunch that these mountainside addresses are among the city's more desirable. As they move up the steep road, Manning—who's not accustomed to running on hills—finds that even their mild pace quickly tires him. In contrast, Neil pumps away with steady strides and deliberate breathing. Manning glances sideways to indulge in the sight of his friend's body in motion.

In spite of the recent rains, the mountain's rocky red earth can support little more than scrub and cactus—except in the rich topsoil trucked up to form carefully nurtured lawns and gardens around many of the houses. The desert environment is hostile toward trees, offering virtually no shade. The blacktopped ribbon of the road, already softening in Arizona's morning sun, winds its way up the mountain in search of greater heights and broader vistas.

The heat, taken for granted by those who live here, is a hedonistic luxury to Manning, who suffered the rigors of a winter storm only yesterday. He gulps lungfuls of warm, dry air while sweat begins to rise from every pore, collecting into salty drops that trickle down his bare skin to lodge in the waistband of his shorts.

Manning has not yet gained his second wind and has fallen several strides behind Neil, who slows his run to pace Manning with measured steps. The pounding of Manning's feet on the asphalt becomes synchronous with Neil's. As Manning follows, he watches the long tendons down Neil's thighs that stretch and contract with each stride, the damp V that creeps further into Neil's shorts and sticks in the crack between his buttocks. Manning has lost awareness of the world around him. His entire consciousness is fixed on the body of the man who runs before him, on his own hard purple-brown nipples that sting hot-cold in the air passing over them, on the lump that comes to life between his legs. He runs easily now, enjoying the euphoric light-headedness induced by overbreathing.

Veering to the edge of the road, Neil directs his feet in a curving path that will reverse the direction of their run. They have reached the road's highest point. To follow it farther would take them down the mountain's other side, a great distance from the house, so Neil is turning back. Manning leans into the same semicircular turn. As they pass each other in opposite directions, each becomes aware of the other's obvious arousal, which intensifies the drives that are building within both of them.

The downward run accelerates into a race for the house. Only moments ago, Manning struggled to climb the road's steep grade; now both men struggle to keep from pitching forward as gravity pulls them through the curves at an all-out sprint, their feet barely tapping the ground while their legs scissor repeating arches like dance leaps. They run in precise unison at each other's side, so close that their arms brush.

About a hundred yards from the house, as if responding to some secret signal, they stop running and begin walking the rest of the way—the "warm-down" that will ease their pulses to a slower, normal rate. Neither speaks as they turn off the road together, cross the courtyard, and enter the front door. Nothing is said as they walk through the main room toward the glass doors in back, still breathing heavily from the rigors of their downhill dash. Without a word, they emerge from the house toward the pool.

Neil descends the terraced decks with a purposeful stride. Stepping onto the canvas-covered mats that edge the water, he collapses on his back next to the bunch of red flowers that Manning dropped there last night. He stares at Manning, his vision blurred by the sun's glare on the sweat that covers him with an unknowable number of tiny lens-like beads. Then, the glare disappears as Manning's shadow crosses over his body.

Manning stands at Neil's feet, their shoes touching at the ankles. He reaches down to push the shorts from his hips. When he steps out of them, his blood-gorged penis springs forward, a drop of lubricant stretching from its tip, dazzling in the sun from over his shoulder.

But Neil sees only the green clarity of Manning's eyes as the naked man drops to his knees, straddling Neil's hips. Manning lowers his chest onto Neil's, and their open mouths meet. Their teeth scrape as their tongues wag within each other, as they exchange a single spent breath and whimper with the dizzying lack of oxygen.

Manning's pelvis grinds in slow circles upon Neil's, his bare penis stabbing at the lump still trapped in Neil's shorts. Manning finally releases his lips from Neil's, sits back, and tears off the shorts with a compulsive swipe. He gazes in wonder at the other man's penis, erect, quivering with each pulse of blood. Cock, he tells himself. *Neil's cock.*

Neil moans a guttural, ecstatic laugh as he feels Manning's lips close upon him. He spreads his legs farther apart. His hips begin to thrash gently, as if wagged by the suction of Manning's mouth.

Without disconnecting from Neil, Manning positions himself to lower his own genitals over Neil's face. Neil reaches with his tongue to tickle Manning's testicles and feels the body on top of him shudder at the contact. Neil draws one of the lumps into his mouth and swirls his tongue around it. Manning groans awesomely as Neil begins to stroke Manning's penis in rhythm with the pumping of his hips. Neil knows he will soon come. His back arches involuntarily as he tries forcing his way deeper past Manning's lips. Manning's grunts are steadily louder. Neil suddenly tenses as the surge of ejaculation grips his body, rips through his penis and into Manning's throat. Manning's moans erupt into a heaving shout as his own semen bursts through Neil's hand and spews like a paste between their chests.

When Manning can move, he crawls around to collapse in Neil's arms, their mouths just touching, panting. The desert sun beats down upon their bodies, upon the bunch of delicate red flowers now scattered at their side and in the pool.

Recovery from their sexual frenzy is slow and serene. The stillness of the morning is pierced only by the peeping of a tiny hyperactive bird somewhere in the nearby foliage. Neil swallows. Deadpan, he tells Manning, "You're supposed to say, 'I never dreamed it could be like this.'"

"I *did* dream about it," Manning assures him, "but you're right—this was far better."

They lie there motionless except for their random exchange of tender little gestures—the touch of a nose, the probing of a fingertip. Then Neil raises one foot high before them, displaying his running shoe, wagging it at the ankle, eyeing it curiously as if not certain what it is. "Hm," he says at last, "that's pretty kinky, Mark. I've never done it with shoes on. Not that it didn't add a certain erotic twist, but it's *highly* unorthodox."

"There was no time to take them off."

Neil concurs, "I noticed a sense of urgency to the whole business."

They both laugh. Neil brings his knee to his chin and reaches forward to unlace and remove the shoe. Then the other. He stands up, his feet at Manning's shoulders. Manning gazes up at him, intrigued by the contour of Neil's body from this perspective. Neil steps over him and lowers himself smoothly into the pool, the water rising to his nipples. Manning rolls onto his side, planting one elbow in the mat to support his head in the palm of his hand. He watches while Neil splashes fistfuls of water over his chest to wash away the sun-baked crust of Manning's orgasm. Manning sits up, removes his own shoes, and slips into the pool.

"Christ," he says, "this water's cold."

"It's December," Neil reminds him. "You *could* be home shoveling snow."

Aware of his complaint's futility, Manning wades forward to embrace Neil. They cling together mouth-to-mouth. Water spurts from between their chests. Their limp penises swim together in the tangle of their legs.

Morning drifts into afternoon. They haven't eaten all day, satisfying their hunger with the exploration of each other's body— on the terrace, in the pool, indoors on the floor, and in bed. Manning proves himself an eager pupil and a quick study in Neil's Berlitz-style version of Safe Sex 101. Their lessons are interspersed with short naps, allowing their bodies to prepare for the next call to action. But when the afternoon sky begins to glow with the first orange streaks of evening, they both, at last, are feeling starved and exhausted. Clearly, it's time to get dressed.

"It's Christmas," Neil announces in a tone suggesting they had both forgotten about it. "I planned a holiday meal—there's a beautiful rack of lamb in the fridge. Will you be in the mood for a late, intimate dinner?"

"That sounds wonderful," says Manning. "I'm famished."

Clad in the running shorts that have come off and on throughout the day, Neil sets to work in the kitchen and sends Manning to the shower.

Standing in the bathroom shaving, Manning leans over the sink and examines himself in the wall-size plate glass mirror. He peers deep into the emerald-flecked irises of his own eyes. They have not changed. He sees nothing unusual within. His face, his entire body, looks the same. The experiences of the day have not marked or scarred him. The labels he has feared have in no way branded him. He can detect neither a superficial nor a fundamental difference.

Except, his happiness. The penetrating ease and warmth defy analysis. He tells himself that these feelings might be logically explained, dismissed as the expected consequence of his escape from winter—or as the afterglow of his sated libido—but he knows that the reasons for his contentment are far more profound. Someone has quietly slipped into his life, changed his life in ways he could never have predicted, taught him pleasures he never knew existed, exposing the sheer, innate rightness of desires he will never again neglect. He proclaims himself a lucky man as he rinses his razor, turns on the shower, and ducks under the steamy spray.

After dressing with inordinate self-scrutiny—khakis (of

course), cashmere sweater (sleeves shoved to the elbow), penny loafers (sweat socks)—he pops into the living room to present himself for Neil's approval. Neil is gone, but his whereabouts are revealed by the hiss of spraying water from the other bedroom wing.

The smell of roasting lamb fills the air, fueling Manning's hunger. He helps himself to a carrot from the veggie tray Neil has set out, then wanders the room, examining it in detail, impressed more than ever by its restrained design, the choice of furnishings—and of course, the Biedermeier console. His eye travels to the dining table, its two elegant settings, a bottle of Bordeaux. He approaches the table to determine the wine's vintage, then notices a folded place card centered on one of the plates. Intrigued, he picks up the card and reads its message, written in Neil's distinctive hand: "Dear Mark, IOU one Christmas gift. FedEx next week. Promise."

Neil's voice says, "Didn't take you long to zero in on *that!*" He laughs while watching from the bedroom doorway, then crosses to the table to hug Manning's waist.

"What's *this* about?" asks Manning, holding the card. "You shouldn't . . . *buy* me things."

"Tut-tut," says Neil, tapping a finger on Manning's lips. "You'll understand soon enough. Now"—he checks his watch, changing topics—"we're just in time. Dinner's going to take a while, but there's something I want you to see."

Manning quips, "I thought I'd seen it *all* today."

"On television, wise guy. It's a church service you don't get in Chicago—I checked when I was there."

"Church?" says Manning. "I'd have guessed you weren't 'into' that."

"Of course I'm not. But this'll be a hoot. Brother Burt, the crackpot evangelist I told you about, is doing a Christmas special on cable tonight. So get comfortable—and enjoy." He ushers Manning to a sofa at the far end of the room, rolls a television out from its hiding place, and switches it on.

The set bursts to life with flashing pictures and the frenetic garble of messages between programs. Then the screen goes black and all is quiet. Faintly, the voices of a choir emerge from the void, accompanied by a piano. The darkness of the screen gives way to hazy-focus sparkles of light reflected from a revolving mirrored ball. Ornate Bible-style text appears superimposed over the disco ball, announcing: The Holy Altar of Mystic Faith.

"What the hell is this?" Manning asks.

"It's the Miss Viola show. Keep watching."

Two cameras pan back and forth across a small choir, cross-fading to give the illusion that the group is ten times its actual size. They wear gold satin robes and sing a homely though rousing hymn about Thy holy law. Verse plods to verse, but at last the final cadence of triumphal chords is banged out on a gleaming white baby grand, an instrument that would appear more at home in a cocktail lounge.

"That's pretty bad," Manning says flatly, objectively.

"Just wait," says Neil through a grin.

The screen fills with the chubby, smiling face of a man who carries a white microphone, sporting a gaudy ring on his plump pinkie. Fifty-something, maybe sixty, his age is made iffy by heavy makeup and the blue gleam of dyed-black hair. He wears a white suit with red contrasting stitching on its double-wide lapels. His brow sweats dramatically as he flourishes his free arm and blusters in an evangelical drawl about the Holy Altar of Mystic Faith. Every other sentence contains the word "Jesus," which he pronounces *Cheee-suss*, protracting the first syllable, wagging his jowls on the second.

"Who *is* this guy?" asks Manning.

"*That's* Brother Burt. He's Miss Viola's archdeacon."

"You mean her sidekick?"

"Sort of. I've heard he's actually the 'brains' behind the whole business, if you can believe it."

While Brother Burt harangues his audience with scriptural citations instructing the chosen people to build a Holy Altar, the cameras entice the viewers with glimpses of the edifice itself.

"Have you ever seen anything so tacky?" Neil comments. "It looks like it was slapped together by the prom committee." Disco balls flash and whirl at random heights before the Holy Altar. Niches enshrine life-size papier-mâché angels, spray-painted gold, some brandishing foil-covered swords with the jerky, repetitive movements of a department store Christmas display. At the center of the altar sits an enormous open Bible, far too big, too perfect, to be real. Behind the Bible loom two arched tablets, clearly of spackled cardboard, "engraved" with Roman numerals to represent the Ten Commandments. Smoke machines puff dry ice around the base of the altar so that it appears to drift on a cloud.

"Wouldn't you love to get a look behind that thing?" Neil asks with a mischievous chortle. "I can just see it—all braced up like a movie set, barely able to support its own weight, held together with staples and tape. Imagine all the motors, the tangle of cords, the big ugly tubes running to the cloud machines. God, I'd love to get back there and cross a few wires!"

Manning asks, "Is this a local show?"

"It sure is," boasts Neil with feigned pride. "It originates at a cable company right here in Phoenix."

"Perhaps we could go down to the studio later and take a peek behind the Holy Altar," says Manning, snickering at the absurdity of the suggestion.

"You may laugh now," says Neil, "but you'll be mad as hell in a minute. Brother Burt is still working up to his pitch."

As predicted, Brother Burt soon mentions a "prayer cloth." Quizzically, Manning draws his brows to the bridge of his nose as Brother Burt reverently displays an oblong piece of terry cloth, about six inches by twelve, with two red circles printed on it. "By now, my brothers and sisters, most of you already have a prayer cloth of your very own, and you have come to know the healing powers, the mystical forces that your prayers can unleash as a result of using this amazing worship aid. Those of you who do not yet have your own prayer cloth—or would like another as a Christmas gift for a loved one—will want to call now." A toll-free number, 1-800-GOD-LINE, flashes on the screen, along with the logos of every credit card known to man. "Miss Viola will send you your very own prayer cloth in return for a hundred-dollar pledge to the work of *Cheee-suss*."

Neil says, "Can you imagine allowing that crap on television? If you or I tried to sell some worthless piece of junk for a hundred bucks and promised it would cure cancer, we'd be tossed in jail and deserve it. But *this* clown can get up there to rob suckers in the name of Jesus, send them a strip of old washrag, explain away—as lack of faith—the fact that the rag won't do a damned thing, and *then* pay no taxes on his profits. Sure, he's just some local clown, a backwater evangelist with his hand in the till, but he's really no different from those network yahoos touting the Christian Family Crusade. They've all got ulterior agendas that are anything but 'religious.'"

He catches his breath before continuing, "I understand, Mark, why Brother Burt is protected, and I realize that this country already suffers from far too much regulation, but *boy* I'd like to punch a hole in that racket."

Manning has nodded quietly throughout the brief tirade, fully grasping the dilemma, fully sharing Neil's frustration.

"And so, my brothers and sisters, let us now pray. In the name of *Cheee-suss*, through the intercession of our beloved high priestess, Miss Viola, let us now kneel upon our prayer cloths with one knee placed firmly on each of the red circles—red from the blood of the Lamb—that we, too, might be cleansed, washed pure in the sacrificial blood."

The choir strikes up a chant of mystical-sounding nonsense syllables as Brother Burt turns his back to the camera and approaches the Holy Altar. He walks with a severe limp, dragging his right foot behind his left . . . thump-slide . . . thump-slide. He lets his prayer cloth drift to the floor, then, with difficulty, drops to his knees upon it. Whiffs of cloud spurt up at his sides to accommodate the intrusive mass of his body. With head bowed and arms raised, with the choir still murmuring, he prays loudly, blabbering about love and Thy holy law, railing against secularists and sodomites with repeated references to "the serpent."

Neil says, "He used to include a bit of snake-handling in his act—honest—but the authorities put an end to it."

The choir stops. Still kneeling, Brother Burt looks over his shoulder at the camera and smiles through the sweat of his religious experience. "And *now*," he announces in the tone of a carnival barker, "the supreme high priestess of the Holy Altar of Mystic Faith: *Miss Viola!*"

He shoots one arm toward the heavens, and the camera follows to focus on a large crescent moon being winched down from the heights of the studio among the disco balls. The moon is ridden by Miss Viola, a svelte, ageless woman with vivid orange-red hair, wearing a fur muff of the same color on one arm. A blue mantle flutters from the collar of her long white gown. Smiling for the camera, she clutches the descending moon with a cautious, uncertain grip. The moon jitters ominously as it lowers, its wires glistening with light reflected from the disco balls. The piano thunders majestically as the moon at last touches the floor with a jolt; Miss Viola becomes visibly more relaxed. She steps off the edge of the moon, her feet disappearing in the cloud of carbon dioxide. With one hand she holds the little fur, and with the other she dismisses the moon, which soars back to its celestial home with a squeaking of cranks and pulleys.

This is the part of the program Neil always enjoys most. Tears fill his eyes as he laughs so gustily that he can barely sit up, gasping for each new breath. Manning also finds it funny, but his laughter is restrained by the incredulity that holds his mouth open in a wondering gape.

The camera zooms inward from Miss Viola's full figure to a tight shot of her face. Her eyes twinkle as she opens her mouth and speaks: "I am the Light of Mystic Faith." The choir wails, *Woo-oo, woo-oo*, while the piano tinkles impressionistically at the upper end of its keyboard. Miss Viola preaches soothing bromides to her followers, extolling the merits of the prayer cloth, enjoining them to send her a hundred bucks for Jesus. As she patters on, the choir continues to warble in the background.

The joke is wearing thin, and Manning is now bored with it. Even Neil's laughter has subsided. And something has apparently gone wrong with the program's sound. As Miss Viola speaks, her words are garbled by loud scraping noises. A second noise begins to overpower the first—a droning sound resembling the putter of an engine. Neil and Manning exchange an annoyed expression that says, Time to turn it off. But as Neil reaches forward and is about to touch the button, the camera zooms back from Miss Viola, revealing the source of the noise. The fur that Miss Viola holds in her arms is not a muff. It is a live animal—a small orange-red cat purring loudly, pawing the microphone hanging from Miss Viola's neck. The camera zooms in tight. It is an Abyssinian kitten of exceptional beauty.

"*Huh?*" gasps Manning, nearly choking.

Neil tells him, "She's never had that Abby on the show before.

Look at that cat—what a magnificent little animal—far more beautiful than any we saw at the show in Chicago."

Manning readily agrees, nodding his head while keeping his eyes riveted to the screen. "Neil," he asks, "in the letter you sent me, you said that you went to a cat show here in Phoenix and saw some fine Abbies. Were they of the quality of this kitten?"

"Yes."

Manning turns to face Neil squarely and tells him, "I've got to talk to that woman. The program must be live; otherwise they'd have cut out the business with the cat. Can you drive me over to the station?"

"Sure," says Neil. "Just give me a few minutes to put our dinner on hold. There's plenty of time to catch her—the program lasts another half hour."

In the car, between bites of another carrot, Manning tells Neil, "I hope this little outing doesn't ruin your meal."

"The lamb will be on the dry side, but I'm sure you'll make it up to me."

Manning reaches across the back of the seat to squeeze the scruff of Neil's neck, winding a lock of Neil's hair around his middle finger. Aroused by the contact, Manning leans over to kiss Neil's ear, inserting his tongue.

"Down, boy," Neil cautions him. "We're here."

The cable company sits near the edge of town in an anonymous building, probably a converted supermarket, with sections of its parking lot fenced off for satellite dishes, all staring blindly at the night sky. The front office is dark, so Neil drives around back, where a few cars are parked near a well-lit metal door bearing a sign: AUTHORIZED ENTRY ONLY.

Manning muses, "We'll soon find out if a Chicago Police Department press pass has any clout in Phoenix."

Neil parks the car and asks, "Want me to wait out here?"

"Please." Closing the door behind him, he adds, not entirely in jest, "And keep the engine running."

"Mark," Neil calls after him through the window, "if you find yourself behind the Holy Altar, don't forget to cross a few wires."

Manning gives Neil a thumbs-up, checks his own pockets for

pen and notebook, then presses the button of an industrial-size doorbell bolted to the cement-block wall.

A tin-badged security guard opens the door a few inches. He's paunchy and genial—hardly intimidating—but he does wear a holster. "Yeah, buddy?"

"Good evening," says Manning. "I wonder if you could tell me if Miss Viola's program has ended yet. I'd like to talk to her."

"Yeah, they wrapped it up a few minutes ago. You don't want a prayer cloth, do you?" The guard laughs. "Some other outfit handles those."

"No. No prayer cloth." Manning flashes his press pass. "I'd just like to speak to Miss Viola."

The guard examines Manning's credentials, impressed. "Sure, buddy. Hold on a minute." The door thumps closed.

Manning turns to look back at Neil, whose expression asks, What's up? Manning shrugs his shoulders. He's so hungry that he feels weak, so he lights a cigarette, hoping it will slake his appetite. While inhaling the first drag, he notices Neil still watching him and wonders if he disapproves. Neil doesn't smoke— they've never discussed it. Does Neil consider it a filthy, damning character flaw? Manning quickly drops the cigarette onto the asphalt. As he snuffs it out with his toe, the door swings open.

"Yes, sir? What can I do for you?" It is Brother Burt himself, waving Manning in, but just over the threshold.

"My name is Manning," he begins to answer as the door closes with a thud behind him. They stand in a big open room—part warehouse, part garage—cluttered with lights, cables, props, and a couple of service vans.

"Of course," says Brother Burt with an obsequious bow of his sweating head, "the esteemed reporter. Whatever brings you to Phoenix—business?"

"No, pleasure. I happened to catch your program tonight and wonder if I could speak to Miss Viola."

"Miss Viola is a very busy and important lady, Brother Mark. Besides, Vi makes it a rule not to speak with the press. She doesn't feel it's in the best interest of her mission."

"I'll bet she doesn't," says Manning. "Let me level with you. I don't give a damn about your 'mission'—though it would certainly make a hell of a story. I'm here only because I have an interest in cats, and I want to talk to Miss Viola about that kitten on TV tonight. Let me see her, then I'll go away. Otherwise, who knows?"

Brother Burt studies Manning with eyes drawn into tight slits, weighs the options, and decides that it will be prudent to cooperate. Wordlessly, he leads Manning off to another part of the building, thump-sliding across the waxed concrete floor. Arriving at the far side of the warehouse, he struggles with an oversize door. Manning tells him, "Let me get that. I'm sorry."

Indignant, Brother Burt asks him, "For what?"

"Well . . . your leg."

"It's not my *leg*," Brother Burt tells him, as if any fool could see. "It's my *foot*. An accident during my youth. My right foot was crushed in a fight with Satan. It never really healed—can still cause excruciating pain." He winces at the words. "A hard-learned lesson in the wages of perversion."

Manning repeats, "I'm sorry."

Brother Burt's tone turns cynically philosophical. "Why dwell on the past? It can be so ugly." As they stroll down a messy hallway, he stops at a door with a dog-eared foil star stapled to it. "Wait. I'll tell Vi you're here." He slips inside the dressing room.

As instructed, Manning waits, hands shoved into his pockets. Hearing a din of activity around the next turn of the hall, he steps to the corner and looks out into the main studio.

A crew of technicians and stagehands scurries about, dismantling the Holy Altar and setting the stage for tomorrow morning's garden show, *Cactus Chat*. Entire sections of the altar, huge slabs of "marble," are turned to reveal panels of a desert landscape painted on the other side of the canvas. A pair of angels—swords poised, cords dangling—lurch toward the warehouse on the prongs of a forklift. Another forklift stops in front of Manning. Whining, it lowers a metal-cased control cabinet, depositing it at his feet, blocking his view of the commotion. He stares directly into the back of the device.

Its innards are a jumble of resistors and other arcane electronics interconnected with a tangle of cords. At the end of each cord is a plug—some black, some red, some yellow—inserted into color-coded sockets. Manning glances heavenward, wondering if maybe someone *is* smiling upon him. Then he checks over his shoulder, whistles nonchalantly, and switches the plugs in a red and a yellow socket.

"Mr. Manning?" calls Brother Burt from the dressing room door. As Manning reappears from around the corner, Brother Burt tells him, "Vi will see you now," and ushers him in.

Miss Viola sits in front of her makeup mirror, its glaring bulbs surrounding her like a halo. Some of the bulbs, though, are burned out or missing, lending to the room's general seediness. She fluffs a matted blue feather boa, thrown on over a dressing gown stained with coffee and rouge. Her hair is in a turban, her reddish wig on the vanity. Curled atop the wig, sleeping, is the kitten.

"Good evening, Miss Viola. My name is Mark Manning."

"Smile-God-loves-you, Brother Mark," she singsongs, offering her hand to be kissed, but he shakes it. "You're here about my Angel?"

"What?" he asks, wondering if she's "on" something—or just nuts.

"My Abby-cat. *Angel.*" She eyes the kitten warmly for a moment. "Isn't she precious? She had a bit of the *devil* in her tonight, though." She laughs maniacally at her play on words.

"Probably just a phase. Nothing that can't be exorcised, I'm sure," says Manning, deliberately ingratiating himself.

"How *clever*, Mark," she twitters. "I must remember that."

Manning steps forward to stroke the forehead of the kitten, who barely stirs. "I've become an unabashed cat fancier myself in recent months. You've got a spectacular Abyssinian here. When did you get Angel?"

Brother Burt's pupils shift beneath his eyelids, following the dialogue with reptilian precision.

Miss Viola tells Manning, "Just this week. I'd been looking for a special pet for a long time, hoping to find a little friend that would match the rather extraordinary color of my hair." She primps, stuffing a telltale lock of gray back into her turban, unaware that the cat, purring at Manning's touch, is kneading its little claws in her wig. "Then I saw a picture of an Abyssinian and *knew* I had to have one. But they're so terribly difficult to find."

"Yes, I know, Miss Viola. I've been looking for just such a pet myself. Could you tell me where you got Angel?"

Brother Burt clears his throat, and Miss Viola glances at him before answering, "I'm so sorry. I'd like to help you—and I know this must sound terribly odd—but I've taken a solemn oath not to identify Angel's breeder."

"I wouldn't think of asking you to break your promise, Miss Viola, but perhaps you could tell me just this much: Did Angel come from a town named Assumption?"

Miss Viola pauses. Then, with a happy, relieved voice, she says, "I suppose I can tell you *that* much, Mark—especially since you already seem to know. Yes, Angel came from Assumption."

Brother Burt's eyes widen with disbelief.

Manning's heart pounds in his ears, but his voice does not betray the importance he attaches to his next question. "This may sound stupid of me, Miss Viola, but where *is* Assumption?"

The woman again bursts into her maniacal laugh. "Oh, Mark," she says, as if slapping her knee, "you *are* a wit. Where is Assumption, indeed!"

"I'm sorry, Miss Viola. I don't understand the joke."

Her laughter breaks off. "Really? I mean, you *asked* about Assumption, and you're *here*, so I presumed. . . . Mark, you're practically *in* Assumption. It's out beyond the other side of town, about an hour off the interstate."

Catching his breath, Manning thanks her, nods to Brother Burt—who says nothing—and quickly leaves the room, closing the door behind him.

In the hall, he pauses to collect his thoughts and jot a few notes. Not a half minute later, his concentration is broken by Brother Burt's voice, screaming inside the dressing room: "Stupid *cunt*—I told you not to tell him a fucking thing!"

Saturday, December 26
6 days till deadline

Driving Neil's car, Manning turns off the interstate and heads down the rural two-lane highway that leads to Assumption. There's never much traffic out here, and even less this Saturday morning, the day after Christmas. The road is his alone.

Both he and Neil awoke early today. They had considered driving to Assumption from the TV studio last night, but it was late, and they were so hungry that Manning couldn't trust his own judgment. Better to eat, sleep, and start fresh. Neil guessed that Manning wouldn't want company on this excursion, so he offered his car, asking Manning to drop him at his office on the way out of town—Neil could get some work done, uninterrupted, on an important project that was "due yesterday."

A road map is spread open on the empty passenger's seat. Miss Viola was right; Manning located, with no difficulty at all, the dot that is Assumption. As he races across the unbending stretch of highway, the whir of the engine blends with the rush of air streaming over the contours of the car—a comforting sound, man-made, assuring. But Manning hears it only subliminally, for his mind is busied by uncertain thoughts. What sort of confrontation might await him out here? Might he at long last find Helena Carter? His preoccupations join with the monotonous landscape to make the trip pass quickly. A road sign sweeps past him announcing a reduced speed limit. He is entering Assumption.

The highway is the main street of the town. A dog strolls along one of the buckled sidewalks, but Manning sees no people. He drives slowly, approaching the crabgrass plot of the town square, the church, the school. Three children walk together near the square.

"Excuse me?" he asks from the window, stopping alongside them.

The youngest of the three, a girl about four years old, hides behind the other two—apparently her brother, about eight, and her sister, about twelve. Manning figures that they don't see many strangers here, and he is charmed by the girl's apprehension.

"Yes, sir?" the boy says boldly.

Manning says, "I'm looking for someone, and maybe you know where I can find her. It's a lady—she's kind of old—and she raises lots of cats. Do you know anyone in town like that?"

"That'd be Mrs. O'Connor," the boy offers at once. Everyone in town knows about Mrs. O'Connor's "funny cats," though few have seen them.

"Can you tell me where she lives?"

The boy opens his mouth to give directions, but a jab from his older sister's elbow silences him. She tells Manning, "You'd better talk to Father McMullen about it." She explains that Manning can find the priest in the rectory, pointing to the big house next to the church.

"Thanks, kids," Manning says with a wink, then he drives around the square and parks in front of the town's only brick house. He gets out of the car and closes the door with a quiet slam that seems to violate the tranquility of this secluded place. Walking up the stretch of sidewalk that leads to the porch of the house, he tries not to shatter again the peace of this little town, measuring his steps deliberately, almost stealthily, as if on tiptoes.

The shady porch is strewn with worn wicker furniture. Windows gape open. Through the screened door, the smell of something in the oven meets Manning's nostrils. What is that?—something he hasn't smelled in years. Then it floods back to him. Tuna casserole. Manning twists an old-fashioned doorbell mounted in the jamb, sending a rusty clatter through the house, making him again feel like an intruder, an invader.

"I'll get it, Mrs. Weaver," a man's voice calls from within. A moment later, Father McMullen appears at the door wearing black priestly slacks and a collarless white shirt unbuttoned at the neck. His years are apparent to Manning from the shuffle of his walk, but his magnificent waves of graying golden hair impart to the man's face a timeless aura that defies description. Saintly,

Manning thinks. No, he reconsiders, it is more the look of a martyr, the look of suffering, smugly endured.

"Ah!" says the priest. "Good morning, Mr. Manning. Won't you come in?" He swings the door open.

Baffled by the greeting, Manning asks, "Have we met, Father?"

"Only on the phone, when we spoke a couple of months ago. I've seen you on television since." He leads Manning into his office and motions that they should sit on either side of the cluttered desk.

Settling in, Manning wonders aloud, "But you seemed to *expect* me."

"Really?" His tone is coy. "Perhaps I did." He gazes at his visitor through the milky blur that clouds his eyes. Picking up a paper clip, he begins to unravel it. There is a long pause. Then the priest closes his eyes and drops his head in a gesture of resignation. The kinked silver wire slips from his fingers and bounces with a tick on the sheet of green-edged glass that covers the desk. Without looking up, he asks, "Why are you here?"

"Because some children on the street told me I should see you when I asked them for directions to 'Mrs. O'Connor's' house."

"I see." The priest picks up and begins to mangle a fresh paper clip. He looks Manning in the eye to ask, "Why do you want to see Helen?"

"I think you know," Manning says. "Or are you asking me to lie to you?"

"You needn't bother," says the priest with contempt. "Money . . ." He exhales the word with distaste. "I don't know which is worse, the greed that produces it or the selfishness that spends it, fritters it away on a cellar full of cats—*cats*, my God—when there's so much of His holy work that could be accomplished with it. Greed and selfishness! I thank the Lord almighty that at least *I'm* not obsessed with the reward."

"Neither am I," Manning says calmly, sidestepping the priest's insult.

Father McMullen breaks into laughter, a snide chuckle of disbelief that quickly blossoms into rude, convulsive guffaws thundering through the dreary house and spilling out through the windows onto the street. When he at last regains his composure, he asks through the spasms that still contort his face, "Then what in the name of heaven are you *doing* here?"

"You could never understand my purpose," says Manning with an even voice, staring at the priest through unflinching, truthful eyes. "The world you've created for yourself is so alien to the one I know, you could never think the thoughts I'm thinking now."

Father McMullen's laughter halts with a jerk of breath that sticks in his throat. Aware that he does not—*cannot*—understand Manning, he feels a sudden and intense awe of the unknown, an awe that verges on fear. Finding his voice, he says, "You may be right, Mr. Manning. I'm sure I don't know. Nor do I care." His arrogance turns pious. "I see no point in imperiling my faith by engaging with you in games of the intellect—in the workings of the merely 'rational' mind."

In a brusque tone declaring an end to their discussion, Manning asks, "Where does Helen O'Connor live?"

"Just a short walk from here, a block past the square." He points the direction. "It's a cottage—stucco, the best-looking house on the street. The mailbox is marked, and there's a statue of a cat crouching under it."

"Thank you," says Manning with a curt bow of his head. He closes the notebook that was folded open on his knee, flipping its cover past the empty page where he has written nothing. He rises from his chair.

The priest rises with him, his face visibly blanched, looking faint. He falls forward to support himself, smacking both palms on the glass top of the desk. Manning watches, unnerved, as one of the priest's hands lands firmly atop the jagged end of an unfolded paper clip. Through a desperate choke, the priest says, "Don't, Mr. Manning . . . please *don't* take her from me." An oily pool of blood begins to spread on the glass from between his splayed fingers.

They have pierced my hands and my feet, Manning remembers, they have numbered all my bones. Manning's eyes shoot back and forth from the desk to Father McMullen's face. For an instant, he sees the priest's golden mane surrounded by a tangled ring of thorns. Barely above a whisper, he asks, "Are you all right?"

The priest falls back into his chair. His wounded hand smears a trail across the top of the desk and disappears in his lap. The paper clip drops to the floor. "Just please don't take her," he repeats.

"I can't 'take' her. I'm not here to 'deprogram' her. Let's not forget about her *free will*—that's a concept you people taught me when I was six—surely it's familiar to you. There's not a thing I could say or do to make her leave this place if she's made up her mind to stay."

"But she . . ." the priest begins, then his voice breaks off as he dismisses Manning with a wave of his good hand.

There is nothing else to say. Manning walks from the room through the front hall and out the door. He darts from the porch to the car at the curb—almost sprinting, no longer fearful of shattering the facade of serenity that hangs over the town like a shroud. He jumps into the car, starts the engine. Though he could easily, quickly walk to the stucco cottage, he does not want to return to the rectory for the car, does not want to leave it as an annoying reminder to the priest.

He finds the cottage within seconds; he sees the mailbox, the statue of the cat. Getting out of the car, he finds that the late morning has turned hot, so he removes his jacket and tosses it through the open window onto the seat with the road map. He hesitates, wondering whether he should close up the car and lock it, then dismisses the notion as ridiculous—of all the dark and dirty sins that may lurk in Assumption, thievery is surely low on the list.

Manning walks up to the front of the house. Raising his fist to rap on the screened door, he pauses. He feels his heart pulsing in his chest, his neck, his hands, as his mind races to recall the long string of events that has led him to this spot, this moment— a situation that any other reporter in the country could imagine only as a fantasy, the crowning moment of a life's work. He has not yet knocked.

"I *thought* I heard someone come up the steps," says a woman's cheery voice from behind the door.

Snatched from his thoughts, Manning feels foolish as he lowers his poised hand, struggling to focus on the woman who stands in the darkness behind the screen. His lips curve into a smile as he discerns the vivid henna hair, the friendly features so much like those of Margaret O'Connor. Manning opens his mouth to speak—there is only one thing to say, and he wonders how the woman will react. Will she scream? Slam the door? He says, "Mrs. Carter? I'm Mark Manning."

"Oh!" It's not a scream, just a squeak. She doesn't seem frightened—merely surprised or embarrassed, as though she has failed to recognize a celebrity standing at her door. "Of course, Mr. Manning," she says with an apologetic laugh, swinging the door open. "Please come in."

The house is small, simply furnished, lacking the expected rummage of advancing years. Manning wonders if the sparse decoration is a reflection of the woman's taste or if her stay in Assumption has not been long enough to assemble fussier surroundings.

A large Abyssinian enters from an adjacent room to inspect the newly arrived visitor. A stately cat of elegant bearing, it moves with slow assurance, thoroughly in control of its household domain. It is without question the most strikingly beautiful cat Manning has ever seen. It leans forward to brush against his leg.

Manning tells the woman, "I'll bet this is Abe."

"You're as clever as I thought you'd be, Mr. Manning. Yes, this is Abe. Here, baby." She picks up the creature, many times a champion, sire to many others, and hands him to Manning. "He's getting on in years, but still, you've never seen an Abby quite like this one."

Manning takes hold of Abe, handling the cat like a long sausage, as he saw the judges do at home. Lanky and muscular, Abe stretches in Manning's hands, purring with a loud, unbroken rumble. "You're right," says Manning, "he's one of a kind."

Manning and the woman sit down and settle into a long, chatty conversation, addressing each other as Mark and Helen. They speak with a candor and humor that would lead an onlooker to assume they were old friends exchanging gossip, as if Manning popped in every weekend to bring her up to date on things back home. Helen asks about her sister, Margaret, about Father Carey, Arthur Mendel, Jerry Klein—grateful for the information Manning supplies, laughing dreamily as she recalls her former life.

Abe has hopped into her lap and nested there, preparing for a nap.

At a lull in their banter, Manning finally says, "When you met me at the door, you welcomed me as though you'd been waiting for me. Why?"

"Eventually *someone* would come. But you were the only one who understood—the only one who hadn't written me off as dead. *That* was reassuring—to know that someone saw my disappearance as anything more involved than waiting seven years to divide the pie. I've read everything you've written about me, but it wasn't till I caught a glimpse of you on TV and saw that determined, calculated look in your eyes—that I knew *you* would be the one to solve this silly mystery, if anyone could. To tell the truth, I've been sort of anxious to hear what you'll have to say about me when you testify at the Houseman Trial next week." She chortles at her own vanity, dismissing the vice as a concession to her age.

Manning laughs with her, then a quizzical look crosses his face. He asks, "What's this all about, Helen? Why did you leave? It's never been clear to anyone—that's why so many people are willing to assume you're dead. It's never been clear to *me*." He uncaps his Mont Blanc.

Helena Carter smiles, then exhales a long sigh. "So we finally get down to it. The story? No wonder it's not clear to you—I'm not sure how much sense I can make of it myself. But I'll try.

"I was looking for something. To be honest, I was running away from something too. Imagine that—a woman turning fifty with no kids, a dead husband, and a hundred million dollars—suddenly starting to question . . . *everything*. Life and death, success and failure, faith itself—faith in all those things we've always been taught were good and pure, unchanging and real. Life really seemed to be *over*, so it was time to turn to God.

"Sure, I'd been 'religious' all my life, but what does that mean? The religious folks you know—the ones who go through all the motions and recite the creeds about what they believe and where their lives are headed—what does their faith actually mean? It's just a badge they wear, another label they slap on their chests with all their other identities: American, liberal or conservative, widow or married, Catholic or whatnot, breeder of champion

Abyssinians, maybe even vegetarian. The list goes on and on. You become the sum of your parts.

"Since some of my parts seemed to be missing, I tried to compensate by working on some of the others. And I turned to God—seriously, for the first time. My life seemed to be waning, and I figured it was high time to get acquainted with the old guy, so I turned to Him. But, Mark"—her voice drops to a whisper—"He wasn't there."

"Of course not," Manning answers softly, shaking his head with the knowing smile of disappointment that accompanies the discovery of a fact that was long suspected and at last admitted.

"So I came to Assumption as an act of faith." She resumes her story with a clear, unemotional voice. "Were you raised Catholic? Remember the 'Act of Faith'? It was a prayer—one of many we memorized—they had one for Hope, too, and another for Charity. For a child, an act of faith is the recitation of words. You feel good and holy when you finally get those words letter-perfect. But for an adult, it's different. Acts of faith have to be *acts*, not words, so I *came* here—simply because I believed that life in Assumption would restore the peace and certainties I knew as a child. It has not. It has slowly begun to confirm my doubts."

Manning tells her, "Confirmation of a doubt is another kind of certainty, isn't it? There's greater peace of mind in truly *knowing* something than there is in merely *believing* otherwise."

"You seem to take comfort in shattered beliefs, Mark—I wish I could. Have you ever felt a label slipping away? Have you ever known the kind of torment that makes a person want to flee—to fly—to take flight from the confusion in search of a dream?"

"I flew to Phoenix just as you did," Manning tells her. "And believe it or not, when I got on that plane in Chicago two days ago, it never crossed my mind that I might be sitting here talking to you now."

"Then why did you come?"

"I flew here for many of the same reasons that you did. I, too, was fleeing doubts and uncertainties of the past. I, too, felt a label slipping away and came in search of something."

"I hope you find it, Mark."

"I already have."

"Then you're a lucky man."

"I know I am."

Manning radiates an infectious joy. In the quiet moments that follow, Helen gazes at her visitor with a wondering stare. Manning finally says to her, "I can understand why you came here, but why all the secrecy? Why the disappearance, the new identity?"

"You've met Father Carey back at Saint Jerome's," she says. "I'm sure he told you that our friendship was rocky by the time I left. I'd convinced myself that the greed I saw in him—which was probably unfair of me—was a symptom of all the changes the church had been through. So I was intrigued by the community that was forming out here in Assumption, thinking that the return to our old ways of worship would automatically bring with it a purity—an escape from materialism."

Manning asks, "How did you first learn about Assumption?"

She pauses uncomfortably before telling him, "It was in the papers a bit at the time, but I first heard about it in a letter . . . from Jamie." Her body tenses. Abe, snoozing in her lap, opens a cautious eye.

Manning looks up from his notebook. "Who?"

"I suppose this will come as news to you, Mark. Jamie—Father James McMullen—is my brother."

Stunned, Manning thinks aloud, "Margaret *said* there were twins at home . . ."

"There were," Helen assures him. "James and Bertrand. They went away to high school, to the seminary, to study for the priesthood together. But something bad happened, and Bertrand died. Jamie changed schools—even his last name—it was such a scandal at the time. Margaret and I never got the whole story; it was all hush-hush at home."

Abe stands, stretching. With his rump aimed at Helen's face, he swipes his tail beneath her chin.

She continues, "I knew that Jamie was later ordained, but then many years passed without hearing from him, until Ridgely died. The inheritance was in the news, and I was starting to get some publicity myself as a breeder. Jamie wrote to express condolences about Ridgely and to tell me of his involvement with Cardinal L'Évêque and The Society. This interested me—because of my troubles at Saint Jerome's—so I struck up a correspondence with Jamie and eventually bought into the whole idea. I decided I wanted to come here, as if 'on retreat,' hoping to nourish my faith."

She leans forward. "But it had to be a secret." Abe is now scrunched between her chest and her lap, so he hops to the floor. "I couldn't just waltz out here announcing who I was, flaunting my wealth to everyone—I was trying to *escape* the influence of my money. I had never told Margaret that Jamie had written in the first place because I thought it might confuse or upset her, so planning the disappearance proved no great challenge. I needed *some* help, though, and Jerry Klein was there for me. He may strike some folks in the business world as timid and ineffectual, but let me tell you, he's a whiz with the numbers, so no one stood a chance of tracing my finances—good thing he's so honest, and he's as loyal as they come. He keeps me comfortable here, and he got some cash to Arthur Mendel a couple of months ago so he could hire a lawyer—I understand that she's a good one, Mark, that she's a friend of yours."

Manning nods, recalling the incident. Abe has circled Manning's chair and now nuzzles his shin. While turning a page in his notebook, Manning gives the cat a quick rub behind the ears.

Helen says, "So Jerry Klein and Jamie are the only ones who know that I'm here. But Jerry has no idea that I'm related to Jamie—no one knows that, except for you. The people in town, they don't know what to make of me. I don't seem to 'fit,' that's for sure, and I know there's a lot of talk that I must have money, but they don't know the details. Morals are pretty strict here, so nobody has a television set—only Jamie and me—because they think it's evil. They haven't seen or heard enough from the outside world to put two and two together. They certainly have no idea there's a second will."

With heightened interest, Manning asks, "What do you mean?"

"That's the whole *point*, Mark. I have no intention of letting Father Carey and his boss, Archbishop Benedict, get their greedy paws on Ridgely's fortune. I came out here in search of a suitable, deserving beneficiary, and in my early days here, I was convinced that I found one—the Society for the Restoration of the Faith. About a year after I arrived, I drew up a new will with Jamie, leaving to The Society everything that was previously going to the Chicago Archdiocese. The plan was simple: After seven years passed and I was declared dead, Jamie would present the new will, the money would go to the townspeople of Assumption and to Cardinal L'Évêque, and I could peacefully live out my latter years in anonymity."

She frowns, sitting back in her chair. "Ultimately, of course, I've always had another option. I could pack up my bags anytime, crate up the cats, and go home—retreat ended, mystery solved, all wills null and void. In my early years here, that possibility seemed remote at best, but lately, I confess, I've had doubts. There's been trouble in paradise, with splinter groups bickering about everything from dogma to doughnuts. These people have shaken my faith in their community. They've shaken my faith . . . in *faith*."

Helen pauses in thought, then leans toward Abe, still stationed near Manning's feet. She beckons the cat with her fingers, he approaches, and she lifts him into her lap.

She says, "Seven years must sound like a long time for a woman of my age to be examining her conscience, but I've been in no hurry. I have little else to do, other than breed my Abbies, and I can do that here as well as anywhere. I'm sorry that my going away has created such a fuss for so many people, and I truly regret that it's been so hard on my sister, but there was simply no other way for me to do it.

"It's been a selfish experiment, I admit, but I don't think I've done anything criminal. The money is *mine*, you know, and I have the right to tie it up any way I wish. My bills and taxes get paid. I haven't defrauded anyone. I haven't even lied about my name, not really. Helena Carter or Helen O'Connor—what's the difference?—they're both me. My name's even in the phone book, but no one ever bothered to look me up."

Manning breaks into laughter. "What a story, Helen! No one would ever believe it—except that it's *true*. What will you do now?"

"You mean now that I've been discovered? I suppose that depends on *you*, Mark."

Manning is jarred by the recognition of what a profound role his own actions will now play in this woman's life. Awkwardly, he tells her, "I plan to do some writing about you—I hope that doesn't disturb you. Please understand that my finding you here is a far bigger story than most reporters ever get a *chance* at. I can't force you to go back home—I don't even especially want to—you're free to remain here as long as you wish. But yes, Helen, I'll surely write about your being here."

"And collect the half million," she adds with a wink, apparently not the least offended by the notion.

Taken aback by her reference to the reward—all the more by her cheery indifference to it—he shakes his head as if to clear his thoughts, then tells her, "I have no intention of claiming that money."

"Oh, *pfoo!*" she says, eyes rolling in disbelief.

He repeats, "I have no intention of claiming it—simply because I have no *claim* to it. The money is yours—you've already said that—not mine to claim and not the court's to give away. I realize that by remaining silent you've passively agreed to the court's offer, but I will not force you to pay me for something— finding you—when all you've wanted is to be left alone. That's not a fair exchange. I haven't *earned* anything. To take your money under those circumstances would be theft. There's a moral order that has nothing to do with law or even religion, and I will not be indicted by it."

Astounded by his words, she asks, "But, Mark—what will you have to show for all your work, your patience, your insight?"

"The story, Helen. I'll have the story, and I've *earned* it. I won't take your money because it's *yours*, but if you asked me very kindly not to print another word about you, I'd refuse, because the story's *mine.*"

"This 'story' sounds like slim reward for your efforts."

He chuckles. "You don't seem to understand how obsessed middle America has become with your disappearance. Of all those who've written about you—and everyone's doing it—I'm the only one who hasn't cried for the blood of your murderer, who hasn't jumped to conclusions and wailed that the public interest be served. Well, damn their conclusions and damn their public inter-est—I was right, and now they'll know it. You call that 'pride'? You *bet* it is—it's the driving force that can take me to the top of my profession and snatch a Partridge Prize. You call that 'vanity' or perhaps even 'lust'? So be it. Others are free to fret about their own deadly sins, but not mine. The slightest amount of clear, unclouded thought tells me this: The last shall never be first, and the meek shall inherit nothing—unless they seize control of their lives and respond to the dictates of reason."

Manning has delivered his words with conviction, giving substance to his innermost thoughts—but without bitterness, not meant to affront the woman sitting across from him. His words, however, have hit Helen like a slap—not from the hand of a malicious aggressor, but from that of a friend attempting to revive her from a lifelong stupor.

"Years ago," Manning remembers, speaking as if to no one, "I was arguing about something with a friend. I was losing, so I dragged God into it—as people often do when logic fails—and I ranted that God would punish this or that. I can't even recall now what the object of the argument was, but I'll never forget the heated reaction of my friend. He looked me square in the eye and told me, 'God is bullshit, and you know it.' His comment enraged me, but not because of its vulgarity or sacrilege. No, it was the second part of his statement, the words he tacked onto the end: *And you know it.* Sure thing. I did."

Manning ponders the weight of his own reflections while Helen sits motionless, her eyes fixed on him, her mind immersed in the issue he has bared so bluntly. Though his words still ring painfully in her ears, she is moved by the mere sight of him—a man at peace with himself, guiltless and confident, in tune with the powers of his own mind. Abe, perhaps offended by the discussion, has leapt to the floor and now saunters out of the room.

"Mark," Helen says at last, breaking the silence, "I understand how important my story is to you, and you're right—the story's yours, you've earned it. But may I ask you a very big favor?"

"What's that?"

"Wait just a short while longer before you print it. You see, I've nearly accomplished what I came here for. From the start, my move to Assumption was meant as a journey to some further destination. I'm almost there. And your visit today has forced a lot of thoughts. But these are thoughts that demand careful consideration, and you've taken me by surprise. If you print my story at once, everything will be pulled out from under me. One way or the other, my life will change radically—I've known that all along. But I won't be prepared for that change until I've put to rest the questions I came here to answer. Mark, please wait a few days, a week at most. By then, my course will be clear. And I promise you this: I'll share my every thought with you, I'll talk to no other reporter, and I'll let it be known that you found me. Here and now, I'll sign any statement you want. Just wait a few days before you publish anything, and I promise to cooperate so fully that you won't have space enough to print it all."

He knows he can trust her, and she is savvy enough to guess that her "exclusive" would entice even the most hard-boiled of reporters. She raises one eyebrow in an impish expression that asks, Well . . . how 'bout it?

He mirrors her grin. "Okay, Helen. Sounds like a fair exchange. I've got some personal business in Phoenix over the next couple of days that I don't care to interrupt anyway. And that'll give me time to work up a scorcher of a draft. But remember—I'm scheduled to testify in court next Wednesday. The questioning should focus on Arthur Mendel, but if they ask me what I know about you . . . well, I won't lie under oath."

"Of course not. I'd never expect that."

He gives her two of his business cards, one for her to keep so that she will know how to reach him. "The other one is for me," he says. "In case anything goes awry, could I ask you to sign and date it, please? Your phone number too." She gladly obliges, and he returns the card to his wallet.

Closing his notebook, he bids farewell to the woman. They exchange a friendly embrace and offer each other words of encouragement for the difficult days that will follow. "I fly back to Chicago on Monday," he says. "I'll be waiting to hear from you."

He returns to the car, starts the engine, and pulls away from the curb. Turning onto the main street, he follows the road out of town and is soon racing toward the interstate, his mind abuzz with the events of the day, anxious to relate his news to Neil. It is midafternoon, and the car is stiflingly hot—funny, he thinks while lowering his window. He remembers that he decided not to lock the car, but he cannot remember closing the windows.

Before long, he sees the main highway in the distance and begins to slow the car as he approaches the entrance ramp. From the corner of his eye, he detects some sort of movement on the passenger's seat. Glancing sideways, he sees his jacket ripple. Then, from under the road map, peeps an inquisitive snake—a big one, judging from the size of its head. The jacket thrashes. The map rustles. The head slides across the seat toward the car's center console.

Manning catches his breath. In a single, fluid motion, he jams harder on the car's brakes, unlatches his seat belt, opens the door, and pitches himself onto the roadway. Hitting the pavement, he winces at the snap of his left arm beneath him.

Neil's driverless car travels several hundred yards down the road before veering off the shoulder and somersaulting sideways into the sandy ditch.

Sunday, December 27

5 days till deadline

With his good hand, Manning fidgets with the controls of his hospital bed until he sits upright, facing the sheriff's deputy. "Did they find it?"

"Yeah. Big fella, four-footer. Damnedest thing, though—it wasn't from these parts, according to the snake guy at the zoo. Good thing, too—they're real mean, poisonous. Can't imagine how it ended up in your vehicle."

"Somebody *put* it there," Manning says testily, stating the obvious.

"Sure looks that way." The deputy scribbles something on his clipboard, then clicks his ball-point and returns it to his breast pocket. "I wish we had more to go on, Mr. Manning. We'll do what we can. You'll probably hear from us after you get back to Chicago. When do you leave Phoenix?"

"Tomorrow, assuming the threatened air strike doesn't muck things up. And assuming they let me out of here—the arm's broken, apparently no complications—they kept me overnight for observation."

"It's a shame to ruin your Christmas trip with something like this. But count yourself lucky—if it hadn't happened so near the main highway, you might *still* be laid-out on that back road." Leaving the room, he turns in the doorway to give Manning a casual salute. "Take care now."

Manning turns to Neil, who sits in a stiff chair wedged next to the bed, and says, "I feel just *awful* about your car."

"Don't worry about the car—it's insured. The important thing, Mark, is that someone tried to *kill* you. Now that you've told me everything you learned yesterday, it's clear there's a lot at stake. Anything could happen. You've got to be careful."

Making light of the warning, Manning tells him, "I'm always careful."

"*Especially* careful." Softly, Neil adds, "I wouldn't want to lose you."

Manning clasps Neil's hand, pauses, then says, "So much has happened over the last two days—first you, then Helena Carter. I'm going home tomorrow—we live so far apart—and there's so much I want to talk to you about. But the whole Carter business is coming to a head now, and suddenly I'm part of it. Forgive me, Neil, but it's difficult to focus on anything else."

"Shhh," Neil quiets him, as if soothing a troubled child, patting his hand. "We have all the time in the world to talk. Right now, you need to concentrate on Carter, on your court date. You've worked too hard and risked too much to jeopardize your story with 'romance.'" Neil snorts a derisive laugh, as if unmoved by the emotions that gnaw at Manning.

They are interrupted by a shuffle in the hall and the appearance of a figure in the open doorway. Manning blinks, breaking the gaze he has shared with Neil, and turns to find Brother Burt standing at the foot of his bed.

"I was making my Sunday-morning hospital rounds," the preacher tells Manning, "and heard that you'd been admitted. Sweet *Cheee-suss*, what a terrible accident . . ."

Manning lifts his broken arm to give Brother Burt a good look at it, telling him, "It was no accident."

"Really," says Brother Burt flatly. But he's not looking at the cast on Manning's arm. His eyes are fixed on Manning's other hand, which still holds Neil's. Brother Burt flexes the muscles of his jaw. Through a tight smile, he tells Manning, "The Lord works in strange and mysterious ways."

Monday, December 28

Silence rings in James McMullen's ears. In the darkness of the confessional, the priest waits to hear the whispers of the next penitent, but there has been very little sinning since Christmas—it's a slow afternoon for contrition. His head bobs. He fumbles to press the button that lights the dial of his watch. He has slept; only ten minutes remain till he can emerge into the daylight. Though not hungry, not yet, he wonders what Mrs. Weaver is concocting for dinner—holiday leftovers if he's lucky, Tuna Helper if he's not.

His idle musing is broken by the thud of the church's front door. He knows from experience how long it takes to walk from the door to the side aisle and then the length of the nave to the confessional. This must be one of the older sheep in his flock—the trip is taking far too long. Waiting, he hears the sound of a limp on the stone floor. Thump-slide . . . thump-slide.

Wooden rings rattle on their metal rod as the frayed velvet curtain sweeps open, then closes again. With a groan of both pain and disgust, the heavy man kneels with difficulty, his face only inches from the priest's, separated by a screen of white pleated linen. In a familiar, sarcastic drawl, he says, "Bless me, Father, for I have sinned," then breaks into laughter.

By force of the sinner's breath, the screen puffs toward the priest, who recoils from its foul odor, covering his own mouth and nose with one hand. As disbelief and anger well within him, his hand slides to his throat and he spits back through the screen, "What in hell are you doing *here?* How *dare* you, Bertrand!"

Brother Burt tells him, "What's the matter—afraid we'll be *seen* together? Not much of a brotherly attitude, Jamie—and to think we were once so close. You didn't seem to mind my being here the other day when I 'lost' one of my pets in that faggot reporter's car. Poor Sasha—I hear she fell in the line of duty, shot by one of the Keystone Kops—God rest her venomous little soul."

"Get *out*," the priest tells him in a loud, panicked whisper.

"I'll leave when I'm damn good-and-ready. We stand to lose everything now. It's time to act, and I'm here to tell you what to do. Think you can handle it? *Cheee-suss*, you were always such a fuck-up."

"*Me?* I'm not the one who brought disgrace to our family. I'm not the one who had to run away, vanish, and 'die.' I'm not the one, Bertrand, who murdered our friend, a classmate—a fellow seminarian, no less—butchered with the stone blade of some heathen relic. Christ, I still have dreams about finding that poor innocent boy . . ."

"Innocent, my ass. That 'friend' was no more than a filthy little queer. He confessed his repugnant 'love' for me, and I was thereby anointed the holy instrument of almighty God's wrath— an avenging angel sent to slay the serpent, to slash his disgusting throat. Satan struggled, maimed me, tangled my foot in the rods of a steel headboard, but I arose victorious from his blood. And God has rewarded me with the bounties of His mission."

"Mission, indeed. The only 'mission' of that TV scam you're running is worship of the almighty dollar. Your insane homophobia is outweighed only by your greed."

"My, my—aren't *we* suddenly self-righteous. You had no aversion to those almighty dollars when I offered you the seed money to start up this pissant retreat—this desert 'paradise' where you and your friends, you bunch of losers, could get together and play old-time religion. The dollars weren't so dirty when they were a gift from God."

"They were never a gift from God, Bertrand. They were a gift from you. Like most gifts, this one had strings attached."

"Damn right. My only interest in helping you get Assumption up-and-running was your promise to lure our dear, long-lost, and very wealthy sister out to this hellhole. *And* your promise to convince her to sign a new will, which I drafted. *And* your promise to enter into a private but ironclad agreement with me that the proceeds of her estate will be divided between our two ministries."

"I have many failings—God knows—but I *am* a man of my word. I've kept all those promises. I owed you that."

"You owe me more, Jamie. You owe yourself more. We've come this far together. We can't just let it all slip away—which it could, since that reporter had found Helen. If she leaves Assumption, she'll never come back."

"But she *hasn't* left," says the priest, trying to assure himself as well as his brother. "In any event, we've got the second will. Sooner or later, the money will come to us."

"You hopeless fool," says Bertrand, "that will isn't worth shit if she's still alive. She has to die, Jamie—*and you're going to kill her.*"

Dumbstruck, the priest watches his brother's hand materialize from the folds of the screen, watches the chubby fingers with dirty nails open to reveal a small glass vial. He inhales the word that springs to his mind, hardly daring to speak it: "Venom."

Bertrand snorts. "Idiot. That would have to be injected. Not very subtle. But this'll do the trick, if you keep it refrigerated. Use it soon. In wine."

Stammering, the priest tells him, "I couldn't possibly do such a thing."

Bertrand's fist jams farther through the screen, striking the priest's chest. Father McMullen has no choice but to take the bottle, holding it in his open, wounded palm, unable to close his fingers around it. With his other hand, he grasps the sacramental stole of purple that hangs around his neck. "Besides," he tells his brother, fishing for an out, "the plan would never work. What about Mark Manning?"

"I'll take care of Manning."

Wednesday, December 30
2 days till deadline

The cab is cold. Manning nestles into his camel-hair topcoat, which isn't buttoned because of the cast on his arm. Clearly, he's in for a period of readjustment.

Manning returned from Phoenix late Monday, lucky to have a confirmed seat on CarterAir, one of the few airlines not affected by a spreading mechanics' strike. His flight arrived on time at O'Hare, and the city had dug itself out of the worst of the Christmas storm. Things were returning to normal, and it felt good to be back—back in the hub of activity, back to work—in spite of the splendid weather he left in Arizona, in spite of the man he left behind, wishing a bittersweet farewell that was peppered with mutual promises to think it through, work it out, get it settled.

Tuesday was hectic—catching up at his desk and preparing for the opening of the Houseman Trial. He spent most of the afternoon with his editor, Gordon Smith, and with Arthur Mendel's lawyer, Roxanne Exner, reviewing background and strategies for their day in court. Both Manning and Roxanne were careful to keep the conversation on a professional level, avoiding personal matters, particularly the trip to Phoenix. Roxanne knew that Manning had been there, but she was not yet prepared to hear any of what transpired with Neil, and Manning was not yet willing to reveal that he'd found Helena Carter.

Roxanne explained that the Houseman Trial—the hearing—would be held in Cook County Circuit Court, presided over by Judge Clement Ambrose, whom she described as "classically crusty-but-fair." When the case was assigned to him, he expressed grave reservations as to whether the inquest was warranted by the known facts of the case, nearly refusing to hear it. He was aware, though, that the publicity surrounding the case would easily entice less scrupulous judges to accept it. There were also the interests—and pressures—of the Archdiocese to consider, so he amended his schedule to accommodate the opening session during the last week of the year.

Roxanne cautioned Manning to be wary of Hank Ferret, Helena Carter's court-appointed guardian *ad litem*. Apparently Humphrey Hasting and his buddy, deputy police superintendent Murphy, invited Ferret out for a "working lunch." Hasting later bragged to a lawyer acquaintance of Roxanne's that it took "precisely two cocktails" to convince Ferret to assume the prosecutor's role in the proceeding, and it is Ferret who has subpoenaed Manning to deliver testimony at the "fact-finding inquest."

In the cab now, Wednesday morning, traffic is slow between the *Journal* offices and the Loop, so Manning burrows deeper into the collar of his coat, slouching with his head resting on the back of the seat. Clearing his mind, he slips into a dreamlike state. His brain is awake, but devoid of words, of syntax, of language itself. His awareness consists only of fleeting images, overarching perceptions. He feels as rested as on that first morning in Phoenix when he awoke to find Neil shaking his shoulder. His trip, he knows, was inevitable—but it wasn't fate that took him out to the desert. It wasn't destiny. He had *decided* to go there. He *willed* it.

He thinks of Neil; his mind blossoms with the textures of their contact, the sounds and smells of their intimacy. He thinks of Helena Carter; he is dazzled by the henna brilliance of her hair, by the truth and wonder in her eyes. He thinks of his own future; his mind is awash with vague options for happiness. The uncertainties that lie ahead invigorate him. He feels no fear.

"Daley Center," croaks the cabbie, yanking Manning from his reverie. Handing the driver some bills, leaving the cab, he reminds himself that the next few days will be the most difficult of his career. With the full assault of reality—to say nothing of the arctic downdrafts that whip through the plaza—Manning suspects that his bout of euphoria should be dismissed as the aftereffect of painkillers he was fed in the hospital. The monumental Picasso bird/woman/dog looks down on him with a wry, shifting glance. Transmitter vans from a half-dozen television stations line the curb.

Manning enters the glass-and-steel monolith of Daley Center and stands still for a moment, letting his senses adjust to the interior space. A commotion at the far end of the lobby stirs his reporter's instincts, drawing him toward the fray. Like bouncers at some trendy night spot, two guards check credentials, allowing some of the people in the crowd to board a single elevator, but turning away others, who howl their protest. Drawing nearer, Manning discovers that the elevator is whisking express to one of the large upper-floor courtrooms where the Houseman Trial will soon begin.

Nudging his way to one of the guards, he flashes his press pass. The guard squints at it, then at Manning's face, then back at the card. He laughs awkwardly and says, "Of course, Mr. Manning, how stupid of me. This way, sir." He clears a path to the elevator door, admonishing the crowd to step aside.

Inside the elevator, the others fall silent as Manning enters and the doors slide closed. The ride is obligingly brief, punctuated by coughs and whispers as they rise twenty-some stories. When the doors open into the upper lobby, Manning strides out from the huddle behind him and into the glare of cameras assembled there to meet him.

A network television reporter charges forward with the ferocity of a quarterback, flashes two perfect rows of capped teeth, and intones, "Can you give us any clues, Mr. Manning, as to what strategy you plan for today's showdown with your opponent, Humphrey 'The Hump' Hasting?"

"Mr. Hasting is in no sense my opponent," Manning begins— while a battery of microphones are thrust under his chin. "I have no idea what motivated his various allegations, but I assume *I've* been called to act as a character witness on behalf of Arthur Mendel. I hope I can help him."

A stunningly attractive woman, dressed more like a fashion model than a reporter, asks, "How does it feel to be on the other side of an interview for a change?"

The cluster of reporters look to him with special attention. He says flatly, honestly, "It amuses me." There is a round of laughter—the laughter of comrades basking in the shared glow of a workfellow's glory, laughter tempered only by their envy.

"Mr. Manning?" says a short young reporter with thick glasses who holds a microphone from one of the local stations. He speaks with an aggressive voice meant to compensate for his stunted height. "Your employer, the *Journal*, has access to the most high-powered legal talent in the city. Who are your editors sending to represent you this morning?"

"I'll stand alone," Manning says. "I'll answer any questions put to me, and I'll speak for myself."

"Did you *hear* that, ladies and gentlemen?" the female reporter coos to her audience.

"An astonishing act of courage," proclaims the network man through his capped teeth.

"But, but . . ." stammers the little reporter who asked the question.

A guard ushers Manning through the doors of the courtroom itself, leaving the gaping and babbling, the glare of TV lights, behind in the hall. Taking his seat in the front row of the gallery, Manning estimates that the room can accommodate perhaps a hundred spectators. It bears scarce resemblance to the movie settings for trials held in turn-of-the-century courthouses. This room has no windows. It's boxy and sterile, painted white, with a ten-foot ceiling composed of acoustical tile interspersed with oblong rectangles of fluorescent lighting. The bench itself is raised—but only a step or two because of the low ceiling—flanked on one side by the American flag and on the other by that of Cook County. A sheriff's deputy, the court clerk, and a stenographer stand gabbing near the bench, sipping coffee from foam cups, waiting for the show to start.

Jerry Klein and Arthur Mendel sit at a table near the front of the room with Roxanne and an assistant, who busily prepare stacks of briefs, notes, and accounts. At a similar table sits a dapper attorney who Manning assumes to be Hank Ferret. He lounges in his chair with his legs crossed at the knees, watching the activity at Roxanne's table with a vague, detached curiosity. In contrast to Ferret's easy manner, his young underling, also at the table, appears jittery and preoccupied, thumbing through a thin pile of notes. Behind them, seated among a group of reporters, Humphrey Hasting picks his teeth with the cap of a ball-point pen.

Cameras are not allowed in Illinois courts, so the hearing will be aired on radio. Technicians fidget with bouquets of microphones placed at the lawyers' tables, the witness stand, and the judge's chair at the bench. Several sketch artists, who will render these scenes in colored chalk for newspapers and television, make quick-study drawings of the room, of the lawyers, of Manning himself. Manning suddenly realizes that he will not be able to report on the hearing because of his own role in it, and he wonders if the *Journal* has thought to send another reporter. Turning in his seat to scour the rapidly filling gallery for a familiar face, he is relieved to spot one of his associates, who waves his reporter's notebook and flashes Manning the "okay" sign.

The deputy announces that all should rise as Judge Clement Ambrose emerges from his chambers to take his place at the bench. He is a shrunken man who walks with a hobble, his robes crossing the floor in jerky black puffs. A thin smile reveals a kindly, fatherly nature, while a glimmer in his eye betrays a smoldering wrath that he sometimes vents in the dispensing of justice. Seating himself, he nods to the others in the room, who then resume their own seats.

Normally absorbed by every detail of an event he is covering for the *Journal*, Manning feels his mind go blank during the opening procedures of the hearing. He is here in court, after all, as a participant, not a paid spectator, and he is concerned with only two questions: What will they ask? How will I answer? Manning consciously shifts his attention to Hank Ferret, who now stands for his opening statement.

Ferret tugs once, briskly at his lapels, then strokes his moussed temples with the palms of both hands. He straightens his tie and steps forward. "If it please the court, your honor," he begins in a deep, booming tone developed for just such occasions, "we have lived for nearly seven years in the anguish of doubt that has surrounded the disappearance—and, alas, the probable death—of Helena Carter." Ferret turns from the judge and strikes a pose for the gallery, prompting an audible scratching of sketch books from the row of artists. "She was a fine woman, a good woman—a woman of faith who was deeply religious, a humanitarian who loved animals."

Humphrey Hasting licks his lips.

"But she has been snatched from our midst," the lawyer laments. "Is there still reason to cling to any shred of hope that she might again grace the North Shore with her benign presence? This is the question we hope to answer through the inquest that begins today. We are not here to accuse, but to learn—not to punish, but to vindicate. We have called here Arthur Mendel, houseman to Helena Carter for many years, that he might share with us any knowledge, any insights, into the circumstances that led to his employer's disappearance. Let us go forward, then, with this fact-finding mission in a spirit of candor and open-mindedness, that the cause of justice may be served, and that Mrs. Carter's estate may be expeditiously settled according to the terms of her will. Thank you."

He ends with a sweep of his arm that could pass for a Shake-spearean bow, drawing a smatter of applause from pockets of the gallery. Humphrey Hasting claps far more loudly than the others, causing Ferret a tinge of embarrassment as he returns to his seat.

Judge Ambrose snuffs the demonstration with a single slam of his gavel, then turns to Roxanne. "Well, Miss Exner?" he says with a smile. "I assume madam counsel has a few thoughts of her own on this matter. Do you wish to respond with an opening statement?"

"I do, your honor." Roxanne rises and turns to the gallery. A gleam of resolution flashes in her eyes as she weighs her thoughts, focusing on the faces that peer back at her. The silence is broken only by the muffled abrasion of colored chalk on paper. She finally says, "I'm directing my comments to you, spectators from the general public and representatives of the press, because there's no jury in this courtroom." Her voice is clear, loud, and deliberately unladylike, delivering her message in sharp, staccato jabs. "There's not a jury because this is not a trial. I urge you all to remember that basic fact and to dismiss the sensational nonsense you've been reading that has led to this opening session of the so-called 'Houseman Trial.' But I repeat: This is *not* a trial, merely a hearing. No one has been charged with a crime, and there's not a scrap of evidence that would warrant charges. Remember that as this inquisition unfolds. Remember that as you observe the techniques of my skilled colleague, Mr. Ferret. Remember that as you witness the unconscionable spectacle of unspecified charges being leveled for unspecified crimes. And remember it, you who hold the power to inform the masses, as you rush from this room to milk 'news' from this hearing—a hearing that was spawned without justification and that will produce nothing of substance except the unprovoked humiliation of an innocent man. *Remember it.*"

She spins on her heel and sits. The crowd stares, stunned. Even the artists have abandoned the drawings that lie in their laps. Arthur Mendel seems more frightened by the lull than comforted by her words of defense.

The *filthy* bitch, Hasting tells himself. Putting down his pen, he decides that not a single word of Roxanne's will appear in the *Post*—not in *his* paper, by God.

"Thank you, Miss Exner," says Judge Ambrose. "Your point is well made and forcefully stated. We'll all try to keep in mind the issues you've raised. Now, Mr. Ferret"—he swings his head—"please call your first witness."

Ferret calls a police detective to the stand. The officer is sworn in, then proceeds to answer a long string of questions from Ferret regarding the underworld connections of many famous—and infamous—horse-racing figures. The questioning is structured to leave the impression that anyone involved in any way with horses, as Mendel was, must necessarily have connections with organized crime. The questioning also reveals, to Manning's amusement, that neither Ferret nor Hasting has discovered Mendel's past gambling peccadillo, which could have been used to build a far more incriminating argument.

Roxanne listens, refraining from the objections she could easily raise. When at last it is her turn to cross-examine the witness, she has but one question: "Do you know of any evidence linking Arthur Mendel to the disappearance of Helena Carter?" The detective answers, "No, ma'am," and Roxanne dismisses him.

Hasting's lips curl into a pout.

Ferret calls a psychiatrist to the stand and questions him on various aspects of the criminal mind, leaving the impression that any man who has spent his career in a role servile to a woman would eventually have to strike out against that woman as a means of asserting his manhood and restoring self-esteem. In extreme cases, murder might well be the unhappy resolution to a situation described by the doctor as "psychologically untenable."

When Roxanne cross-examines the witness, she again poses the question: "Do you know of any evidence linking Arthur Mendel to the disappearance of Helena Carter?" The doctor answers, "No, ma'am," and is dismissed.

Hasting fumes.

Ferret then questions the county coroner on techniques for disposing of a body under various circumstances, failing to include—Manning notes—the possibilities presented by concrete or construction sites. The coroner describes an array of grizzly procedures glossed over with technical jargon, rendering his morbid expertise unemotional and businesslike. He leaves the impression that if a person set out to destroy the mortal remains of a victim, it is a task that any clever child might accomplish.

Roxanne again asks her sole question. The coroner responds that he knows of no such evidence. He is dismissed.

Similar examinations and cross-examinations take place with a bank president, a priest, a jockey, a forensic pathologist—a parade of "expert witnesses." Roxanne begins to wonder if Ferret will ever call Mark Manning or Arthur Mendel. She herself is determined not to call them to the stand, but she is surprised that Ferret has not yet lunged. It's nearly one o'clock, and the proceeding has grown sluggish. Attorneys and witnesses alike are getting hungry and irritable.

Judge Ambrose finally asks the two lawyers to approach the bench. He asks how many witnesses they still intend to call, wondering if they should first break for lunch.

A murmur swells from the gallery. Humphrey Hasting, straining to hear what is being said, slips from the edge of his chair. Fumbling, he spares himself the ignominy of landing on the floor.

"Before calling our star witnesses," Ferret confides with a wink that makes Roxanne want to slap him, "I'd like to question Mrs. Carter's sister, Margaret O'Connor, but I'm amazed that I haven't seen her—"

"Your honor," Roxanne interrupts, "Miss O'Connor is not here today. Jerry Klein tells me that she preferred not to attend, finding the proceeding too painful. If called, however, she will willingly testify."

The judge turns from Roxanne to Ferret. "Well, counsel," he says, "it seems you won't be questioning Miss O'Connor today. Do you wish to go ahead and call Arthur Mendel?"

"No, your honor. That can wait."

"How about you, Miss Exner? Any witnesses you wish to call today?"

She begins to answer in the negative, then stops herself, reconsidering. She says aloud, for all to hear, "Yes, your honor, I *would* like to call a final witness—Mark Manning."

The murmur from the gallery immediately surges into a cross fire of excited discussion. Judge Ambrose raps for order and calls Manning to the stand. An expectant smile spreads across Humphrey Hasting's face, and he watches with a predatory stare as Manning is sworn in and seated.

Roxanne asks her witness, "Is it true, Mr. Manning, that in the course of your investigative reporting of the Carter case, you've had occasion to interview the family houseman, Arthur Mendel?" Roxanne's delivery sounds cool and prosaic, as though she has never met the man she now questions.

"Yes, Miss Exner, I spoke with Mr. Mendel at length on two occasions in October." Manning's mind snaps into focus as he falls into the expected pattern of questions and answers.

"And what was the purpose of those interviews? Did you plan to write a story about him?"

"No, I wasn't planning a specific story. They were background interviews. I had reported events surrounding the Carter disappearance since the day after it happened, and though I'd met Arthur, I'd never interviewed him because there was no reason to think he was involved. But since his name kept popping up as a possible suspect—"

Roxanne asks, "You mean, in Humphrey Hasting's articles in the *Post?*"

"Exactly. Because the *Post* repeatedly named him as a suspect, I decided to talk to Arthur simply as a means of confirming—in my own mind—his noninvolvement."

"You've been reporting for the *Journal* for how long, Mr. Manning?"

"Nearly twenty years. I joined the paper right out of college."

"Your reputation for the work you've done there is widely known among the press. At the risk of embarrassing you, Mr. Manning, would it be accurate to say that you are generally respected for your fairness, your thoroughness, your judgment?"

"That would be accurate," he replies, not at all embarrassed.

"You think of yourself, then, as a good judge of character—that's an important part of your job, isn't it?"

"Yes, Miss Exner."

"Tell us, then, what conclusions you drew from your discussions with Arthur Mendel."

Manning smiles. "After some initial doubts, I found it inconceivable that he could be in any way involved with Mrs. Carter's disappearance. In fact, I know that he is innocent."

Hank Ferret shoots to his feet. "Your honor, the witness is expressing opinions. Mr. Manning's statement is irrelevant to this proceeding."

"Don't be silly, counsel," the judge snaps at Ferret. "All character witnesses are called to express their opinions, and Miss Exner has demonstrated that Mr. Manning's opinion in this matter is indeed relevant. Objection overruled. Sit down, Mr. Ferret." He cracks his gavel and turns to Roxanne. "Please continue."

Taking an unexpected turn, she asks, "Mr. Manning, has your involvement with this case proved in any way threatening to your health?"

Ferret is again on his feet. "Your honor, I *must* object. Madam counsel's transparent attempt to dramatize the witness's bandaged arm is obviously a sympathy ploy beneath the dignity of this court!"

With a menacing leer, Judge Ambrose tells him, "Overruled. I'm intrigued by the question. The witness will please answer."

Manning says, "Yes. My life has been threatened. Twice." His words are met with astonished mutterings. "My arm was broken a few days ago in an auto accident resulting from potentially lethal mischief that seems clearly related to the Carter case; I do not know who was responsible. Earlier, on October nineteenth, I received a death threat in the mail; I have never taken the October incident seriously, however."

Roxanne asks, "Do you still have this letter?"

"Right here," Manning answers, producing the envelope.

Roxanne has Manning read the insipid note into the record, then she has it entered into evidence and hands it to Judge Ambrose, who studies it closely.

The judge asks Manning, "Do you have any idea who sent this?"

"Yes, your honor, I know exactly who sent it."

The judge's eyes pop. "*Who?*"

Manning tells him, "Humphrey Hasting, reporter for the *Post.*"

Pandemonium. The crowd's whispers explode into whoops of dismay. Reporters scribble ecstatically—*this* is the stuff they've been waiting for!—and a veritable cloud of chalk dust rises over the heads of the sketch artists. Hank Ferret screams his objections. Judge Ambrose hammers over the din. And Humphrey Hasting sits with his mouth agape—a numbed, quivering blob in a bow tie.

When a semblance of order has been restored, the judge asks, "Can you substantiate this charge, Mr. Manning?"

"Indeed I can," says Manning. Everyone in court listens, engrossed, as Manning recounts the events of the day when he received the letter. He points out the *Post*'s watermark on the stationery. He notes certain tendencies in Hasting's writing style—including overuse of the word "modicum." He explains the distinctive little E's typical of old newsroom typewriters, adding, "Mr. Hasting once told me at a party that he writes all his stories on 'an ancient Underwood.' I'm certain, your honor, that if you impound his typewriter and examine its type, you'll find that it produced the letter in evidence."

Judge Ambrose instantly dispatches two deputies to the *Post* building to confiscate the machine, making the order official with a pound of his gavel.

A hush falls over the courtroom. All eyes turn to Humphrey Hasting, who hasn't moved, hasn't spoken. He peers at the judge for a moment, then shifts his gaze to Ferret, to Manning, to Roxanne, then back to the judge. Moments pass. Silence reigns. The room closes in on him.

"**N**o," wails Hasting, "*it wasn't signed!*" He flails both arms at the heavens. "You can't prove it—you can't prove a thing!"

In a comfortable chair in a little stucco house in Assumption, Helena Carter listens to Hasting's outburst on the radio. Abe, the greatest of all champion Abyssinians, lies curled in her lap. Abe's tail, tipped with hairs of purest black, just touches his brick-red nose. The cat's slow, easy breathing gently parts the black tuft of fur with machinelike regularity.

The woman sits perfectly still, except for one of her thumbs, which strokes Abe behind the ears. She is the picture of contentment, but her mind is troubled. She hears the uproar that now fills the courtroom. She hears Judge Ambrose hopelessly gavel for silence. She hears the words of an announcer describing the scene. She hears the churning of her own brain, burdened for days with the decisions she must soon reach.

"Your honor!" Hank Ferret's voice barks through the mayhem. "I most strenuously object to Miss Exner's line of questioning. I *demand* that the witness's testimony be stricken."

"Overruled!" the judge blasts back at him. Then, in a civil, normal tone, he asks, "Miss Exner, have you any more questions for this witness?"

"No, your honor."

The judge asks Ferret, "Well, counsel, I suppose you'd like to cross-examine."

Soft-voiced but eager, Ferret replies, "Indeed I would." There is a moment's quiet while the lawyer approaches the witness stand. "Mr. Manning," he asks, his tone suggesting that a new thought has occurred to him, "do you feel, as you implied by your testimony, that it was somehow improper for the *Chicago Post*—which happens to be your employer's principal competitor—to name suspects in the Carter case?"

"It was highly improper," says Manning, "to publicly accuse a man without evidence—even if motivated by the so-called 'public interest.' That's not the function of journalism."

"I see. Could you share with us, Mr. Manning, your more highly *evolved* philosophy of journalism?"

"It's not a philosophy, but simply a matter of definition. The reporter's job is to report the news—not to make news. He deals only in facts, striving to report them in a concise and intelligible manner. It is the reader's task to understand those facts and to interpret them."

"But we don't always have the facts, do we, Mr. Manning? Sometimes we have to rely upon our beliefs."

"Not in news reporting. Beliefs are always personal, usually meaningless, and sometimes dangerous. Beliefs are never knowledge. By their nature, they refute knowledge and dismiss facts."

"Come now," clucks Ferret, as if he has trapped a child in a ridiculous fib, "are you trying to tell us there is no room in the world for belief or trust or . . . *faith?* Do you never act on a hunch?"

"Of course I do—sometimes we're forced to. When we don't have sufficient facts that would allow us to act on the basis of knowledge, we must make decisions and take actions based on our best judgment. That's acting on a hunch, a 'belief.' But my point is this, Mr. Ferret: When I'm stuck with a hunch, *I don't write about it.*"

A stir of muted voices affirms that the crowd in the courtroom has been swayed by Manning, but Ferret presses on. "It's easy to point the finger, isn't it, Mr. Manning? But fingers point both ways, you know. You have upbraided Humphrey Hasting for accusing Arthur Mendel in his columns, yet I distinctly heard you say of Mendel, 'He is innocent.' Isn't that a *belief* on your part? Haven't you acted on a hunch in so judging him?"

"No." Manning's voice is clear, his manner resolute. "The innocence of Arthur Mendel is not a belief on my part. It is knowledge."

"Oh, *really?*" says Ferret with a sneer. "Do, please, enlighten us with the precious facts that enable you to make such a judgment."

Manning pauses before answering. "For seven years I have reported details suggesting that Helena Carter is not dead, but has disappeared of her own willing. No one else has followed this reasoning or drawn this conclusion. Now I *tell* you: The woman is alive. This is a fact—but those who would profit from her death are no more likely to accept facts than they are able to understand reasoning."

Ferret says, "What makes you so certain that Mrs. Carter is alive?"

Manning replies, "I could tell you that Helena Carter has not been murdered. I could tell you that I've recently seen her, sat with her, spoken with her at length. I could tell you all these things, but you wouldn't believe me. I could swear to these things, but you'd accuse me of perjury. I could tell you precisely how I know the things I know. But I won't."

Ferret says slyly, "A wise decision. No, Mr. Manning, I wouldn't believe you. Yes, I'd accuse you of perjury. If the things you said were true, there'd be no need for this hearing today. If your words were true"—Ferret breaks into loud laughter—"you'd be a very lucky, rather *wealthy* man!"

The crowd laughs nervously with Ferret, shifting its fickle allegiance. Judge Ambrose raps his gavel, and the disturbance is quickly quelled.

"Your honor," says Ferret, his voice still shaky with waning spasms of laughter, "I believe the 'credibility' of this witness has been sufficiently demonstrated. I have no further questions."

The judge addresses the assembly: "Ladies and gentlemen, these proceedings have taken far longer than planned. It's well past my lunchtime, and Mr. Mendel has yet to testify. To the parties who have an interest in Mrs. Carter's estate, it is important that we resolve these matters before New Year's Day, so we will meet again tomorrow afternoon, December thirty-first, at one o'clock. At that time, Mr. Manning, you will substantiate your fantastic claims to Mr. Ferret, or you will be held in contempt of this court. We stand adjourned."

At the sound of the gavel, background jabber fills the room, and the hush-toned announcer begins his needless summary of what the listening audience has just heard.

"Excuse me, Abe," Helena Carter tells the cat as she lifts him from her lap and sets him on the floor next to her chair. She rises, crosses the room, and switches off the radio. When she returns to the chair, Abe leaps into her lap and resumes his nap, bearing no apparent grudge for the intrusion.

The woman gives a chesty sigh as she settles back with her thoughts. She tells herself that Mark Manning's life has been threatened as a result of her soul-searching escapade. She thinks of Humphrey Hasting—a man she does not know, but instinctively dislikes—and feels a pang of sympathy even for him, aware that his wrongdoing was inspired by an overzealous response to her disappearance.

She thinks of her sister and Arthur Mendel—my dear, yes, Margaret and Arthur—soon to be questioned in court, like *crimi-*

nals. What effect would that have on them, especially after living through the uncertainties and the bleak suspicions of the past seven years? Arthur has been a steadfast friend of the family for over thirty years. And Margaret—well, that indiscretion was long ago forgiven—she's still the little sister, and she's going through hell.

It's gone too far, Helen tells herself. It's gone on too long. It's time to put an end to this nonsense.

She knows what needs to be done. She must speak to her brother, Father James McMullen, and she knows when to do it. The priest sent a note to her today, asking her to come to the church tomorrow morning—*early,* at five o'clock—to celebrate with him "a private Mass of thanksgiving for the good fortune that is about to befall Assumption." Odd, she tells herself. The first Mass of the day is normally at six. Why is it so important for them to be alone? Just as well, though—their discussion is not apt to be pleasant.

Secure in her thoughts, she rolls her fingers under Abe's chin and ponders the conclusions she has reached. Abe purrs.

"**N**o," wails Humphrey Hasting, *"it wasn't signed!"*

At home on a mountainside in Phoenix, Neil crouches before his television set, watching an evening news report of the Houseman Trial. Earlier, at work, he tried to follow the live radio coverage, but he was busy today, and the constant interruptions made it difficult for him to make sense of the disembodied voices. He wanted to close his office door, clear his desk, and just *listen,* but an important project was still overdue—Manning's belated Christmas present—and he had to hustle to get it finished in time for the four-thirty FedEx pickup. It will arrive tomorrow morning—something to perk up Manning's day before things get ugly in court.

Neil sits cross-legged on the floor now, no more than three feet from the picture tube. "You can't prove it—you can't prove a thing!" The recording of Hasting's outburst continues to play while a sequence of chalk drawings flashes on the screen, depicting the dramatic moment as a smidge more dramatic than it actually was.

Neil watches vacantly as a panel of "law and journalism experts" analyzes events of the day's hearing. They all agree that as far as Manning and Hasting are concerned, the results of tomorrow's court session will surely "make" one of them and "break" the other. They then play the portion of Manning's testimony in which he hints that he has recently talked to Carter herself.

One of the panelists comments, "It seems to me that Mr. Manning was indulging here in a bit of gaming with Hank Ferret. Manning stated, after all, that he would not swear to his outlandish claims concerning Mrs. Carter—shrewdly avoiding the possibility of perjury charges, yet at the same time managing to tantalize both Ferret and Judge Ambrose. What did Manning *mean* by this cryptic exchange? I'm afraid that's anyone's guess, but one thing is clear: It is now presumed with near certainty that Mrs. Carter has been dead since her disappearance seven years ago, so it's unlikely that Manning meant for us to take literally his claim of having spoken with her. Perhaps he has had a mystical experience. Perhaps he is himself clairvoyant or has spoken with the deceased heiress through the aid of a medium. I doubt if we shall ever know the exact meaning of Mark Manning's words."

Neil knows the meaning of Manning's words—they can be taken literally, at face value, with no hidden message whatever. These idiots on TV have been told point-blank the answer to this whole trumped-up mystery, and they don't even have the presence of mind to recognize it. But Neil knows that Manning is right, that Manning would not expect anyone to accept his words on faith, that Manning must have a plan. Neil certainly *hopes* that Manning has a plan—because at this moment his prospects appear chancy at best.

Neil leans back, supporting his weight on his elbows, and breathes an impatient sigh. The news program ends, followed by a Fox Network jiggle rerun from the pre-beefcake era, beloved by the masses for its wet T-shirts, sniggering innuendo, and precocious smart-mouthed kids. But Neil is not aware of the show. Not even the noisy, strobe-flashing commercials are able to steal his attention and penetrate his thoughts.

Neil tells himself, Mark has been gone from Phoenix for only two days. Now, without him, the four days we spent together seem like the compression of a lifetime—as though we were always so near, as though it could never have been any other way, as though nothing could ever change. But things *have* changed. Mark is gone. We're going to think things over. We'll torture ourselves with a separation intended to clear our minds and make our true desires known, unclouded by momentary passions or the urgency of lust. These things take time. These things take a level head. Infatuation is a poor foundation for decisions that change a person's life. We'll have to endure this a little longer. Another month? Perhaps a year? And then what? Either I go to him or I stay—in a month or in a year or not at all.

The waiting no longer makes sense. Neil knows his mind. He knows what he must do.

"Oh, *Daddy!*" yells the busty adolescent on the screen. She's been helping wash the family minivan, and now Daddy's getting tricksy with the hose.

Neil snorts a derisive laugh. With his toe, he reaches up and punches the button that blackens the screen.

Thursday, December 31
1 day till deadline

The early-morning air is cool, almost frosty. A few minutes before five, Helena Carter steps out of her house wearing a bulky cardigan to protect herself from the chill. She will soon leave this climate, and she likes the idea of strolling outdoors in a sweater on a dark winter morning. Besides, the church is only two blocks away. She is a vigorous woman—a brisk walk will do her no harm.

She didn't sleep well overnight. Yesterday's hearing spawned thoughts that kept her addled and awake despite her self-assurances that the long period of uncertainty had ended. Now, though, as she walks past the town square and approaches the church, her trepidation gives way to a sense of relief, as though the dreaded confrontation with her brother were already behind her.

It feels strange to touch the big gnarled handle of the church door—unfamiliar and foreign, without the significance that the act of entering church has held for her in the past. She walks through the vestibule, strolls down the center aisle, and sits in a front pew. The candles on the altar are already lit—tongues of fire aglow in the dimness of the sanctuary. Muted voices drift from the sacristy as the priest instructs an altar boy in details of this odd private Mass. She hears the clink of heavy glass cruets being prepared for the Eucharist—one filled with water, the other with wine.

As she waits for the service to begin, her gaze travels to the stained-glass windows, normally radiant, but inky black at this early hour. Then her gaze crosses the aisle to the windows on the opposite wall, and she can just discern the figures depicted in the glass, enlivened by the grayish light that begins to fill the eastern sky. East, she thinks—that's home, beyond the windows, beyond the mountains.

Her musing is interrupted by the clang of a bell as Father McMullen and the boy appear in the arched sacristy doorway and walk to the foot of the altar. As they mutter their Latin dialogue, Helen does not follow in her missal as she always has, but allows her mind to stray again to other matters, rehearsing the conversation she must soon have with the priest.

Forever unchanging, like a relic embedded in stone, the Mass continues along its prescribed course. The woman in the front pew sits, stands, and kneels, blessing herself with the sign of the cross, as she has done countless times during her life. But she participates without emotion, through force of habit. She feels suddenly, irreparably detached from these surroundings, as if her mind had floated from her body and were looking down upon her from a remote corner of the vaulted ceiling.

She sees the room as if with new eyes. She sees the statues no longer as models of virtue, but as gaudily painted plaster. As for the scenes still brightening in the windows, she no longer views them with the comfort and ease of meeting old friends; she is jolted by the quaint, mythical nonsense of doves and dragons, reverent camels and warring angels. Then she peers at the priest, her brother, who stands before the altar. She no longer sees Father James McMullen as the man of deeply rooted beliefs who has dedicated his life to a holy mission; she sees him with instant clarity as a pathetic earthbound creature with his mind in the sky who has doomed himself to live a lie. In the solitude of her conscience, she weeps at her recognition of the real world, then she laughs—with a child's ecstatic joy, a joy that stems from the rational consistency of seeing things, really *seeing things*, exactly as they are.

The service wears on predictably, with its age-old verbatim sameness, toward the climactic moment of transubstantiation. The priest bows low over the wafer of bread and summons God's presence, Christ's body, as the altar boy lifts the silver bell from its velvet cushion and rings it with three sharp snaps of his wrist. The priest bows low again and peers into the gold chalice. *"Hic est enim calix sanguinis mei,"* he utters—This is the cup of My blood. Over the years, he has performed this rite daily, surely ten thousand times. But this time, the wine is cloudy, tainted. This time, when he dreams the waking nightmare of his twin brother's crime, he is not haunted by it, but inspired.

He eats the bread—but does not drink the wine.

Instead, he turns to his sister and descends the stairs to the edge of the sanctuary. "Come," he bids her. "Drink from the cup of our Savior's blood."

She rises from the pew as commanded and steps toward him. They stand on opposite sides of the communion rail, their faces a foot apart. He raises the chalice and touches it to her lips. She stares into the wine for a moment, then into his eyes. With the tips of her fingers she nudges the cup back toward the priest and tells him, "I'm going home, Jamie."

His nostrils flare. He steadies the shaking chalice with his free hand.

She adds casually, almost flippantly, "I thought you should know."

"I . . . don't understand," he stammers. "Tomorrow the estate can finally be settled. We've waited so long—you and I—seven years. This is what we both wanted. We agreed. To back out now would be betrayal. It's a sin!"

"Never mind *my* sins," she snaps. "What of your own? What Christian motive led you to entice me out to this desert? I've hurt people who love me, I've stripped away my very identity, I've spent seven years with you in this squalor—and for what? *Do I have to say it?* Do I have to say that you're no better than the rest? Face it, Jamie—your only interest in my 'immortal soul' has been my money and its service to your bullheaded mission."

He backs a step away from her, speaking rapidly. "Be careful, Helen. Judge not, that you may not be judged. Let him who is without fault cast the first stone."

"*Stop* that!" she says, venting a fierce frustration. "That's drivel. You can't just quote your way out of every tight corner. You can't get through life on slogans."

"*Slogans!*" he says, backing to the first step of the altar. "Your words border perilously upon sacrilege, Helen, while the words of Christ are the words of *life*. 'I am the way,' He said. 'I am the way, the truth . . . '"

"Stop it, Jamie." Her voice is now calm as she leans over the rail that separates them like a wall. "That won't work anymore—

not on me. You can believe anything you wish, but wishing and believing won't change reality one iota. Here I am, fifty-six years old, and I spent all those years hoping and praying and worrying about the depth of my faith. And what has all that anguish accomplished? What *could* it accomplish?"

The young altar boy, terrified by the priest's reaction to the confrontation, has sidestepped out of the sanctuary and peers back through the sacristy door.

Helen continues, "I'm fed up with the sniping and craziness I've found here, and I've come to question the purpose of it all—to say nothing of *your* motives, Jamie. I no longer find The Society worthy of my husband's hard-won fortune. Not another dime. If I hurry, I can get myself—and my cats—on a plane to Chicago this morning. Mark Manning needs me there."

"*Manning* needs you?" shouts the priest, aghast, backing up another stair toward the altar. "What about the needs of Holy Mother Church? For God's sake, what about the needs of your own flesh and blood?" He clasps the chalice close to his chest, sloshing wine down the brocade of his chasuble. "Manning is responsible for this betrayal. The sin of your infidelity rests upon *his* blackened soul—may it burn in hell for eternity!"

Helen is still restrained in the face of the priest's raving. She tells him, "Mark Manning is a friend. He helped me. But I made up my *own* mind. I accept full responsibility for my actions—and it's high time."

The priest trembles as he glares at the woman who watches him serenely over the communion rail. With anger still mounting, he extends an accusing finger. "You blaspheme!" he bellows, his ire matching that of any judge of the Inquisition. "Saint Paul tells us plainly that man is justified before his God *by faith alone.*"

Backing up to the top stair of the altar, he drops the chalice—it bounces and clanks on the marble. He crosses both arms before him as if to ward off an evil presence. "Only faith has the power to heal and make us whole—faith in a God we can never know and only dare to love. Faith alone is what raises man from the filth and mire where he wallows with the other animals. Faith permits him a fleeting vision of the divine." The veins pound visibly up his neck and through his temples. "Almighty God is a merciful judge, but the wrath of the Lord will be upon those who have heard His words yet fail to believe. Woe to the unfaithful!" he cries. "Woe to the infidel!" he screams again, enraged—but this time he chokes on his words.

Suddenly breathless, he feels a crush of pain against his chest, like steel bands tightening around his torso, his arms, his neck. He felt this pain once before and recovered, but now it assaults him ruthlessly. "My . . . my *God*," he gasps as he struggles to inhale, fingers clawing to loosen his collar. His legs can no longer support the weight of his body, and he collapses before the altar. His head cracks soundly against an edge of the stone steps. His foot kicks the consecration bell from its cushion and sends it skittering across the polished floor until it crashes with a final, mangled clatter against the wrought-iron base of the pulpit.

"Go!" says Helen to the ashen-faced youngster as she fumbles to open the gate of the communion rail. "Run to the rectory. Tell Father's housekeeper to call an ambulance." As she steps into the sanctuary, the boy darts from the church, but she knows that his efforts will be futile.

The priest's eyes are barely open, squinting with agony and fright. One hand still flails lamely at his neck. The other beckons Helen to his side.

She kneels on the steps next to him, opens his collar, and takes hold of his hands. Trying to speak, he drools blood from the corner of his lips. She leans close to his mouth, and he whispers several sentences to her.

He shudders, then exhales his last breath.

A couple of hours later in Chicago, Roxanne gulps coffee from a mug at the table in Manning's loft. She wanted for them to meet—"it's *imperative*"—before the afternoon court session, so Manning invited her to his home, since the office would surely be chaotic today.

She slaps a folder closed and tosses it atop one of several stacks of files on the table. "Please be aware," she tells him, "that you could be in bigger trouble than Humphrey Hasting if Judge Ambrose holds you in contempt."

Manning isn't listening. He's busy unwrapping an oblong parcel, a three-foot tube that has just been delivered to his door.

She continues, "Your elusive testimony about Helena Carter yesterday made great headlines, but I'm afraid you're going to find yourself in some very hot water because of it."

He's got it open. Clumsily, working with only one good arm, he pulls out a roll of papers that springs open on the kitchen counter, smelling distinctly of ammonia. He grabs various cooking utensils to anchor the curled corners.

It's a set of architect's blue-line prints. The top page is a floor plan, vaguely familiar but largely meaningless to Manning—a cryptic profusion of symbols and lines with overlapping arrows that mark dimensions. He turns to the second sheet, a similar plan, probably another level of the same building. He pages through more of these technical drawings, then a sequence of elevations that look like walls, and finally a perspective—a detailed, colored rendering of a large interior space drawn three-dimensionally. Manning turns the page and finds another perspective, as if looking at the same room from its opposite corner. Glancing up from the drawings and into his unfinished loft, the plans suddenly make sense. He has his bearings.

Roxanne says, "Mark, this is important—and you haven't heard a word. What on *earth* is so interesting over there?"

"Christmas gift from Neil." His nose is buried again in the plans.

"*Ohh?*" She rises from the table to join him, looking over his shoulder.

"Can you believe it?" he says, more to himself than to Roxanne. "Neil has been here only once, and he knew I was at a loss for ideas for the place. Just *look* at this!"

The empty, boxy loft space has been transformed into a sculptural network of platforms and balconies, creating a complex interplay of masses and voids. While the overall composition of the room is boldly artful, this has not been achieved at the expense of function, for the distinct areas of the space are thoughtfully suited to their various purposes—conversation, reading and writing, sleeping and bathing, cooking and eating, storage. Though the aesthetic is decidedly modern, the effect is neither stark nor sterile. On the contrary, rich detailing and knowledgeable, playful allusions to styles of the past lend an inviting, livable atmosphere to the design. Even the Clarence Bird painting is sketched on a prominent expanse of wall, where it appears comfortably at home.

Roxanne says, "God, Mark, it's fabulous."

"Maybe a little *too* fabulous. How could I possibly build this?" He flips through the final sheets of the plan, where there are detail drawings of cabinetry, trim, and light fixtures—all custom—followed by a materials list that includes granite and beveled glass. "Reporters aren't *that* well paid."

Then, at the bottom of the last page, he spots a yellow Post-it note. In Neil's forceful hand, it says, "Together, I'll bet we could swing it."

Manning freezes, stares at the note, reads it several times, catches his breath. Then he realizes that Roxanne has also seen it, and he turns to face her, braced for the worst.

"Congratulations," she says quietly, without inflection. "Or should I say, 'Much happiness'? One *tries* to be politically correct, but the protocol of these modern relationships isn't quite hammered out yet."

Manning can't read her tone. The words are genial enough, but their sarcastic edge is ominous. He suspects she's ready to blow. "Roxanne, I . . ."

"Mark"—she stops him—"I'm over it."

A pause of relief. He takes her fingers into his hand. "I'm sorry you were hurt. I never meant to lead you on."

"You didn't. I was playing with fire, and I knew it. My passions were real enough—you're a hot man, Mark—but the booze had me out of control."

"I was tempted to say something," Manning tells her.

"I wish you had. But it was ultimately something I had to deal with myself. I binged on Thanksgiving and screwed up royally with a client after the long weekend. That's when I knew I had to stop. I'm doing much better now, but withdrawal was a bitch."

"*Tell* me about it. I haven't had a cigarette in five . . . no, six days. Neil never said anything about my smoking, but I was sure he didn't like it. So I decided to quit because of him—then I realized I was doing it for myself."

"Good boy," she tells him. "Hang in there. That's *next* on my list—but one vice at a time!" They share a laugh of understanding.

Roxanne's tone turns lawyerly. "Now that we've cleared the

air, let me make my stand on one particular matter perfectly clear." She can't suppress a smile. "If you ever decide you're tired of guys, Mark, *do* let me know."

"You'll be first on my list." He kisses her. It's not passionate, but sufficiently physical to rekindle in her a momentary pang.

Fanning her lips with her hands, she says, "We'd better get back to business," and returns to the table.

He follows, saying coyly, "As long as we're baring souls, can I trust you with some highly relevant—but confidential—information?"

She eyes him askance, intrigued. Her look tells him, Well, let's have it.

He sits. Facing her directly, he says, "My speech in court yesterday about Helena Carter—the 'elusive testimony' that has you so worried—is all true. I had a long talk with her last week, just outside of Phoenix."

Roxanne says nothing. Her unwavering stare suggests that she can't decide whether to believe him. He pulls a business card from his wallet and shows it to her, saying, "She signed this for me. That's her phone number. Want to call her and say hello?"

Roxanne studies the card, suspicious. "I don't get it. If you've actually found her, why don't you just . . . *turn her in* and be done with it?"

"Let me start at the beginning." Manning pauses, takes a deep breath, then carefully recounts the whole story, from the point when he arrives in Phoenix for Christmas, sees Brother Burt on TV, then Miss Viola's Abyssinian kitten, which leads him to Assumption, Father McMullen, and ultimately the missing heiress. He concludes by explaining his pact with Mrs. Carter—her full cooperation on an exclusive story in exchange for his temporary silence.

"What I don't understand," says Roxanne, trying to sort through the details, "is the motive of the priest, her brother. Why would he get messed up with all this? The contents of Carter's will are widely known—there's nothing in it for him or his band of reactionaries."

"That's exactly what threw *me* off course, at first. But when I finally talked to Helen, I learned that she has signed a *new* will, drawn up with Father McMullen, leaving nearly everything to

The Society and zilch to the Chicago Archdiocese. When Helen is declared dead tomorrow, McMullen plans to present the second will and collect the loot, allowing Helen to live out her remaining years in blissful anonymity."

With instant comprehension of the legal thicket described by Manning, Roxanne blurts, "But that's *absurd*. Both wills would be moot, since the second one was written after she disappeared. It would prove that she had not died—unless, of course, they produced a body with the document and ..." Roxanne stops short. She and Manning stare at each other, realizing that Helen is in danger.

Manning grabs the business card, rushes to the phone, and dials Helen's number. There is no answer.

He tries calling Neil. The phone rings and rings. Manning glances at his watch; it's barely eight o'clock in Phoenix, and Neil doesn't go to the office till nine. Where *is* he? What's he *doing?*

After a dozen rings, Manning replaces the receiver, feeling the unmistakable welling-up of an emotion that has played, till now, no role in his life. What *else*—he asks himself, guessing a likely answer—what *else* would Neil be doing away from the house so early in the morning?

Neil is in fact settling into his seat near the front of the coach section of a CarterAir jet. Because of the mechanics' strike, this is the only flight from Phoenix to Chicago this morning, so it's packed. For Neil to get booked on such short notice, his travel agent must have owed him a whopper of a favor. Neil grins as he buckles the seat belt.

A few rows in front of him, a bunch of businessmen in dark suits are making a fuss. Flight attendants and official-looking airline factotums attempt to mollify the surly executives. As a stewardess hustles down the aisle with an armload of pillows for them, Neil nabs her and asks, "What's going on?"

"It's the craziest thing, but really sort of funny," she confides in a whisper. "The gentlemen in front of you are—or I should say, *were*—our first-class passengers. Not long before we started boarding, the head office informed us that some lady—some eccentric, I guess—had booked the entire first-class cabin. I don't know *who* she is, or *what* she paid, but they actually gave it to her and bumped these guys back into coach."

"Why would anyone need the entire cabin?" Neil asks with a laugh.

"That's the screwiest part. She's traveling with fifteen or twenty *cats*. Some rare breed. They're loading them now." She points beyond the closed curtain. "You should see it—they're all in their little travel cages, each strapped into a seat. It looks like a pet shop in there."

Neil blinks. Is it *possible?* He asks, "Does the woman by any chance have red hair?"

"Matter of fact, she does. Don't tell me you *know* her."

"Sort of. I wonder—if I wrote a note—could you take it to her?"

The stewardess bites her lip, checks her watch. They will take off soon. "Certainly, sir," she says to Neil, "but I should warn you that she left instructions not to be disturbed by *anyone.*"

Neil quickly writes out his message: "Mrs. Carter? I, too, am a friend of Mark Manning's, flying to Chicago to see him. I feel that I already know you. I met your sister last fall at a cat show, and I've seen some of your wonderful Abyssinians. I would very much like to talk to you." He signs the note, folds it, and hands it to the stewardess.

She takes it, drops off her pillows with the bickering businessmen, and disappears through the curtain that hides the first-class cabin.

Shortly after the plane is in the air, she peeps through the curtain, looking surprised. Catching Neil's eye, she smiles, then motions with her finger that he should come forward.

"**I** see," Helen tells Neil, offering another glass of champagne. "Then Mark should have gotten your drawings by now—I'll bet he's delighted."

"I hope so," says Neil, sipping his drink, petting the kitten that has slept in his lap for the last hour. "But Mark has plenty *else* on his mind right now—I guess we all do."

"*Don't* we?" says Helen with a pensive sigh. "You've been

sweet, Neil, to listen to all my rambling. May I bore you with the rest of the story?"

"It hasn't been boring at all," he assures her.

"Yesterday I got a message from my brother Jamie, asking me to meet him in church early this morning." She tells Neil about the Mass of thanksgiving, the difficult thoughts she was thinking during the service, the confrontation over the communion rail, and finally, the priest's heart attack.

"How terrible," says Neil. "I'm so sorry."

"But the worst was still to come," she says. "After Jamie fell, he waved me to his side. I thought that at last he would speak to me honestly, without the hidden motives that had come between us. I expected something of a deathbed confession, but instead, he whispered words of spite: 'Our brother Bertrand is still alive, Helen. He's become that TV heretic, Brother Burt. He killed a boy in school, and now he'll kill Manning. Manning deserves it—he's destroyed all our dreams.'"

Neil swallows hard. "Was your brother clear-witted? Or delirious?"

"I don't know," Helen tells him. "I'd already lost faith in anything Jamie told me, and I've never even met this 'Brother Burt' character—unless, of course, he *is* my brother Bertrand."

"I'm worried," says Neil. "I *have* met Brother Burt, and I wouldn't put anything past him. I wanted my trip to be a surprise, but I'd better call Mark—he needs to know what's happened." He sets down his glass, hands the kitten back to Helen, swipes his credit card through the phone at his seat, and dials, guessing he can reach Manning at home today.

Within moments, Manning answers, "Hello?"

"Mark!" says Neil, relieved to hear his voice. "I know you must be half nuts getting ready for court, but there's something you should know."

"Neil? Is that *you?* I got the floor plans—they're wonderful. Hey, we've got a fuzzy connection."

"I'm on a plane," he speaks up. "On my way to Chicago."

Neil hears Manning laughing through the static on the phone. "I *wondered* where you were. So you took off early for a long weekend, eh?"

"Not exactly. I've made an appointment with our Chicago office for first thing next week—to talk about transferring—if you think that's a good idea."

There's a long pause. Neil holds his breath, unsure of Manning's reaction. Then a quiet, deliberate answer comes over the phone: "That's the best idea I've ever heard in my life."

"Mark . . ." says Neil, "there's so much for us to talk about, about 'us,' but that's not why I'm calling. You see, I'm sitting here with Mrs. Carter. She's on the plane too . . ."

Helen warbles in the background, "Hello, Mark," while pouring herself a fresh glass of champagne.

Manning asks, "Is she okay? Roxanne just figured out that she's in danger from her own brother."

Neil says, "She's had something of a rough morning already, but she's fine. My point, Mark, is that *you* may be in danger." Neil tells him about Father McMullen's heart attack—and his dying revelation of Brother Burt's true identity, murderous past, and threats against Manning.

"Thanks for the warning," says Manning, "but I'm not too concerned. Lots of things get said in the heat of passion. Besides, I'm *here* and Brother Burt's out *there*—how could he hurt me?"

Helen taps Neil's arm. "Tell Mark that he's earned his story. I'm all his." She stifles a petite champagne belch. "I'll be at his disposal as soon as we land—he'll probably want me to go to court with him."

Manning's voice sounds over the phone, "I heard every word, Neil. When do you arrive?"

"A few minutes after noon."

"Terrific. That'll give us just long enough to get downtown in time for the hearing. I've got to call my editor and ask him to hold page one. And I'll need a photographer at the airport." Containing his excitement, Manning pauses. "Neil," he says, refocusing his thoughts, "I love you."

"I love you too, Mark. I want to build a future with you. So please be careful."

"Don't worry," Manning tells him. "I can take care of myself. I'll meet you at O'Hare, kiddo. We're home free now."

*   *   *

But in the back of the plane—the only plane from Phoenix to Chicago this morning, wedged into a middle seat between two other passengers—Brother Burt dozes. Troubled dreams play through his mind like a cinematic pastiche of the lifelong events that have nudged him toward this moment. Through the copious folds of his jacket, his hand reflexively gropes the blade of a sacrificial Indian hatchet.

It is the same tomahawk that he has treasured since he was a little boy, when he terrified his younger sister by using it to decapitate a garden snake. Margaret was always the timid one, easily frightened, and Bertrand wasted no opportunity to prey on her weakness—the silly bitch. Helen was a problem, though. Older, smarter, gutsier than Margaret, she never hesitated to stand up to Bertrand. Snakes didn't scare her. Blood didn't scare her. Bertrand didn't scare her—the contemptible cow, the apple of their daddy's eye, the rich-ass whore who married for money and lucked out, widowed young. Women are such . . . serpents. Writhing, lame, deadly. He's spent his whole life wanting what Helen has, hearing of her fortune from afar, dreaming of the power of her wealth.

Dreaming, Brother Burt strokes the handle of the sacrificial hatchet.

It is the same tomahawk, the same deadly weapon, that he kept at the seminary, where he used it to slaughter a friend who dared to love him. Kyle was an athlete, a year younger than Bertrand, the apple of Monsignor's eye. Kyle was everyone's friend, but he had a special affection for the twins—Jamie, with his devout manner and scholarly focus, and Bertrand, quite the opposite with his outgoing personality and adventurous sense of curiosity. That curiosity led him to explore with Kyle a depth of friendship that broke a Commandment or two. For weeks, they had hinted to each other what was on their minds, and late one afternoon, behind the field house, they kissed, then groped. That was all. It was a secret, of course—no one must know. But someone saw, or heard, or told. "Bertrand loves Kyle," someone wrote somewhere. "It's a damnable lie!" Bertrand insisted to others, then sneaked Kyle to his bed, fucking the boy's mouth before cutting his throat, injuring his own foot in the scuffle. Bertrand fled. Both he and the murder weapon disappeared. Many accused him of the crime. Others conjectured that he, too, had been murdered. There was talk of suicide. It was never resolved, and though the police never closed their file, Bertrand, the affable young seminarian, was indeed dead—to the family he disgraced, to the school he terrorized, even to himself. He had to reinvent himself, dreaming up a new past, new future, new mission.

Dreaming, Brother Burt crosses his arms, hugging the sacrificial hatchet closer to his chest.

It is the same tomahawk that came to rest proudly on his desk in the office of the ministry he developed, the Holy Altar of Mystic Faith. Though the ministry has been widely ridiculed as the flagrant scam of a hack preacher, Brother Burt has quietly chuckled at such criticism, for he knows a truth that is shared by only a handful of other men—respectable men, powerful, influential men who speak with drawls and call the shots at the Christian Family Crusade. They know that the Holy Altar was founded as a cash-mill for the CFC, secretly funding the efforts of a far-right anti-gay political agenda. Buoyed by the success of their stealth campaigns at the local and state levels, the CFC has been preparing to flex its muscle in Washington. They've got legions of committed followers, they've got God on their side, and they've got cash. But they need more, lots more, and Brother Burt—their man in Arizona—has promised to deliver. Fifty million dollars. That's enough to buy him a seat on the CFC national board of commissioners. It's enough to buy some self-respect. And it's enough to turn back the clock on gay rights. But now, it's not going to happen. His sister and his brother have failed him, and a reporter—a filthy fag reporter—is to blame. He dreams of sweet revenge.

Dreaming, Brother Burt snores, lips sputtering, head bobbing. His chin nudges the sacrificial hatchet. Microscopic flecks of blood, hardened and blackened by the years, still cling to the pitted surface of its primitive but well-honed blade—a stone blade of featheredged flint that passed through the airport metal detectors without causing so much as a blip.

Dreaming, Brother Burt hurtles through the sky. Thirty thousand feet below, the plane's shadow darts eastward across the

Mississippi River. Almost imperceptibly, the plane's nose dips, beginning its long, gradual descent over Illinois.

Gordon Smith, managing editor of the *Journal*, paces his office. Days like this jibe his easygoing nature. He unbuttons his vest, peers at his watch. Eleven thirteen—no more than a minute has passed since he last checked. He exhales an impatient sigh, stops in front of the window, and gazes vacantly into the white sky.

His phone trills, and the voice of his secretary rasps over the speaker, "It's Manning. Line one."

Smith slides into his chair and grabs the receiver. "What's up, Mark?"

"I put a story in the system two days ago, Gordon. It's not finished, but I'll wrap it up soon. You've got access—why don't you call it up?"

"I'm one step ahead of you," says Smith, typing codes into his computer. Manning's directory appears on the monitor. "Which slug?"

"AbbyCat."

Smith cursors to the title, enters, and a story fills the screen. Its headline reads, EXCLUSIVE: HELENA CARTER LIVES!

Smith begins scrolling through the text, spellbound. His mouth hangs open. His eyes sparkle. He has just been handed the plum of an editor's career. The article stops at the point where Manning finds Carter in Assumption.

"My God, Mark," Smith says into the phone, "you've actually *done* it—but how does it *end?*"

"It ends at the hearing today when I march Mrs. Carter into the courtroom. She's on a plane now, due at O'Hare around noon. But it's even juicier than I thought." Manning tells him about Father McMullen and Brother Burt, the second will, the death threats.

Smith howls with delight. "Long-lost brothers, *evil twins*— too damn delicious to be true! *Unsolved Mysteries* even did a segment on this Bertrand nut. Imagine our headline: SEMINARY SLASHER VOWS VENGEANCE . . ."

"Whoa, Gordon," Manning tells him, laughing. "First things first. The afternoon edition—can you hold page one?"

"For the biggest story of the year? You betcha, Mark. Need a photog at the airport?"

"Sure do. And a limo with a phone."

"Got it. Now get your butt out there—sure as hell wouldn't want to miss *that* plane! Call me from the car as soon as you've snagged the ol' gal."

Smith hangs up. He wrings his hands with glee. He literally skips around the office before returning to his desk and punching an extension number into the phone.

"This is Smith," he tells the secretary upstairs in the tower. "Let me talk to Nathan." Pause. "Of *course* it's important."

Nathan Cain, publisher of the *Journal,* a living icon of Chicago newspaper lore, is a man of few words and vast power. He is never seen in the newsroom, and not many of the people who write and edit the paper have ever spoken to him. Sardonic humor colors his voice as he picks up the call. "Morning, Gordon. Sad to observe, Mr. Manning's hourglass seems to be running on empty. Anything to report?"

Smith tells him . . . everything.

With no audible trace of excitement, the publisher says, "Pull out the stops. Give it the works. If those union loons down in production give you any crap about what 'their people' can or cannot do, just let me know." Dryly, he adds, "Please extend my personal thanks to Mr. Manning. And have a happy New Year, Gordon."

Manning is waiting at O'Hare. Because of the strike, and in spite of the approaching holiday weekend, the terminal is calm—in sharp contrast to the mayhem he found here only a week ago on Christmas Eve. Pockets of people cluster near the gates that serve CarterAir flights, but the long corridors are deserted. A noon radio newscast plays throughout the halls from unseen speakers:

Early reports confirm that the threatening letter sent to Mark Manning two months ago was in fact written on Humphrey Hasting's typewriter. Chicago Post publisher Josh Williams has called a news conference for later this afternoon, during which he will make a public apology while announcing stiff reprisals for the paper's flamboyant and best-known columnist.

Manning makes a few notes describing the scene inside the airport, which he will use to add color to the ending of his story. A *Journal* photographer waits with him, chomping on a big wedge of pizza that he got at one of the concessions in the concourse. At the gate, Jerry Klein directs airline personnel in various matters—it is he, of course, who arranged for Helen's return after she phoned him earlier this morning.

He has also arranged ground transportation for her and the cats. Outside, three matching limousines are lined up at the curb, sputtering exhaust into the cold air. It seems the cops have been alerted that something's about to happen—they don't even bother to shag the cars away from the door.

Meanwhile, a wondering public awaits the opening of today's session of the Houseman Trial, set to begin in about an hour. Contempt charges will surely be leveled against Journal *reporter Mark Manning, stemming from yesterday's stunning but groundless claims that he has recently spoken to Helena Carter, the missing heiress who will be declared dead by the end of this afternoon's hearing.*

Manning watches the horizon through the glass walls of the terminal. There are so few planes in the air today, it's easy to spot the CarterAir flight as it appears low in the sky and touches down on a distant runway. Within a couple of minutes, it taxis up to the gate and stops.

"Right on time," Jerry Klein tells Manning, tapping his watch with fatherly pride. He ushers Manning and the photographer through the crowd of onlookers to the door of the ramp that leads to the plane.

The door swings open, admitting the whine of engines, smell of fuel, and patter of approaching footsteps. Then, from around the corner, emerges Helena Carter. She carries one of the cages—it's Abe. Neil, at her side, carries her coat, a voluminous red fox that matches her hair.

"Mark!" she says. "So tickled you could come—I *do* hate fussing with cabs."

Manning can tell she's a little tipsy as he steps forward to greet her, kissing both cheeks. "Smile," he whispers. "We'll be all over the next edition." The photographer snaps frame after frame, capturing every nuance of the moment.

We will forgo our regular programming for the remainder of the afternoon in order to bring you live coverage of the hearing from Daley Center. Between now and the opening gavel, we're happy to feature this station's own celebrity commentator, Bud Stirkham, who will interview an expert witness not called to testify yesterday—a clairvoyant who's had startling dreams of late, revealing the grim details of Mrs. Carter's death.

Manning goes to Neil, who has stood out of range of the picture-taking, and hugs him with his good arm, sandwiching the fur coat between their bodies. Tousling Neil's hair, Manning tells him, "My *God*, I'm glad you're here."

Airline personnel file out of the plane carrying the cages; Manning and Neil step aside to let them pass. Jerry Klein, who's been hugging Helen, takes Abe's cage from her, hands it to one of the attendants, and directs them down the concourse toward the cars. People waiting for passengers at the gate exchange confused shrugs, then someone figures it out. "Look, everybody, it's *them*— that reporter with the dead woman!"

Some laugh, some wave, some begin to nudge toward them, so Manning, Helen, and Neil start walking toward the exit. The coach passengers are only beginning to get off the plane, and the crowd stays put to greet them.

Friends, this is Bud Stirkham. We're going to open up the phone lines soon and try to determine the consensus of the common man. We'll ask: Is Mark Manning guilty of perjury? And how should he be censured? For just two dollars a call, you can be judge and jury. Dial 1-900-U-B-JUDGE to phone in your verdict.

The threesome strolls down the corridor, arms linked, Helen in the middle. Manning explains that he will phone his editor from the car to dictate the final paragraphs of his story; another reporter will cover their appearance in court.

Other passengers from Phoenix—most conspicuously the corporate types who were bumped out of first class—begin rushing past, anxious to claim bags or attend meetings. Then, out of the Jetway hobbles a crazed-looking man from the rear of the plane who jostles and weaves, in spite of his limp, through the throng.

But first, we're honored to share the microphone with Adam X, a renowned psychic who has come to the rescue of baffled police forces in Copenhagen, Tangiers, Singapore, and now finally Chicago. Tell us, Mr. X, how these visions first came to you.

Helen says to Manning, "I understand you received a Christmas gift this morning. Your young friend here must be very talented."

"Indeed he is," replies Manning with a broad smile. Then to Neil, "The plans are incredible. I'd start the project tomorrow if I could, but it's a *tad* ambitious." He laughs at the understatement.

Neil asks, "Did you see my note on the last page?"

"Sure did. Nothing would make me happier than building it with you. But even if we pooled our resources ..."

Helen interrupts, "The half-million bucks ought to get the ball rolling."

Manning stops them in their tracks. "Now Helen, you already know how I feel about that."

She plants her hands on her hips and faces him nose-to-nose. Being shorter, she rises on her toes. Her no-nonsense tone is firm: "You told me last week that you wouldn't accept the reward because it would be like forcing me to pay you for something I didn't want. Now it's clear to me that I *did* want to be found, and I needed someone to shake some sense into me—which you did, Mark. I've already spoken to Jerry Klein about it. The check is written. It's yours."

Like all reputable psychics, I keep a diary of my dreams, and I began to notice a pattern of irregularities in them, a clear signal that someone from the other side was trying desperately to make contact.

Sweaty-browed, panting, Brother Burt spots his quarry through the shifting crowd.

Because these atypical vibrations always occurred during otherwise pleasurable flight dreams, I drew the irrefutable conclusion that they were a sign from the missing—and alas, dead—airline heiress.

Now, when Manning at last feels that all crises have passed—when he dares to imagine for the first time in his life that an elusive joy, born of total self-acceptance, may at last be within grasp—his thoughts are broken by the shriek of a woman passing behind him. Brother Burt lunges into view from the line of travelers, knocking Neil to the floor. He brays insanely, "Yea, the Lord God rained down fire and brimstone from the heavens upon Sodom and Gomorrah!"

Stunned, Manning is easy prey for Brother Burt, who pins Manning's good arm powerfully from behind. The demented cleric raves, "He smote those cities and destroyed all the plain—with everyone that liveth there and everything that groweth in the ground!" He twists Manning's head to bare his throat and in one swift movement pulls the ancient hatchet from his coat and arcs it to the top of his swing.

Everyone watching screams, not knowing how else to react.

But Manning knows. Remembering what he learned on Christmas night at the cable studio—that the injury suffered during Brother Burt's youth can still cause excruciating pain—Manning jerks his knee upward, then smashes his heel onto his attacker's deformed right foot. Brother Burt's ear-piercing wail silences the horrified onlookers as he collapses in unspeakable agony, dropping the hatchet, shattering its blade on the terrazzo paving.

The *Journal* photographer has captured it all, and security guards now arrive (better late than never) to restrain Brother Burt with handcuffs.

While he thrashes on the floor, Helen steps over and looks down upon him. Wistfully she says, "This isn't Bertrand. Bertrand died many years ago. So did my brother Jamie. Something bad happened."

I have succeeded in establishing contact with Mrs. Carter on the other side and have had many conversations with her. I am saddened to report that she has at last revealed the shocking truth of her brutal demise.

Neil has rushed to Manning, and they hold each other tightly. Unable to fathom the loss that was so narrowly escaped, Neil nuzzles his head against Manning's, telling him, "I had no idea that *reporting* could be so hazardous."

Manning's tone is casual. "Not to worry. It's really just a desk job. Such an incident could never happen twice in one man's career."

Neil gives him a skeptical look. "Promise?"

Manning doesn't answer. Instead, he kisses Neil—it's no mere "airport peck," but a fairly serious lip-lock.

Helen watches them. Turning impish, she says, "There'll be time for that later, boys. Right now, Mark, *you're* due in court."

Manning tells her, "So is my surprise witness."

"Race you to the car!" She winks, then takes off down the concourse at a surprisingly spry clip.

Manning and Neil exchange a bewildered glance, then trot off together after her, soon catching up.

I see these things so clearly. Such a ghastly fate . . .

They laugh, running all the faster. Their footfalls echo in the sprawling halls of the terminal.

Epilogue
3 months later

Winter has ended. It was a rough one, but now, in late March, there are signs of spring in the city—shrinking snow drifts reduced to runny black ice, buds here and there, a bird or two. A few hearty souls even frolicked in Lincoln Park when the clouds broke last weekend, but the weather is still cold enough to keep most people indoors.

In a loft near the park, overlooking Lake Michigan, Manning and Neil work in tandem to position the antique Biedermeier console along a wall beneath the contemporary painting by Clarence Bird. Stepping back to inspect the new arrangement, Neil proclaims, "Perfectly mated."

"They were *made* for each other," Manning agrees.

Some of Neil's furniture was shipped to Chicago earlier this week, and he and Manning have spent recent evenings dressing up the all-but-raw loft space. It's a temporary decorating scheme, a stopgap till summer, when the interior construction project will get under way. The floors are still bare concrete, but the place is starting to feel like home—for both of them.

"She'll be here any minute," says Neil. "Are you sure this is a good idea?"

It's just past six on a Friday night, and Manning has invited Roxanne over for drinks after work. The three of them have not socialized since Neil's permanent arrival in the city in February, when he was transferred to his architectural firm's Chicago office.

"I mean," Neil continues, "she might think we're trying to rub it in."

Facing him squarely, Manning places his hands on Neil's shoulders and tells him, "She'll be fine. She's already dealt with 'us.' Now we need to deal with *her*. She's been a great friend to both of us—and hey, we owe her a lot. I thought she'd enjoy seeing a semblance of order here before this place gets completely torn up, and I could tell from her voice that she was happy to be asked."

Neil hugs Manning. "Okay," he says over Manning's shoulder, "you're right. But it's a little awkward."

"How so? Ashamed to be seen with me?"

"Hardly!" Neil takes Manning's face into both hands and kisses him. His tone turns suggestive: "Do you suppose we've got time . . . ?"

But the door buzzer squelches Neil's carnal notion.

It is indeed Roxanne, who makes a grand entrance wearing a fur-lined trench coat and a big-brimmed hat. Neil takes her coat, but she keeps the floppy hat, which seems attached to a new hairdo. If she harbors any grudges, they're not evident, and it's clear from the outset—from their instantly animated discussion— that the three friends have a lot of catching-up to do.

She asks Manning, "When did they chisel that cast off your arm?"

"Weeks ago," he tells her, stretching and flexing his mended limb. "Good as new."

"Before we settle in," Neil says to Roxanne, "can I get you something?"

"Just water, thanks. But don't mind me, boys—the cocktail hour is nigh."

Manning offers, "I think we've got a Pellegrino. Maybe a club soda?"

"Whatever," she says. "The important thing is, we're all here." She strikes a pose against the Biedermeier console, the rakish rim of her hat juxtaposed against the oil painting. Sobriety has been good to her—she looks fabulous.

Neil fetches their drinks, and Manning suggests they get comfortable on some of the new furniture (new to him, anyway). "I'm not used to living with upholstery," he quips. "What a luxury."

When they are all seated, Roxanne offers a toast. "To your new home—and your new life together." It's a gracious gesture, but with bittersweet overtones. After they drink, there's a clumsy pause.

Changing the subject, Roxanne tells Manning, "I see that your pal Brother Burt is back in the news."

"From behind bars, no less." Manning shakes his head. "It seems the charges just keep mounting. Most serious, of course, is the murder of his fellow seminarian. Then there's his attempt on *my* life. And now he's under investigation for fraud—one of those 'Expose the Right' watchdog groups figured out that his so-called 'ministry' was no more than a fund-raising machine for the strictly *political* agenda of the Christian Family Crusade. His connections appear to run so deep and so dirty that he just may bring down the whole organization."

"And did you hear how they figured it out?" asks Neil. His tone is gleeful, his expression beaming.

"Something to do with his cable program," says Roxanne, whirling a hand as she tries to remember the details. "Wasn't there a . . . mishap?"

"*I'll say.*" Neil licks his lips before continuing. "Brother Burt was arrested here in Chicago on December thirty-first. His weekly cable show, *The Holy Altar of Mystic Faith*, was scheduled for live broadcast the next day, New Year's, from Phoenix. So Miss Viola had to go solo, attempting to explain to her followers how their archdeacon had managed to land himself in the slammer. At the start of the program, she always descends from the 'heavens' on this chintzy crescent moon, but that night, something went wrong. The smoke machine, the mechanical angels—everything was out of whack. Miss Viola's moon was within a few feet of landing on the floor, when it lurched. She carries this cat, and it freaked. It leaped from her arms, and in midair, snatched the wig off her head! So then *she* freaked and jumped off the cardboard moon. In her scramble to get out of camera range, she snagged her gown on the moon's pointy tip, ripped off her skirt, and ran screaming from the studio in a pair of black lace panties."

Neil laughs so hard, he can barely talk, so he pauses before explaining, "It was such a hoot, the tape aired everywhere on network news. That's how it came to the attention of the watchdog group."

"Talk about a fortuitous blooper," says Roxanne.

Catching his breath, Neil tells her, "And they *still* don't know what went wrong. There's an electronic console that runs the program's gadgetry, and the CFC issued a statement that the device may have been tampered with. 'An unknown saboteur,' they moaned, 'has scuttled the Crusade's holy war against the powers of perversion.'"

Manning smiles sheepishly.

Roxanne asks him, "Have you stayed in touch with Helena Carter?"

Eager to switch topics, Manning tells her, "After our splashy court appearance, and then my series of stories about Helen, I was on the phone with her every day for a while, but that tapered off. Now she's traveling the cat-show circuit again, with Margaret and Arthur in her retinue. She seems to have forgiven Margaret for that long-ago fling with Ridgely; Margaret, in turn, has forgiven Helen for pulling her seven-year stunt. You might say they've traded transgressions."

"All's well that ends well," says Roxanne. "How's Arthur adjusting?"

"Arthur is . . . well, *Arthur*. He's still the loyal manservant, good-natured as ever, in spite of Humphrey Hasting's attempts at character assassination."

"I'd almost forgotten about the Hump," says Neil. "We haven't heard much from *him* lately."

"Nor are we apt to," says Manning. He can't help grinning as he tells them, "His sister—wife of the *Post*'s publisher, you'll remember—sentenced him to Siberia in one of their suburban bureaus. Elgin, I think." Manning chuckles. "Writing obits." He explains through a laugh, "That's about as low as you can go." He laughs even harder, having thought of something. "I hear they even drummed him out of the cat club."

"Poor Fluffbudget," says Neil, "innocent victim of her master's sordid past."

Roxanne leans forward to refill her glass from a green bottle. Cocking her head to eye Manning from under the brim of her hat, she says, "Speaking of publishers, you've been skirting the topic of—"

"Nathan Cain," Manning finishes the sentence for her, no longer laughing.

"You had a lot of suspicions about him," Roxanne reminds Manning. "Obviously, he didn't murder or abduct Carter—no one did—but do you think he knew more than he was letting on? After all, he's so . . . *connected.*"

Manning sighs. "I was getting paranoid, that's all. Cain's quirkiness fed that paranoia. Yes, his ultimatum seemed inscrutable, but let's face it, he's an odd man. I guess he was just *pushing* me. He's taught me a lesson too. It should have been self-evident, and I won't forget it: Never let objectivity be clouded by speculation."

Neil offers, "He's really not such a bad guy, Rox. When Mark solved the case and got the story, Nathan Cain was the first to admit he was wrong. Mark got the page-one series, a nice bonus—"

"*Plus,*" says Manning, "the Partridge nomination. The forms went up to Cain's office this afternoon."

"Congratulations," says Roxanne.

"That's a bit premature," Manning cautions her. "It's only a nomination. Coming from Cain, it'll have extra weight, but the decision rests with the national committee, and I'll be up against the stiffest competition in my field."

Roxanne rolls her eyes. "You're a shoo-in, Mark."

"Maybe," he admits.

The buzzer interrupts their conversation.

"Oh?" says Roxanne, looking toward the door. "I thought it was 'just us' tonight."

"It *was,*" Manning assures her.

"I'll get it," says Neil, rising. He crosses the single vast room, leaving Manning and Roxanne to talk.

They don't, though. Their eyes follow Neil to the door.

He opens it and tells someone in the hall, "Yes, he's here." Then Neil signs for something, closes the door, and returns with a document-size package. Handing it to Manning, he says, "They sent a messenger from your office."

"Ahh," says Manning, picking at it, "this must be the Partridge Prize nomination. My editor knew I'd like to have a copy— thoughtful of Gordon to send it over."

Manning's eager expression changes to one of curiosity, though, as he opens the large envelope and finds another one within. "No . . ." he says, "this has nothing to do with the coveted Brass Bird. It's a FedEx, addressed to me at the *Journal.* From a lawyer's office. In Wisconsin."

He's got the second envelope open. He skims the document within. Then his eyes pop.

Neil asks, "Well?"

"For Christ's sake," snaps Roxanne, "what *is* it?"

Manning drops the paper to his lap. "An uncle of mine died. He's left me his house in central Wisconsin. I saw it only once, when I was a kid, and I was spellbound by it. The place is a whopper—I'm sure it's worth plenty."

"Wow," says Neil. "Your uncle had no kids?"

"As a matter of fact, he had three."

Roxanne asks, "Then why would *you* inherit the house?"

"I'm not sure," says Manning. "I have an inkling." He pauses, smiles. "But that's a whole other story."

❑